AC

THE

RED

ACROSS THE RED

BY

KEN FARMER
&
BUCK STIENKE

BOOK #4 IN THE NATIONS SERIES
THE BASS REEVES SAGA

Cover by Ken Farmer

THE AUTHORS

Ken Farmer – After proudly serving his country as a US Marine, Ken attended Stephen F. Austin State University on a full football scholarship, receiving his Bachelors Degree in Business and Speech & Drama. Ken quickly discovered his love for acting when he starred as a cowboy in a Dairy Queen commercial when he was raising registered Beefmaster cattle and Quarter Horses at his ranch in East Texas. Ken has over 41 years as a professional actor, with memorable roles *Silverado, Friday Night Lights, The Newton Boys* and *Uncommon Valor*. He was the spokesman for Wolf Brand Chili for eight years. Ken was a professional and celebrity Team Penner for over twenty years—twice penning at the National Finals—and participated in the Ben Johnson Pro-Celebrity Rodeos until Ben's death in '96. Ken now lives near Gainesville, TX, where he continues to write novels.

Ken wrote a screenplay back in the '80s, *The Tumbleweed Wagon*. He and his writing partner, Buck Stienke adapted it to a historical fiction western, *THE NATIONS*—a Finalist for the Elmer Kelton Award. They released the sequel, *HAUNTED FALLS*—winner of the Laramie Award for Best Action Western, 2013—in June of 2013. *HELL HOLE* was the third in the Bass Reeves saga written by Ken alone.

Buck and Ken have completed twelve novels to date together including the westerns.

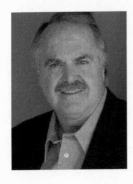

Buck Stienke is a native Texan originally from Houston. He spent many of his formative years in the Texas hill country, and lived on the LBJ ranch when Lyndon Johnson was president.

His love of almost all things Texan extends to movies, books as well as music. He's an accomplished guitarist and singer / songwriter. In fact, a country song he wrote inspired this novel. Buck has an extensive knowledge of guns, modern gunsmithing and ballistics.

Buck and his writing partner, Ken Farmer, have published twelve novels to date. *Devil's Canyon* was Buck's first solo effort.

ISBN-13: - 978-0-9904389-8-4 - Paper
ISBN-10: - 0990438988
ISBN-13: - 978-0-9904389-9-1 - E
ISBN-10: - 0990438996

Timber Creek Press
Imprint of Timber Creek Productions, LLC
312 N. Commerce St.
Gainesville, Texas

ACKNOWLEDGMENT

The authors gratefully acknowledges T.C. Miller, Brad Dennison and Doran Ingrham for their invaluable help in proofing and editing this novel.

Contact Us:
Published by: Timber Creek Press
timbercreekpresss@yahoo.com
www.timbercreekpress.net
Twitter: @pagact
Facebook Book Page:
www.facebook.com/TimberCreekPress
214-533-4964

DEDICATION

ACROSS the RED is dedicated to all writers of the Western Genre. With special notice to Louis L'Amour, Zane Grey and Edgar Rice Burroughs.

This novel is a work of fiction…except the parts that aren't. Names, characters, places and incidents are either the products of the author's imaginations or are used fictitiously and sometimes not. Any resemblance to actual persons, living or dead, business establishments, events or locales is entirely coincidental, except where they aren't.

First printing - 1 Feburary, 2015

HISTORICAL FICTION WESTERN

THE NATIONS by Ken Farmer and Buck Stienke
Www.tinyurl.com/the-nations-Bass
Audio version: www.tinyurl.com/TheNationsAudio
HAUNTED FALLS by Ken Farmer and Buck Stienke
Www.tinyurl.com/haunted-falls-Bass
Audio version: www.tinyurl.com/HauntedFallsAudio
HELL HOLE by Ken Farmer
Www.tinyurl.com/hell-hole-Bass3
Audio version: www.tinyurl.com/HellHoleAudio
DEVIL'S CANYON by Buck Stienke
http://tinyurl.com/devils-canyon-B

Coming Soon

MILITARY ACTION/TECHNO
BLACK STAR BAY by T.C. Miller

HISTORICAL FICTION WESTERN
BASS and the LADY by Ken Farmer & Buck Stienke
Book five of the Bass Reeves Saga

TIMBER CREEK PRESS

CHAPTER ONE

COOKE COUNTY, TEXAS
DELAWARE BEND

Texas Ranger Bodie Hickman instinctively ducked when he saw a puff of rifle smoke from across the Red River. Approximately one second later he heard the crack of a bullet just as it clipped the top of his gray center-creased Stetson and took it from his head—followed immediately by the boom of a big gun.

The big rawboned redhead dove from the back of his line-back dun mustang, Lakota Moon, rolled to a crouch, still holding on to the reins and tapped the horse's left front foot in the signal to lay down. Moon dropped to his knees and rolled over on his right side.

"Git down, Billy!" he shouted at the young posseman behind him as he reached over and jerked his brand-new '86 Winchester lever action rifle from its boot. The warning came too late as the second booming report of the distant big gun was followed by the sickening *twack* of the round striking flesh.

Bodie turned just in time to see a cloud of red explode from Billy Malena's chest as the young man flipped backwards out of his saddle and fell to the ground. His panicked horse lunged up the side of the draw and into the woods on the south.

The two lawmen had been riding single file—tracking some rustlers moving a small herd of horses—down a shallow three foot deep wet-weather wash that headed west toward an area known as the *breaks* along the Red River, still some three hundred yards away.

The heavily wooded section close to the wide, but usually slow moving border river between Texas and the Indian Nations, had become a sanctuary for the lawless, allowing the malefactors to head into the Chickasaw Nation if the Texas Rangers got too hot behind them.

The sweeping six square miles of the bubble-like Horseshoe Bend on the west side of the much larger Delaware Bend of the Red was ten miles south east of Marietta, IT and twenty miles northeast—as the crow flies—from Gainesville, Texas. It had been a past haven to the likes of the guerrilla chieftains of the south, Charles Quantrill and Bloody Bill Anderson, as well as the James gang and now was a crossing point for stolen cattle and horses bound for the Nations—especially in early summer when the water level was going down.

"Billy!" Bodie shouted in vain at the motionless body of his young friend and brand new posseman four yards behind him in the gully. Another *boom* sounded and a slug slapped the sandy bank just above his head a half-second later. "Son of a bitch!"

He raised his head just enough to see over the edge of the gully and could make out a small cloud of gunsmoke coming from atop a forty foot bluff just across the river. "Damnation! Purtnear a quarter mile…Gotta be .45-70…Got a shooter up there, Moon. Stay down…That bastard don't know I got a little surprise for him."

He belly-crawled forward—his rifle cradled across his arms—in the wash as quickly as he could about fifteen feet to a low scrub bush over the northern lip of the bank. Bodie adjusted his Lyman tang sight up to where he saw the four hundred yard range notch was marked and took a deep breath. He levered in a long .45-90 round and brought the rifle snugly to his shoulder. He rose up slightly, found the desired sight picture on the slowly dispersing cloud of smoke, concentrated on the front sight, exhaled half his air and fired.

The big round—originally created for taking buffalo at long distance—bucked hard, but he paid it scant heed as he quickly cranked another into the chamber and shot again. Both rounds were discharged in less than a second with the distinctive roar of the big bore echoing up and down the Red River valley. "Bet you weren't expectin' that, were you, asshole?" *Not like I had a chance of hittin' anything, but maybe I scared 'em off.*

The cloud of his own gunsmoke gradually drifted away, but not before he had smelled the pungent aroma of burnt sulfur from the black powder load. Bodie drew a pair of the cigar-sized cartridges out of his custom-made gun belt and shoved them past the loading gate as he contemplated his next move.

He waited for return fire for a good five minutes—nothing. *White man…Injun would have the patience to wait me out.* Just to be safe, he crawled back to his horse. "Git up, Moon."

The big mustang got to his front feet, followed quickly by his back—he shook, as horses will do after getting up from the ground. The young ranger led him over to the woods on the side near Billy's mount, ground-tied him so he could graze a bit and solemnly walked back to his friend's body.

His hat lay near Malena. He picked it up, slapped the dirt off on his thigh and stuck his index finger through the hole in the top of the crown. "Yep, .45." He jammed the Stetson firmly back on his head and knelt down beside Billy and caressed the side of his face.

"God, I'm sorry, boy…Yer first day, too…What in the world am I gonna tell yer mama?" He slipped his arms under the still warm body, easily lifted the wiry teenager and carried him over to the horses.

DEXTER, TEXAS

Bodie slowly walked Moon—leading Billy's blood bay with the young man draped across the saddle—down the dirt main street of the dying little north Texas town.

At one time, Dexter had been larger than Gainesville, the county seat, until the highly anticipated Santa Fe Railroad went south through Woodbine, instead of Dexter, to Gainesville.

He passed by Ed Stein's Sugar Hill combination store and saloon with two cowboys leaning against the porch posts smoking roll-your-owns. One—a reed-thin man in his twenties—touched the brim of his dark Montana pinch hat, gave the young ranger a surreptitious grin and blew a cloud of smoke in his direction.

The two working cowboys sported batwing chaps—as opposed to the shotgun style preferred in Montana and Wyoming—because they were cooler and gave greater freedom of the lower leg when mounting—each wore store-bought white boiled cotton work shirts without vests. The thin one had a Colt Peacemaker strapped to his hips and his shorter, heavier friend sported a Smith & Wesson Schofield in a cross-draw.

Bodie noticed the two out of the corner of his eye, but didn't acknowledge or even look their way. He was able, however to see that both the horses tied to the hitching rail in front of the saloon were lathered. *Hmm, interesting.* He knew who they were and would bet money they were involved in the rustling ring that was plaguing north Texas and the Indian Nations across the Red. He just couldn't prove it—yet.

Every step Lakota Moon took increased his dread, not of the two ne'er-do-wells he just rode past, but of having to tell Billy Malena's mother what happened. *Damn, I'd rather git whipped with a wet rope...but I ain't got no choice.*

He drew rein in front of a small, but well-kept, white painted clapboard house—with a galvanized standing-seam roof and flowers along the front porch—on the outskirts of Dexter. Bodie stepped down and quickly moved to Billy's body. *Hope I can git him down 'fore she comes out the door...Don't want her seeing her son draped over his saddle.*

He slid the young man down and cradled him in his arms like a baby, turned and stepped toward the porch only to see the widow Millie Malena standing on the stoop, both hands to her mouth. She was a very attractive, 5' 2" brunette in her late-thirties—widowed at the age of twenty-eight when her bank teller husband had been killed in a robbery.

"I'm powerful sorry, Miz Malena, we was bushwhacked near the Red…"

She dropped her hands and said in a soft, but steady voice as her eyes filled, "Bring him in the house…Need to get word to Father Miller…He'll need…need his rites read…proper." She choked back a sob and held her head up as she opened the screen door for Bodie.

"Yessum, I'll see to it right away."

"Lay him there." She directed him to place her only son on his bed against the wall and then grabbed Bodie's arm after he gently laid Billy on the patchwork quilt cover. Millie lifted her chin in resolve even as the tears continued to course down her cheeks. "You find who did this, Bodie Hickman...You hear me?...You find them."

He nodded.

"I want them punished...he was just a baby...my only baby. But he was a man...Wanted more than anything in this world to be a Texas Ranger...You catch 'em...and I want to be there when they put the noose around their neck."

A lump built in Bodie's throat and he rasped out, "You can count on it, Ma'am." He swallowed and headed to the door. "I'll fetch the priest."

Even the closed door couldn't keep him from hearing the anguished wail from the bereaved mother inside as she couldn't hold back her grief any longer. He wiped his own tears with the back of his hand, mounted, reined Moon in the direction of the small Catholic chapel and Father Thomas Miller. He bumped the gelding into a hand gallop—it was less than a mile away.

GAINESVILLE, TEXAS
COOKE COUNTY SHERIFF'S OFFICE

"Damn shame on Billy...Boy had the makin's of a fine lawman," said Sheriff Wacker—a trim thirty-three year old man, with a full head of light sandy hair and mustache—as he filled his cup from the coffee pot on the wood burning stove in the corner.

"Pure out and out dry gulchin', Tal...uh, Taggart...Didn't have a chance. Shot from near 400 yards away..."

"Takes a hellova gun to do that. A .45-70 you think?"

"I mind that would be it. But it was a repeater...weren't no fallin' block or trapdoor, I can tell you that."

"I'll give Sheriff Colcord up to Oklahoma City and that new Sheriff at Ardmore...Uh, Pullman, a call and have them check their area for sales of .45-70 ammunition. We can do the same here."

"I reckon there's quite a number out there since the '86 Winchester came out."

"True, but it at least would narrow the field."

A messenger from Western Union came through the front door. "Got a telegram here for Ranger Hickman."

"That would be me, son." He took the yellow flimsy and flipped the young man a dime from his tan canvas vest pocket.

"Thank you, sir. Ya'll have a nice day, hear?" he said over his shoulder as he closed the door.

Bodie stared at the envelope for a moment.

"Well, you gonna open it?"

"Oh, yeah, sure…Just wasn't expecting a telegram. That's all."

"You know what they say about a guilty conscience?"

"No, what?"

Wacker paused for a second and grinned. "Damned if I can remember…but if I think of it, I'll let you know."

"Cain't wait." Bodie ripped open the thin paper and unfolded the message. "Well, butter my butt and call me a biscuit."

"What?"

He chuckled. "Listen to this…'Finished arrangements for the church and the preacher. Stop. Preacher has never done a double wedding before. Stop. Mama and Father are en route by train from Alabama. Stop. Sent telegram to your mother. Stop. She will contact you when she will arrive in Gainesville. Stop. Sent telegrams to Marshals Reeves, McGann, Lindsey and Hart. Stop. Wedding is June 18. Stop. You don't show up…Texas isn't big enough to hide in. Stop. Love, Annabel. Stop'."

"Wonder what she means by that?" Wacker said with a smile as he pulled out a cigar from his shirt pocket.

"Guess…Hell, she's a better shot than I am. Reckon I better show up."

"Ya think?" He lit the end of the hand-rolled stogie from Virginia, drew the fire into the broad leaf burley tobacco and blew a cloud of blue smoke over his head. "What's that about a double wedding?"

"Colcord's deputy, Willie Agee…told you about him gittin' shot an' all…and Annabel's best friend, Theresa Chadwell…"

"Ah, the other girl in the kidnappin'."

"Right…Well, anyways, they're tyin' the knot too."

"Don't that beat all…Sounds like ya'll are gonna have a hellova chivaree."

FORT SMITH, ARKANSAS

The young teenage messenger hopped up and stabbed his boot in the stirrup after he had sucked up his cinch. The telegram he had placed in his saddle bag was addressed to Deputy US Marshal Bass Reeves. The boy knew exactly where the famous black lawman lived. He had delivered telegrams out there a half dozen times before and had always been rewarded by one of Bass' signature tokens—a shiny Morgan silver dollar that was worth more than his daily pay of seventy-five cents.

He turned the brown grade mare up the street from the Western Union office and quickly brought her up to a road trot.

REEVES FARM
VAN BUREN, ARKANSAS

Mame Reeves, Bass' tall blond adopted daughter, was visiting after teaching school in the nearby town. She heard the knock on the door as she and her dad sat drinking iced tea and enjoying one of their infrequent visits. Riding the Indian Territory for Judge Isaac Parker—known as the *Hanging Judge*—did not give the big man much time for a home life.

"I'll get it, Daddy. You deserve to sit back for a change."

"Much appreciated, baby girl," he said as he settled his 6' 3" frame back in the overstuffed chair. His yellow and black catahoula dog, Buttercup, lay back down at his feet and sighed.

"I'm not a baby girl anymore," she said over her shoulder.

"You are to me."

She smiled, opened the front door and saw the eager messenger waiting outside on the porch.

"Telegram for Marshal Bass Reeves."

She opened the screen door. "Come right in, young man. I do hope it's not a call for him to come back to work already. He just got home two days ago."

The boy shrugged. "Couldn't say, ma'am. Ain't allowed to read 'em." He held out the envelope as well muscled man got to his feet—he had a full mustache and always kept his curly hair cropped very short. Reeves took the message and handed it to Mame, as the former slave had never been taught to read—that was a privilege his owner had denied him.

She opened it quickly and read it aloud. Bass beamed as he glanced over at a Dr. Thomas'-Eclectric Oil calendar on the wall.

"That falls smack dab in the middle of my time off, I reckon. Looks like me and Momma have us a little trip to Oklahoma City a comin' up." He fished into his pocket for some money and handed it to the messenger. "Send this reply, if you would be so inclined, son...Mister and Missus Reeves will be most proud to attend your wedding."

The young man jotted down the missive on his note pad, grinned, put the dime, a nickel and the silver dollar in his pants pocket. *Boy, oh boy, oh boy, made a dollar fifteen tip today.* "Thank you, Marshal! I'll be sure the message gits sent soon as I git back to town."

He nodded politely to Mame, donned, and then tipped his short-billed baseball cap, spun around and headed for the door. Once he was gone, she smiled at her dad. "Are those the two young girls you were telling me about? The ones you rescued out in the Glass Mountains?"

He nodded. "Yes, honey...Got there just in the nick of time. A few more seconds and they would'a been goners, fer sure."

"And you get to see Jack again...And this time, nobody will be takin' pot shots at you."

He laughed. "We can only hope, baby girl...We can only hope."

McGANN CABIN
ARBUCKLE MOUNTAINS
CHICKASAW NATION, IT

Deputy US Marshal Jack McGann sat in a slat-backed rocker on the front porch of his and Angie's spacious log cabin next to Honey Creek. He was holding a bottle for his adopted daughter while she nursed. His big white wolf/dog lying beside the chair got to his feet—his tail wagging. "Somebody comin' you know, Son?'

He looked over at his master with his unique golden eyes, danced on both front feet and wagged his tail harder.

Jack glanced back up to see Marshals Selden Lindsey and Loss Hart round the wooded corner from the wagon road and jog trot up to the hitching rails set outside the whitewashed slat fence.

"Hey, Jack," the broad shouldered, mustachioed Lindsey said as he dismounted, loosened the girth on his big black stallion, Dan, and looped the reins around the shaved hickory rail.

"Hey, Selden, Loss. Ya'll come in…You lost or in trouble?"

"Neither," Lindsey said as they climbed up the four steps to the wide front porch. "I'd shake hands, but looks like you got yers full…how's Baby Sarah doin'?"

"Aw, growin' like a weed…Gonna be knee high to a short frog 'fore you know it."

Jack's wife, Angie, opened the screen door and stepped out onto the porch. "Well faith and wouldn't ye know the worst pair of hooligans in the Nations would be showing up at lunch time," said the attractive fiery redhead.

Loss looked at Selden. "You mean to tell me it's noon already?...I gotta git my watch fixed."

"The divil fly away with ye, Loss Hart. Don't try to spread the blarney with me. I've known ye too long...Well, just so ye know, I fried up a big hen to go with some creamed new potatoes, so best ye wash up...Would ye be wanting me to take Baby Sarah, husband?"

"'Spect so, she's finished her bottle. She burps better fer you than fer me."

She took the squirming child from his arms. "Ye think she's a bag of grain."

"Aw, do not."

"Do to." Angie draped the child on her breast with her head on a clean cloth she had placed on her shoulder and rubbed three circles on the middle of her back, and then gently patted her just below her shoulder blades and was immediately rewarded with a long burp. "See, husband. That's how ye do it."

"Balderdash, you jest know how to hold yer mouth right." He turned to the grinning Selden and Loss. "And what brings you boys out to our neck of the woods...'sides lunch time?"

Selden pulled a Western Union envelope from his coat pocket and handed it to Jack. "Come this mornin'."

"Hope it ain't from the judge." He ripped it open and read the telegram. "Well, well, well...Knowed this was a comin'."

14

"Loss and I got one just like it," Selden said as he grinned. "Woman of the house!"

Angie came back to the screen door. "What husband? Do ye need me to teach ye something else?" she said as she stepped out on the porch.

He handed her the message.

She quickly scanned it and grinned. "Well bless Paddy!"

DEXTER, TEXAS

Bodie was one of six men asked by Millie Malena to serve as pall bearers at her son's funeral. He was the second oldest, as Billy's favorite uncle, Earl Russell—Millie's older brother from Gainesville—was, at age 39, the most senior member serving in that solemn capacity. All the rest were teenage friends or cousins, each dressed in black as was the custom in those days.

The grave had been dug at the Orlena Cemetery just south of town—on the east side of the dirt road between Dexter and Callisburg. A few mature live oak trees dotted the premises, offering shade for those attendees not inside the 15' x 15' off-white tarp that had been erected near the grave site itself. It was a spot selected next to Billy's father's resting place—one he himself had visited many times since his father's passing, back when the young man had been just a lad.

The men lifted the simple wooden casket from the glass-sided hearse, as the two magnificent shiny black Thoroughbred horses—festooned with dyed black ostrich plumes on their browband headstalls—stood quietly in their traces. A skinny beanpole of an undertaker held the rear door open and whispered cautions to the men as they slid the box out and took their assigned places at the brass handles—three on each side.

Father Thomas Miller, the smallish local priest, finished the service and invited the small throng gathered to pay their respects to Millie. Most of them did so, although a couple of them simply turned and made their way to their horses and departed.

Sheriff Wacker stood in line behind a few of Billy's distant cousins and finally got to address the grieving mother personally. They had never met before and he was immediately taken by the beauty of the thirty-eight year old widow. Despite the strain of burying her only son, her flawless alabaster skin, classic bone structure and gorgeous dark eyes caught his attention, even through the mourning veil she wore.

"Ma'am, I cannot tell you how sorry I feel for your loss. I knew Billy through Ranger Hickman and I felt he had the makin's of a fine lawman." He took her hands in his and gave them a gentle squeeze as she nodded, but said nothing. The sight of tears streaming down her cheeks caused tears to rim his own eyes as well. "If there is anythin' I can do for you...anythin' a'tall, Miz Malena...please contact me over at the Sheriff's office."

She squeezed his hands in return, touched by his sincerity and managed to whisper out a weak, "Thank you, Sheriff Wacker. So kind of you to offer," as their eyes locked on one another for a few more seconds.

He released her hands and tipped his hat as he moved to speak with the other relatives.

Bodie stayed until the service was over and the relatives were escorting Millie home. Earl approached him and stuck out his hand.

"Thanks for coming, Ranger. Billy meant a lot to us...Would you like to drop by the house for a bite? I'm sure there's plenty to go 'round. You know how it is...Well meanin' folk always seem to bring enough food for a month, thinkin' the family won't feel like cookin'."

The Ranger shook his head as he gripped the uncle's hand firmly. "Thank you kindly, but there's somethin' important I got to do." He swallowed at the lump that had been in his throat since the service started. "Nice meetin' you, Earl. Just wish it coulda been under happier circumstances."

"Likewise," Earl replied as he released the handshake. He watched as Bodie tightened the cinch on the dun and stepped into the saddle.

The lawman nodded once and reined Lakota Moon west and single-footed up the dusty road.

He's headed back up where they ambushed him and Billy. Man's got sand, I grant you that, Earl thought as he watched him ride away.

He unshucked the big Winchester—just in case—stepped down and let Moon's reins fall. The mustang stood still, except for an occasional swish of his tail to try to keep the flies at bay and cropped some of the early summer grass growing along the tree line.

Keeping a sharp eye on the bluffs on the far side of the Red, Bodie made his way down to the wash and found his footprints where he had bailed off after the first shot.

He studied his tracks as he played the memory of the awful event over and over. *Here's where I was crouched down. Billy fell over yonder on the second...and the third hit right about...there.*

His eyes found a small depression in the sandy wall of the wash. He took one more look back at the bluff from which the deadly shots had come. *I wonder if somehow those jayhawkers knew we were comin'?* Bodie shook off his question and reached for the sheath knife he wore on the left side of his gun belt and began to slowly dig at the sand under the obvious point where the bullet had impacted. The loose sand eventually fell clear of the disturbed surface, leaving a clear tunnel about a half inch in diameter. *Now we're gettin' somewhere.*

He searched around for a small stick to probe with, but the wash was pretty barren. *Dummy, you got a pencil in your coat.* He pulled it out and stuck it in the hole, but didn't make the contact he was expecting. He left the pencil inside the hole and resumed digging beneath the bullet bored tunnel, carefully taking the outer layers of moist dirt away. After another minute of digging, he tried probing again and felt something solid this time.

Coming up from underneath, he was rewarded with his persistence by a long heavy bullet dropping into his hand along with some tightly packed sand and his pencil. *That's what I came here for.* He cleaned off the slug and examined it carefully, and then took another look up at the bluff. The bullet itself was not exactly what he had expected to find. It lacked deep lubricating grooves and certainly was not as big as the .45-70 round that had knocked off his hat or the one that killed his posseman. *This here slug was paper patched and ain't no bigger than .40 caliber.* The evidence in his hand told a story, and one he didn't much care for as he came to the most logical conclusion. *Two.*

COOKE COUNTY, TEXAS
CALLISBURG

The waxing gibbous moon that had just risen above the tree line offered the only light inside the old abandoned Butterfield Stage depot just a block from Billy Rousseau's Dry Goods and Grocery store. The faces of the three men inside were hidden in the dark shadows broken only by the pale moonlight streaming through the broken window panes and by the meager glowing ends of their handmade cigarettes. One was wearing a dark hood over his head with round holes cut for his eyes.

The Butterfield Overland Mail was a stage line that carried passengers and mail from two eastern termini, Memphis, Tennessee and St. Louis, Missouri to San Francisco, California. The trail merged in Ft. Smith, and then curved south through Texas, New Mexico and finally terminating in San Francisco, California. The line only operated from 1857 to 1861. The US Government revoked the contract of the company in anticipation of the coming conflict, but the operation continued on a limited basis for the Confederacy through 1862. A few abandoned way stations still stood along the route—the building in Callisburg was one.

"That ranger is going to be gone for a while I hear," said one.

"Gittin' married, is he? Haw!" said another. "She might be gittin' widdered purty soon when he gits back."

"Maybe you'll do a better job the next time," said the man in the mask.

20

"Hey, wadn't our fault...He ducked."

"Not worried about that...just now. But it is an opportune time to move that herd of horses we been collectin'. My buyer in Love County has been ridin' me to take possession and to move those cattle south from Sorgum Flats."

"When's the ranger leavin'?" asked the first man.

"My understanding is next weekend...Saturday, been told."

"We'll move the herd the followin' week...Be a full moon," said the second man.

"You don't get paid 'til both herds are delivered."

"Yeah, yeah, this ain't our first rodeo."

***

CHAPTER TWO

COOKE COUNTY
BROWN'S CROSSING

Bodie nudged Moon out into the slow moving current of the red mud tinted water that gave the river its name. He slipped his feet from the brass-lined, flat-bottomed stirrups. *No need in gittin' my boots wet.*

The sixteen hand mustang pushed through the water shoulder deep until he was just past midway of the ever changing channel. Hickman raised his feet a little higher, extending them out past the neck of his mount. "Damn, son, you coulda picked a spot that wadn't quite so deep."

Moon blew through his nostrils, stopped, sucked in a gallon or so of water and then waded upon a wide sandbar that extended out from the Chickasaw Nation. The big horse shook to free himself of the water dripping from his underside—rattling Bodie like a doll on a string as he tried to stick his feet back into the stirrups. "Godamighty Moon, wish you'd warn me when yer gonna do that…Damn near loosened three of my teeth."

He squeezed the big dun up into a road trot and headed almost due north paralleling the river toward the westward most loop of Delaware Bend—the originating point of the ambush.

He had picked the ford across the river adjacent to cattleman David Brown's Circle B ranch because it was the nearest to Delaware Bend to the east and far enough away that he wouldn't be noticed. The crossing was almost a mile east of the Gulf & Colorado railroad trestle connecting Texas with the I.T.

Two miles due east of Thackerville, I.T., he reined to the northeast and followed an old abandoned logging trail to the bluffs overlooking the Red.

Bodie dismounted, dropped his reins—to allow the horse to graze—loosened Moon's cinch and pulled his field glasses from his saddle bags. He walked near the edge of the forty foot high cliff and scanned the far side of the river until he found the wash where he and Billy had been. Plotting back from their position, he moved sideways a little bit at a time. *Uh huh…that should do it.* He refocused on the spot where he fired back at the bushwhackers. *Line's just about right, I reckon.*

He let the glasses hang from his neck and began to slowly look around. Bodie glanced behind him keeping on the line of fire and finally spied an old hickory log that was almost two feet in diameter—set back around fifteen feet from the edge of the bluff. *That looks kinda promising.* He walked to the massive deadfall and squatted down in the grass in front. *Son of a bitch.*

Two chunks of loose weathered bark had been blasted away. The exposed wood areas—each the size of a saucer—were not over six inches apart. The off-white bare trunk, protected for years by the rough bark, sported a pair of almost identical bullet holes. He stuck his index finger inside one of them up to the first joint and smiled. *Forty-five caliber, I would say. Not bad shootin'...If I had been just a few inches higher...*

Bodie stood up and glanced on the far side of the old trunk. It was plain that two people had lain prone—side by side—for some time, flattening the grass. One shooter had even scooped out a slight depression for his right knee. *No wonder they didn't stick around...Bet I made 'em lose their water.*

He reached down and picked up two fired .45-70 Government casings and another long skinny one in .40-90 Ballard. *Hells bells...That's a dang buffalo rifle cartridge! Gotta be from a Winchester High Wall or a Ballard. Ain't many of them heavy boogers around any more.*

He noticed six hand-rolled cigarette butts and picked up two that looked a little dissimilar and took a sniff of each. *This one's Bull Durham,* he paused at the other darker one. *Prince Albert. Yep, no question...just like daddy smoked.* Bodie slipped out his small pocket tablet and made a couple of notes. Folding one of the sheets into an improvised envelope, he tucked the butts inside, and then placed them and the brass in his shirt pocket along with the spent bullet.

He looked across the river again at the wash. *They had to know we was comin'. Only damn place with a clear line of fire...Got a snake in the woodpile.*

Walking up the hill a ways, he found where two horses had been tied. He knelt down and studied the tracks as well as the boot prints that offered a wealth of clues—the left rear shoe on one was a bar shoe—designed to correct a split hoof. One of the boot heels was missing a small *V* shaped chunk. He sketched the two on another piece of paper from his pad for later dissemination to the US Marshal Service.

Bodie turned, walked back where Moon was cropping the low growing yellow hop clover and cinched him up. "All right, son, found out what we needed to know...Gonna have to wait, though." He stabbed his boot in the stirrup and backed the gelding away from the trees. "A purty little blond-headed gal is expectin' my presence...Ain't a chance in hell I'll disappoint her...You git a little vacation too."

Lakota Moon bobbed his head and chuckled.

"Don't need to act so pleased."

GAINESVILLE, TEXAS
COOKE COUNTY SHERIFF'S OFFICE

"Now, God dammit, Wacker! I'm damn tired of losing stock, you hear me?" Tom Sullivant bellowed as he leaned over the sheriff's desk. He was a stocky, ruddy complexioned horse breeder with thinning auburn hair and a full mustache. "I've lost forty head of prime horseflesh in the last two months to those damn wire-cutters! I'm just a frog hair from goin' busted in the horse business."

"Settle down, Tom. Settle down. Just have a seat and I'll pour you a cup of coffee…"

"Settle down, my ass…I don't want any damn coffee…I want results."

"Doin' what we can, Tom. The ranger lost a posseman trackin' the thieves near the Red just last week…"

"Sorry as hell about that, but it ain't solvin' my problem. I got fifteen pure bred Morgan mares I just got in to breed with my Saddlebreds…just what the cavalry wants. Cost me a pretty penny, don't mind sayin'…I need protection from those thievin' sons-of-bitches…I'll take that coffee now," he said as he finally sat down in the bow chair across the desk from the sheriff and let out a big breath.

Wacker grinned, stepped over to the cast iron potbelly stove in the corner and filled a white ceramic cup. "Sugar?"

"Nah, don't want to ruin it." He took the coffee, blew across the top and had a sip. "When you drink coffee, drink coffee…Want sugar, eat a pie."

"Got a point…How's Francis Ann?"

"'Bout to drive me to the drink. That's why I'm here, Taggart…to pass along the ass-chewin' I'm gittin'. She's better with the horses than I am. Hell, even got names for every one…No clue how she keeps track of 'em all." He blew on his coffee again.

"How many men you have on the payroll?"

"Probably not enough, but it's all I can afford now…Ten all told. Rotate 'em out in two shifts watchin' the brood stock."

"Oughta be enough…Don't think it's big gang."

"Purtnear a full moon next weekend…prime time."

"Keep your eyes peeled. Want me to send my chief deputy, George Rudabaugh out?"

"Nah, he'd just be in the way."

GAINESVILLE, TEXAS
SKEANS BOARDING HOUSE

Bodie had dropped Moon off at Clark's Livery and Wagon Yard—a block down at the corner of Pecan and Rusk, next to the jail and fire station—and was climbing the concrete steps to the boarding house. "Afternoon, Miz Faye, Miss Floyd." He tipped his hat.

The attractive dark blond-haired owner of the large two story Queen Ann style red brick house was sitting in the shade of the big wrap-around verandah having tea with another of her tenants, Roberta Floyd—an English teacher at the high school. Faye was widowed and Miss Floyd was what was termed an old maid, even though she was only in her late fifties and had been afflicted with a condition known as Bell's Palsy in her twenties. The left side of her face was paralyzed giving her a somewhat frightening appearance which had the tendency of putting the fear of God in her students.

"Afternoon, Ranger. Would you like some ice tea?"

"Yessum, I surely would…with a sprig of mint, if you have it."

"Well, you can just turn around, go back down the steps and look to your left. There's a whole bed of it…Just pinch off what you think you want while I go in and fetch your tea…Sweet, right?"

Bodie grinned, ducked his head and stepped over to the mint bed. "Yessum." He grabbed a sprig with three of the long leaves on it and snapped it off.

Missus Skeans came out the screen door with his iced tea in a quart mason jar at the same time he hit the top step. She held the jar out and looked at it. He was confused.

"Do you want me to put the mint in it too?"

"Oh! No, ma'am." Embarrassed again, he took the jar, which had already begun to sweat, poked the herb in and stirred it with his finger.

She grinned and sat back down in her slat-back rocker. The back was draped with a dark green knitted throw. "Well, light and set."

He whipped off his hat and picked one of the other rockers that were scattered about the wide porch. "Yessum and thank you Ma'am." Bodie turned the jar up, took a long drink and wiped his red mustache with the back of his index finger. "Mighty fine tea, Miz Faye. Mighty fine."

"I think *excellent tea* would be a more proper choice of words, don't you, Mister Hickman?" corrected Miss Floyd.

"Oh, yes, Ma'am. Sorry."

Roberta turned to Faye. "Humph! These youngsters tend to obfuscate the Queen's English on a consistent basis."

Faye grinned.

"Yes, ma'am, my fi'-ann-cé..."

"You mean, fiancée, young man. From French; fiancée is the feminine of fiancé," corrected Miss Floyd.

"Uh, yes, ma'am, that too...My Annabel is constantly correctin' my grammar."

"As well she should."

"When is the wedding?" Faye asked.

"Uh, yessum, I was just goin' to mention that...It's June 18."

"Goodness, that's just next Wednesday...Are you getting nervous?"

"Yessum, just a tad...I'm meetin' my mama at the station and we're headin' on up to Oklahoma City in the mornin'...We're goin' to have a short honeymoon in Hot Springs, Arkansas, and then come back here...We, uh, could use a larger room...if you have one, ma'am." He took another sip of tea.

"Of course. There's that suite of two rooms down the hall. Bedroom and a side parlor...I'm so looking forward to meeting her, aren't you, Roberta?"

"Certainly. It's always a pleasure to have a conversation with someone of letters...What did you say her degree was in, Mister Hickman?"

"Uh, literature, Ma'am. English Literature. She wants to teach."

"Marvelous, I know we'll have many long hours discussing the classics, Plutarch, Shakespeare, Montaigne, Homer, Chaucer. I could go on and on."

"I'm sure you could," Bodie said under his breath.

"What was that?"

"I said I better bring in some wood…for the kitchen stove."

"How very nice of you, Ranger. The box is getting a bit low."

"Yes, Ma'am." He reached in his coat pocket and removed a stamped envelope. "Would you see that this letter gets posted tomorrow, Miz Faye? I know the carrier won't be by until after I leave."

"Why certainly."

Bodie got to his feet, tipped his hat again to the ladies. "Guess I better get on about splittin' that stove wood if we're gonna have supper." He went down the steps and headed around to the back of the big house removing his coat as he walked.

Faye glanced at the address on the front of the envelope.

Captain L. P. Sieker
Quartermaster Frontier Battalion
Texas Rangers
Austin, Texas

She furrowed her brow, turned her head and watched as the young Ranger disappeared around the side of the house.

GAINESVILLE, TEXAS
SANTA FE DEPOT

A northbound Gulf & Colorado train was parked alongside the long building—the coal-fired 4-2-2 black with red trim locomotive was slowly bleeding off steam. The ranger walked down the platform carrying his carpet bag—his eyes searched the disembarking passengers.

"Bodie!"

He spun on his heel at the sound of his name coming from behind him. "Mama!" He spied his attractive middle-aged mother—Lollie Hickman—stepping down the steps from the first passenger car, waving to him.

She wore a light blue gingham travel dress with a small matching forward-fitting hat and held her arms out as her youngest son ran up to greet her. He grabbed her around the waist and lifted the tiny woman off her feet.

"Boden Reese Hickman, you put me down this instant!" She swatted him across his shoulder with the dark blue clutch attached to her left wrist by a braided silk strap.

He laughed and dutifully set the 5' 1" woman back on the platform, leaned over and wrapped his arms around her in a big hug. She threw hers around his neck and held him close.

"Missed you, Mama."

She stepped back. "Missed you, too, son...If I didn't know better I'd say you've lost a bit of weight. That woman at the boarding house not putting out a good table?"

31

"Oh, yes, ma'am...not as good as yours, of course, but I've been awful busy chasin' some rustlers and...I...I lost a man last week."

"I am so sorry...Bushwhacked?"

He nodded and looked toward the caboose. The blue clad conductor was walking in their direction. He had just finished supervising the unloading of five head of Morgan horses for the Rafter S Ranch. The railroad yardmaster had removed the ramp and was closing the sliding door to the livestock car.

"All aboard! All aboard for Ardmore, Oklahoma City and points north! All aboard!" He waved his arm at the engineer looking out at him from the cab of the big black locomotive.

"Guess we better get on. I brought us a basket lunch...your favorite. Fried chicken, buttermilk biscuits, hogshead cheese and carrot cake."

"Love your fried chicken, mama."

"I know."

He helped her up the steel steps just as the steam whistle blew a shrill blast and engine gave out its first chug to start the five foot tall drive wheels turning.

"I just can't wait to finally meet Annabel."

"You're gonna just love her to death, Mama."

"As long as you do, son, that's what counts...What I think doesn't mean a hill of beans."

Tom Sullivant, his red-haired daughter Francis, and the ranch foreman, Shorty Hall mounted their horses. One of the other hands, a black cowboy named Jefferson White, took the string of brood mares, all tied together in a daisy chain and led off toward the Rafter S. The others followed along behind—the ranch was only eight miles to the northeast of town toward Callisburg.

"Fine lookin' mares, Francis Ann. You did a great job."

"Thank you, Daddy. Sorry I took so long down at Elgin. I wanted to spend some time with the herd, study their offspring and demeanor. Don't want any crazies."

"They's all got good eyes, Miss Fran. Good eyes."

"I thought so too, Jefferson...Tell a lot about a horse from looking at their eyes..."

"Yessum, shore can. Eyes'll never lie to you...jest like folks."

COOKE COUNTY, TEXAS
CALLISBURG

The three-quarter moon was already high in the night sky, but thick clouds were scudding across the face, muting the reflected golden glow—the occasional breaks were almost like rays of sunshine in comparison to the darkness. The clouds were a portend of a coming storm.

Four men gathered in the darkness of the old stage waystation, again their faces lit only by the feeble glow from cigarettes and one cigar except when the moon broke through for brief moments.

"Want you boys to hold off a day, Pink."

"What the hell for?"

"Word is that Sullivant got himself some new high dollar breedin' stock in. Picked up five head from down near Austin just this mornin' at the station." He drew on the cigar and blew a cloud over his head. "Thought we might add 'em to the herd."

"Hells bells, the old bastard is gittin' dicey. Got night guards out now," said Pink's brother, Jim Lee.

"And the point is?"

"Somebody might git themselves kilt," said a reed-thin cowboy as he crushed his smoke under his heel.

"Well, now, that's really an astute observation there, Windy...Didn't seem to bother you any when you shot that posseman...Or is it that you just have a problem when they might be shootin' back?" said the man in the black hood.

OKLAHOMA CITY, OT
LEE MANSION

Nearly a hundred people filled the large ballroom of the spacious six column, two-story quondam plantation style white house. Almost all of the attendees were relatives of the Lees, Holcolms, Hickmans, Chadwells or the Agees—the rest were close friends of the various families including the four Deputy US Marshals mingling with the crowd. Jack had been Bodie's best man and Bass was Willie's at the ceremony.

It had taken almost two hours for the assemblage to make the trip from the First Baptist Church to the home of Bartholomew Lee—Annabel's uncle—for the reception.

The room was amply lit by the series of nine foot windows along the east wall. The entire opposite wall was taken by white linen draped tables, covered with hors d'oeuvres of all types. Jack picked up one of the small smoked turkey sandwiches and was looking it over.

"Man would have to stand here fer mor'n a hour to make a meal on these little scudders."

"Don't think they're designed to make a full dinner on, Uncle Jack," said Bodie with a grin. "Think you're supposed to just sorta git a sample of a bunch of stuff and put it on those little plates there."

"Well, now see. There you go again...I'd call them saucers, not plates. Why ain't hardly big as Bass' hand."

"You talkin' 'bout me agin, Jack?" the big man said as he walked up.

McGann turned. "Not you...These tiny little things." He held up one of the finger sandwiches.

"Believe yer supposed to try one of everything."

"That's what I told him, Bass...Hell, git one of those little sausages wrapped in bacon...I'd take the stick out first, though."

Jack cocked his head. "You think?"

Bodie glanced around and noticed that everyone else was gathered around the two beautiful brides. He nudged the two marshals and motioned with his eyes toward the French doors leading to the outside. The three ambled out onto the patio at the back of the house. The ranger turned and leaned on the white railing that surrounded the deck.

"Got a problem."

"Well don't choke on it, sunshine," said Jack as he popped the tiny sandwich in his mouth.

"Got a rash of rustlin' goin' on down in my country…cattle and horses. They'll grab a bunch and head across the Red into the Chickasaw Nation…Playin' the border like a violin…Been goin' on for a couple of months now…"

"Damn, hate to hear about yer man…'specially from a drygulch." said Bass after Bodie had finished filling him and Jack in.

"He was a good kid."

"Sounds like somethin' we oughta git involved with, Bass."

"I 'spect yer right…Believe the US Marshals service an' the Texas Rangers needs to join up forces."

"Was hopin' ya'll would see it that way." Bodie reached into the inside pocket of his new black broadcloth cutaway wedding coat, pulled out an envelope and handed it to Jack. "I wrote everythin' down…names, maps, ranches that are bein' hit the most…"

"We'll go in undercover as ranch hands lookin' fer work," interrupted Bass. "No idee who's behind it?"

"Not a clue. Got my eye on a couple of fellers that hang out at Ed Stein's Sugar Hill store and saloon…Just hired help…Got nothin' I can hang my hat on though. It's rumored that Stein is a supplier of whisky that's smuggled into the Nations…Hell, may all be linked together."

"Cain't rule nothin' out," said Jack.

"Go ahead and enjoy yer honeymoon…Give us a chanct to work our way in and scout around a mite 'fore you git back."

"I can give you one little piece of advice."

"What's that?"

"There's two ways to argue with a woman…and neither one works," Jack finished with a bob of his head.

"Yeah, already found that out." Bodie grinned. "Hate leavin' ya'll to do it yourselves, but got no choice. That little Alabama gal would peel my head like an onion."

"Believe Bass and I kin handle it…ain't our first fish fry…specially with that help you mentioned."

They looked around as Annabel—Bodie's waspwaisted, blond, blue-eyed bride—swept through the glass-paneled double doors in her white satin and lace wedding gown and slipped her arm inside his. "Thought I might find you scoundrels out here. I know how you are about crowds…Just what kind of mischief are ya'll working up now?"

"Oh, nothin', sweet-pea, just gittin' some air." He kissed her on the cheek, winked at Bass and Jack over his shoulder as they turned to the doorway.

"Well, come on back in. I'm not cutting the cake by myself, you know."

Bass and Jack watched them go back inside.

"What say we send a telegram to that new marshal workin' fer the Judge, Brushy Bill Roberts? Met him a while back in the Judge's chambers. Hear tell he worked for the Anti-Horse Thief Association and the Pinkertons 'fore Parker hired him on," said Bass.

"Yeah, heard of him. Supposed to be handy with a gun."

"More important is he's done horse thief work. Git him to scoutin' the north side of the Red...see if he can find out who it is that's buyin'."

"Mind that's a good idea. Everbody in that part of the country knows what Selden and Loss look like," Jack said.

"What say we meet in Denison in two days?...Go on horseback from there. Don't need to be goin' into Gainesville by train."

"Wouldn't think so, Bass, wouldn't think so."

COOKE COUNTY, TEXAS
GAINESVILLE

A long, lanky cowboy—wearing a once white boiled shirt with green suspenders—astride a blood bay, ambled into the south side of Gainesville on the Denton road which became Grand Avenue. His gelding's head was low and he was shuffling his hooves, showing his fatigue as their shadows from the afternoon sun tracked alongside. He turned left onto tree-lined Pecan Street and pulled rein just west of Pecan Creek at Clark's Livery and Wagon Yard.

The owner, L.D. Clark—a smallish balding man in his late sixties, wearing bib overalls and a battered fedora—came out from inside the barn, wiping his hands on a rag. "Welcome to Clark's...Folks just call me Pap."

38

He stepped down from the saddle and stuck out his hand. "Well, Pap, I'm Walt, like to stable my horse. His name's Pepper. What do you charge?"

"Two bits a day, forty cents with grain...Two dollars fer the week."

"Give him a bait of grain an' check his feet...He's purty tuckered."

"Noticed...Give him a good brushin' too."

"Much obliged...Place to stay round here?"

"How long you gonna be in town?"

"Lookin' for work...Could be here a spell."

"Skeans Boardin' House, just a block over on Dixon." He pointed. "Sets a hellova table...Nice widder lady. Reasonable rooms...Damn sight better'n stayin' at one of the hotels...less you're partial to girls of the line."

"No time, ner money." He nodded, grabbed his bedroll and saddlebags and headed toward Dixon Street.

SKEANS BOARDING HOUSE

The cowboy climbed the steps to the front door of the boarding house and knocked on the jamb.

"It's not locked," came a melodious voice from inside.

He removed his hat, opened the gingerbread trimmed screen door and stepped inside. "Howdo?"

"I'm in the kitchen, come on in. Up to my elbows in dough."

"Yes, Ma'am."

He headed through the parlor toward the open doorway the voice had come from and stepped into the large, well-appointed kitchen. "Name's Walt Durbin, Ma'am."

She looked up from kneading the yeast dough at a central table, picked up the large ball, placed it in a clean white ceramic bowl, covered it with a dish towel and set it on the counter next to the black wood burning cook stove. "Gonna be dinner rolls...Has to rise for a couple of hours, though..."

"Shore smells good. Nothin' like hot yeast rolls slathered in fresh churned butter."

"Be ready for supper. I'm Miz Skeans. Folks just call me Faye. How can I help you?" She started to hold out her hand until she looked at it still all covered with flour.

"Lookin' fer a room, Ma'am. Pap Clark sent me this way."

"You came to the right place. Got one vacancy. A Texas Ranger had it, but he's off getting married and will take the two room suite down the hall when he and his bride get back...Five dollars a week."

"Sounds reasonable, I'll take it."

"Don't you want to look at it first?"

"No, Ma'am, figure if it's anythin' like the rest of the house, it'll do fine...'Sides I ain't about to miss out on them rolls."

"You'll do." She grinned.

MUSKOGEE, IT
CREEK NATION

"Marshal Roberts? Marshal Bill Roberts?" asked the young Western Union messenger boy of the two men in dark suits leaning back against the wall in front of the marshal's office in ladderback chairs.

Marshal Bud Ledbetter tipped his hat back on his head and nodded toward the other man also with his hat down over his eyes. "Bill. Wake up."

The other man leaned forward, set his chair down on all four legs and pushed his hat to the back of his head. "Damnation. Man can't catch a few winks anywhere these days...Whatcha got, boy?"

"Telegram for Marshal Bill Roberts, sir. You him?"

"Guess I am today." He took the flimsey from the boy.

"Will there be an answer, sir?" The young man took out his pad and a very short pencil.

"Hells bells, boy, give me a chance to read the dang thing first." He stuck a finger under the edge of the yellow envelope flap, ripped it open and read the missive. He nodded to the lad. "Meet you in Denison, stop. Brushy Bill." He reached in his vest pocket next to the US Deputy Marshal badge, fished out a quarter and flipped it to the messenger.

"Wow! Thank you Marshal Roberts." He turned and took off at a run back toward the Western Union office down the street.

"Meet who in Denison?" asked Bud.

"Bass Reeves. Something to do with horse rustlin'."

"Ever work with Bass before?"

"Nope, only met him once in Fort Smith in Judge Parker's chambers. Mentioned to him I used to work with the Anti-Horse Thief Association and the Pinkertons. Reckon that's why he's callin' on me for assistance."

"Better stock up with ammo, you goin' to work with Bass."

"So I heard." The slight built 5'8", 165 pound thirty-six year old lawman with the bright blue eyes, grinned, got to his feet and straightened his coat. He had small hands, disproportionately large wrists and twenty-five bullet and knife scars on his body. He was born William Henry Roberts, December 31, 1859. "Mind I'll go down and check on the train schedule."

Marshal Ledbetter watched Roberts saunter down the street in the direction of the Katy Depot. *Strange man. Moves like a cat…More to him than meets the eye.*

As Brushy Bill walked down the covered boardwalk, he pulled a black cheroot from his vest pocket and stopped. Fishing out a strike anywhere match, he scratched it on a canopy post, lit up, blew a cloud of blue smoke over his head and mused: *Good thing I've had some experience at this…Wouldn't Big Casino just have a hissy?*

***

CHAPTER THREE

RAFTER S RANCH
COOKE COUNTY

"Come and git it 'fore I throws it to the hogs," said the skinny black man from the cook fire.

The other four cowboys pulling night watch on the main Sullivant brood mare herd, shuffled over with their tin plates and cups. The sun had disappeared beyond the purple horizon after the men settled the horses in a swag where there was plenty of grass. They had all ridden into camp to get their supper before the long night.

"Ain't got no hogs, Fats," said Fletcher.

"I know. Jest somethin' my mama used to say…God rest her sweet soul."

"Yer mama teach you to cook, Fats?" asked Shorty Hall as he filled his plate with a beef, onion and potato hash.

"My grandmaw. Mama was sick most of the time and we lived with her mama..."

"If she could cook like this, how's come you're so skinny? Damned if I don't believe you could take a bath in a gun barrel."

"A .44 or .38, Shorty?" quipped Bosco, a large, somewhat thick waisted cowboy.

"Aw, ya'll cut it out. Don't seem to matter how much I eat...just seem to burn it off," said Fats as he filled the coffee cup of the only Mexican caballero working for the Rafter S, Pancho Renaldo.

"*Usted necesita más frijoles con queso de cabra doble y tortillas de harina Fats. Ponga un poco de carne en las costillas.*"

"Dang, Pancho, you couldn't put meat on Fats' ribs with horse glue."

"Be easier to nail some more leg to the bottom of yer feet, Shorty...Haw!" said Bosco.

"What's chances of gittin' some of that goat cheese, Pancho? I kin do the beans and pat out some tortillas, fair good."

"I bring you some...next time I go see my girl in town."

"How's come you don't speak English all the time?"

"I forget, Fletcher. Sometime it sounds same to me whether it's English or Español."

A shot rang out—Fletcher McFadden grunted and fell forward on his face.

The others threw aside their plates, drew their side arms and peered into the brushy shadows. Four men on horseback charged out of the scrub oak trees, shooting on the run while two others fired from the darkness with Winchesters.

Fats took a hit to the side of the chest and went down, followed quickly by Shorty. Pancho dove beside a log and returned fire to the men on horseback. Bosco stumbled and fell across the back of Renaldo.

"I'm hit, Pancho."

The Mexican caballero twisted out from under the bigger man and snapped off two more shots, knocking one of the raiders off his horse as they rode through the camp. He got to one knee to fire again and caught a round in the middle of his back from the trees—and then the silence was deafening.

The riders wheeled around and trotted back into the firelight. Bosco rolled over and held up both hands.

"I'm shot, boys. No more, please, no more."

The reed-thin outlaw shot him between the eyes. "What'd he say?"

"Damn if I know, Windy. Sounded somethin' like he said he was shot," said black outlaw Bully July.

"Do believe he was right," added Pink Lee. "Twice...Alright, let's git out and round up them brood mares. They woulda heard them shots over to the ranch house...Somebody check on Emerson."

"Dead, Pink," said Dallas Humby, a burly man a little over six feet tall.

"Sling him over his saddle and tie him on." He looked to the east. "Moon'll be comin' up in about thirty minutes, let's ride."

Fifteen minutes passed when the group of riders from the Sullivant ranch headquarters slid to a stop just outside the still burning campfire. Francis Ann was first to dismount as she hit the ground running—quickly going from body to body.

"Damn! Dirty rotten bastards!"

"Francis!" admonished her father.

"I'm sorry, Daddy, but these were good men...That's how I feel," she said as she bent over the cook. "Daddy! Fats is still alive!" Francis leaned close to his face. "Can you hear me, Fats?"

His eyes flickered and he groaned. "Yessum, I hears...hears you."

Francis took her kerchief from around her neck, folded it and pressed it against the wound in his side.

"Cain't hardly...hardly breathe, Miss Francis." He reached up and grabbed her shoulder.

"You've got some busted ribs, Fats, but the bullet ricocheted off...didn't go through. You were lucky."

He groaned again and released his grip. "Yessum, been known to be...be lucky. But it hurts like...like hell."

Tom knelt down beside Francis. "Did you see anybody?"

Fats nodded. "They was four...on horseback an' a couple more in the trees...Heared one call one skinnier'n me, Windy...ahh, an' another, Pink...Pancho got one of 'em."

"You just try to relax, Fats. We'll send for a wagon...Mo, you ride back to the house and get a buckboard." She looked around at the four bodies. "Better make it two...The rest of you go see how many of the mares they got." She glanced at the huge yellow orb that had just risen above the tree line. "With the moon coming up, there should be plenty of light."

"Yessum, Miss Fran," said Jefferson as he led C.J. and Buck in the direction of the swag.

She rose to her feet, got her blanket-covered canteen from her saddle, knelt back down beside Fats and let him have a couple sips of water. "That's enough. With those ribs, you durn sure don't want to choke."

He nodded. "No, Ma'am."

"You're going to be fine, Fats."

"Yessum, jest hate like hell we couldn't stop 'em. They jest...jest come out of nowhere."

"I know, Fats, I know." She stared out into the moonlit night as a single tear rolled down her cheek.

COOKE COUNTY

"Still gonna ford downstream from the regular crossin'?" asked Bully as they rode along at a jog trot through the moonlit tree-shrouded coolie.

"Yeah, ain't too boggy. We kin water at Brown's Springs, then head to Thackerville and bed down at my brother's place nearby."

"How's come Jim has a place in Indian Territory?" asked Windy.

"Married a Chickasaw woman...Gives him rights in the Nation."

"Makes it kinda handy, don't it."

"It do...We kin git supplies at Oce McCage's grocery store in the mornin' and then slip over to Wolf Hollow and add these to the others." Pink Lee twisted in his saddle. "Dallas, how many we git?"

"Twelve. Lost four in the brush...Didn't think it was smart takin' the time to look for 'em."

Lee grunted. "Probably right 'bout that."

RAFTER S RANCH

The ranch buggy with Tom and his daughter, Francis Ann, clopped across the bridge over Elm Creek at the entrance to the ranch headquarters—the matched set of blaze-faced sorrel Saddlebred's steel shod hooves made hollow thumping sounds on the wooden planking. They were followed by ten ranch hands, all dressed in their go-to-meeting clothes.

"Who's that, Daddy?" Francis pointed to the tall slim cowboy leaning against the hitching post in front of the rambling ranch house. Tied next to him was a blood bay gelding.

"I have no idea, Francis." Sullivant pulled back lightly on the ribbons as they reached the white picket fence surrounding the yard. "Whoa up there boys." He set the brake, flipped the leathers around the handle and stepped down—followed by his daughter.

The cowboy moved forward, unfastened the lead rope and tied the team to the hitching rail on the other side of the gate. He turned and stuck out his hand. "How do. Name's Durbin, Walt Durbin."

"Tom Sullivant and this here's my daughter, Francis Ann," he replied as he shook the man's hand. *Good grip.*

Walt removed his dark gray, sweat-stained Stetson and nodded. "Ma'am."

"It's Miss."

He grinned and turned back to her father.

"What can we help you with?"

"Lookin' for work, Mister Sullivant. Horse wrangling...I can break, train to rope, teach gaits, pull a wagon..." He glanced over the team as a horseman would—from the feet up. "Nice Saddlebreds...or cuttin'. I never allow a horse to realize he can pitch...Ain't good for them or the rider...I teach trust, first off...and I ride for the brand."

Francis' eyebrows went up. "Some of our hands couldn't teach a hen to cluck...You're hired." She continued to appraise the long drink of water.

Tom turned, glanced at his daughter, grinned and shook his head. "What she says goes, Mister..."

"If my daddy had named me 'Mister', I think he woulda told me...It's just Walt."

"Walt...She runs the horse operation...what there is left and we are short handed. Gotta be straight up with you...Just had four men murdered and one more is laid up in the bunkhouse mendin' from a gunshot. Rustlers...Got twelve good brood mares the other night...Thought you oughta know."

"We just came from the services at Rest Haven cemetery...They only got one herd of twelve...Mostly Morgans...Our best, plus the new ones we just brought in, we had up in a trap here at the house."

"'Preciate the information, Miss. Sorry to hear 'bout yer men...Dealt with rustlers before. Man's just gotta watch his back."

"We pay sixty a month and board."

"That'll do."

"You can move your gear into the bunk house...plenty room. Put your horse in with the remuda. We keep it up close to the barn."

"'Preciate it, Mister Sullivant. Been staying at Miz Skeans over in town."

Tom nodded. "The chow's not as good as her's, but it's fillin'."

"She does set a fine table, I grant you that and a right handsome woman, too."

"Daddy's kinda sweet on her." Francis nudged her father in the ribs.

"Francis Ann, when are you gonna learn to keep your mouth shut?"

"Daddy, you should know by now, if I have something to say, I'm going to say it...and by the way, I think she likes you too."

Walt grinned.

Tom turned and looked at his daughter. "Really?"

KATY RAILROAD YARD
DENISON, TEXAS

The yardmaster and his swamper led the two saddled horses down the cleated ramp from the livestock car. One was a tall—sixteen hands—light grey Standardbred stallion and the other was a red and white Overo paint gelding.

"Bass, Jack!"

The two lawmen waiting on their horses turned as one at the salutation.

"Bill!" said Bass as he stuck out his hand.

Jack quickly followed suit and shook hands with the slightly built man.

"See ya'll made it in good time. I been here since last night."

"Almost didn't recognize you, all duded out like that," Jack said as he took in Brushy Bill Roberts' dark green bowler, green three piece suit and yellow cravat.

He laughed. "Figured if I was goin' to be a big time horse buyer from back east, oughta a least look the part...Right? 'Sides, when I change into my trackin' clothes, folks won't be so quick to remember me."

"Some say clothes don't make the man...But then in our line of work, sometimes it does...Carryin', ain't you?"

"Now, Bass, I know we only met once before, but if I ain't carryin', I'm either dead or in the bath...and then there's a shooter in close reach. Made a few enemies in my time…Got a bird's head Colt .38-40 in my shoulder holster and a three inch barrel cut down Thunderer ankle gun."

"Ain't we all…Partial to .38-40 myself, but Peacemakers." Bass opened his lightweight tan canvas jacket.

"Crossdraw. How's that work for you?"

"Well, 'parently, purty good…so far." He grinned a big toothy smile.

"I heard that…Either hand?"

He nodded. "Never pay much attention…just grab the one that's closest."

"I don't care much for left hand shooting…How 'bout you, Jack?"

"Well, I prefer my .45-70 Marlin fer long shootin' and my .44 Russians fer up close an' personal…hip an' a back up shoulder holster gun…cain't hit a bull in the butt with a broom usin' my left."

"Fine weapon, the S & W Russian. Carried a Schofield a time or two myself…So what's the plan?"

"…So, there you have it. You know what we know. There's no question these curly wolves won't hesitate to kill," said Bass as he finished filling Bill in a few minutes later.

"Always go in figurin' as much…Eliminates surprises."

"We'll communicate through Marshal Lindsey's office in Ardmore. Reckon we should check in…say ever three days?"

"Hear tell Selden's a good man."

"He'll do to ride the river with," said Jack. "He's just too recognizable around these parts."

Bass turned as the yardmaster and his helper approached with their horses. "Much obliged, gentlemen." He flipped a silver dollar to each.

"Thank you, sir," the two railroad employees said together.

They watched as Bass and Jack tightened their chinches, mounted and rode off while Brushy Bill walked back toward the depot.

The men looked down at the shiny new Morgan silver dollars in their hands.

"Who was that man?" asked the swamper.

The yardmaster just shook his head, flipped the dollar up in the air, caught it and put it in his vest pocket. "But he can come back anytime."

CHISHOLM TRAIL
CHICKASAW NATION, IT

Pink Lee and his men slowly walked the herd of fifty brood cows south, down the old Chisholm Trail toward Red River Station—the opposite direction of the big cattle drives some twenty-five years earlier. They had traded the stolen horses with their buyer outside of Healdton, IT for the cattle—mostly Herefords crossed with Longhorns stolen up in the northern Nations.

A group of five mounted soldiers—a sergeant and four enlisted men—approached the gang in the distance. Behind them they were leading a two-horse caisson with a .45 caliber Gatling Gun mounted on it.

"Soldiers," said Bully as he looked through his field glasses.

The other outlaws reacted with varying degrees of excitement.

"Soldiers?" asked Windy.

Pink pulled a bag of Bull Durham from his vest and rolled himself a smoke. "Stay calm. They ain't after us." He struck the match on the butt of his Winchester sticking out of its boot.

Bully handed the glasses to Dallas. "Ain't that a Gatling Gun they're a pullin?"

Humby looked for a brief moment through the binoculars. "Do believe that it is, Bully...Yes, siree, do believe it is."

"Where you reckon they're goin' with it?" asked Windy.

"Fort Washita is the only place I know of in that direction...But I thought they closed that place down," commented Dallas.

There was a pause, and then Pink exhaled a cloud of smoke. "When you'as in the army, did you ever use one of them Gatlin's, Windy?"

"Some...in the last Comanche uprisin'."

"Well, now...Think I just figured out how to improve our situation. Let's just hold the herd here on this side of the creek 'til they go past."

"What're you aimin' to do?"

"You'll see, Windy, you'll see...Ya'll jest foller my lead."

"You wanta bring the whole U.S. Army down on us?"

"Shut up, Bully, and do like I say."

The soldiers, looking hot and dusty, approached the sixty foot wide creek. Grade 5 Ordnance Sergeant Charles Watts was the only one wearing a sidearm.

Pink and the gang were on the opposite side—the cattle spread along the bank downstream for a hundred yards watering. Lee stood with his horse between himself and the soldiers, pretending he was adjusting the cinch while his horse drank.

A couple of the soldiers dismounted and gathered canteens to fill. Sergeant Watts remained astride a chuckle-headed sorrel gelding. He looked across the stream at the outlaws.

"Afternoon, gents."

Pink, peered over the back of his horse, threw up his hand in a quick salute. "How do, Sergeant. Pleasant day, ain't it?"

"Is…Makes a body glad to be alive. Startin' to get a mite warmish, though…Got some good lookin' mama cows there."

"Yeah, movin' 'em to some fresh pasture…Where ya'll headed?"

"Fort Washita."

"Thought it was closed down."

"It is. Our company is just bivouackin' at the old site an' fixin' to do some field exercises in the wooded countryside 'round there."

Lee held his revolver in his hand, hidden from the sergeant's view by his horse—he cocked the hammer.

Bully July was shielded by a tree—his Peacemaker in his hand also.

Dallas and Windy nonchalantly led their horses back from the water toward some rocks behind a thicket. Once out of sight of the soldiers, they pulled their Winchesters from their saddle rigging.

Private Dugan straightened up from where he had been filling a couple of canteens. He crossed to the sergeant and handed one to him and then stepped over to his horse. The last two troopers mounted up and turned the government issue animals around, while Watts—bringing up the rear—twisted in his saddle to call back to Lee.

"You fellers take it easy, now, you hear?"

He threw up his hand in a good-bye wave and rode on after his troopers.

Pink brought his pistol up, rested it across his saddle and took careful aim.

Windy and Dallas both eased theirs up for action from their cover in the rocks.

The sergeant nudged his horse into a lope and as he rode by his men, growled a quick warning command, at the same time digging his spurs in harder for a gallop. "Clear outta here, fast!

All the soldiers responded, their horses simultaneously breaking into a run. Private Dugan brought up the rear, leading the team pulling the caisson.

Lee, Bully, Windy and Dallas opened fire with a fast volley.

One of the troopers, hit from behind, tumbled forward and to the side of his mount. His comrades bent low over their horses' necks—riding for their lives—as the outlaws continued their murderous fire.

Another soldier was knocked from his saddle and still another somersaulted to the sloping ground, rolled over several times as his mount stumbled. Trooper Dugan reined in his panicky animal, utterly confused. The sergeant's horse was shot out from under him and they went down together, but he immediately got to his feet.

Dugan let go of the lead rope to the horses pulling the caisson, jumped from the saddle and sprinted toward the sergeant as did the trooper who was thrown.

Sergeant Watts grabbed the latter soldier by the arm and pulled him to the ground beside him, behind a small clump of rocks which offer very little protection. He drew his Army Colt .45 and cocked it, glancing quickly toward Dugan.

"Sarge, what's happening?"

"Get back on that horse, Dugan, and get the hell away!"

Dugan whirled and headed back for his mount. As he started to chase the frightened animal, trying to catch it, Bully squeezed off a shot and the young trooper fell to his knees, He struggled to his feet as bullets kicked dirt all around him and turned toward his sergeant in a half-stumbling run.

Windy drew a bead on the soldier from his cover up in the rocks, grinned and triggered off a round from his rifle.

Dugan jerked from the impact of the .44 caliber slug, sprawled awkwardly and went down for the full count.

The sergeant saw the private get it and threw a shot blindly in Windy's general direction. The young trooper beside him who had never been under fire before, was seized with sudden hysteria. He began to sob and whimper as bullets continued to splatter around them.

"Sarge, what's goin' on? Why are these men shootin' at us? Please help me! Fer God's sake help me."

Watts ignored the boy's babbling, raised his pistol carefully, trying to find someone to aim at. A rifle shot sounded—the pistol was ripped out of his grip and spun away. He held up his hand to see a couple of bloody stubs where two fingers used to be. "Sonafabitch!"

A twelve man patrol unit trailing a mile and a half behind Sergeant Watts' Gatling detachment had stopped their horses at a small stream to water. Their Chickasaw scout, Cyrus—Red Eagle—Maytubbi, glanced at Lieutenant Pitt.

"You hear?"

"Yeah, sounds like it come from where Watts oughta be."

The troopers pulled their horses up from drinking.

"Forward at the gallop...Ho!" commanded the young West Point graduate as they splashed across the small stream.

The patrol, led out by Pitt and the guidon bearer—with the D Company red and white pennant flapping—charged in the direction of the gunfire.

Lee's gang continued to reload and fire—puffs of smoke came from the slopes where the outlaws were concealed.

Sergeant Watts and the young trooper crouched as flat as they could get among the too-small rocks. Bullets splattered all around them—some ricocheting away with mournful screams.

The sergeant finished wrapping a makeshift bandage from his yellow bandana around his bloody hand. He gritted his teeth against the throbbing pain of his wound and the hopelessness of their plight. "Hold your fire!...For God's sake, stop shootin'!...We're unarmed!

Windy, with a thin sadistic smile, drew a careful bead on the man.

"Hey, I know that sergeant...Name's Watts. He caused me to git throwed in the stockade oncet," said Dallas with a grin. "I got 'im." He sighted slowly, carefully, along the rifle barrel.

"Hold your fire! We cain't fight!" Sergeant Watts grimaced again.

The young trooper beside him was beyond being mortally terrified as the bullets continue to pepper around them. "What'll we do, Sarge? What're we gonna do?" The panic rose again in his voice.

"I expect we'd better say our prayers, boy...We're about to get killed."

Dallas smiled and squeezed off his shot.

The bullet struck Watts in the center of the forehead and he slumped down dead. The young trooper—spattered with the sergeant's blood and gray brain matter as the rifle ball exited out the back side of his head—panicked. He jumped up and bolted screaming, down the coolie as bullets whistled around him.

Dallas, still smiling, drew a bead on the running figure.

"Let him go, he ain't no older'n you," said Bully.

Humby shot him a look of contempt, and then turned back to the business at hand. He squinted carefully through the sights.

"I said…let him go!"

A certain something in the black man's voice caused Dallas to hesitate—he glanced over uncertainly at Bully.

The trooper ran frantically up one sloping wall of the wash. A shot rang out, he pitched forward and rolled back down to the bottom—dead.

Pink lowered his smoking Winchester. He and Windy exchanged glances as they got to their feet.

"Grab them army horses!" Lee commanded as he and Humby mounted up and started across the creek.

Bully and Windy took off down the creek after the animals on foot. July grabbed the lead rope of the horses pulling the Gatling gun.

Lee and Dallas started after the cattle that had moved away from the gunfire—not far, as they had found some succulent late spring grass to graze on.

Dallas noticed something in the distance, hesitated, looked hard, and then stepped up on the top of the gully to get a better view. He saw the army patrol a half mile away—coming on hard in a cloud of dust. He jumped back down into the ravine and yelled. "Ferget the horses! Cavalry patrol comin'!"

Bully came to a stop, turned and started running back toward the others letting Windy take over the gun horse team.

Pink turned in the saddle to reply to Dallas, "How close?"

"Close enough to spit on."

Thinking fast, Pink's eyes fell on the blued barrels of the Gatling Gun. "Windy, any ammo in that thing?"

He hurriedly checked the big round drum mounted at the back and above the deadly ten barrel rapid fire gun. "Full drum!" He grinned.

"Git it over in them bushes...fast! The rest of you...back where you were."

Windy pulled the horses toward the copse of willows next to the creek as rest of the outlaws scurried up the sides of the gully to take their places. Pink took a quick look around, and then spurred up the slope on the far side of the creek.

At the top of the ravine, Dallas was back in the rocks he and Windy used before. Lee rode up, tied his horse over in the trees, pulled out his rifle and stretched out beside Humby. The patrol was not over a hundred yards away. Pink turned and signaled to Windy.

Folsom had tied the horses up short to a small tree and crouched behind the Gatling, his hand on the crank handle—he peered intently through the bushes with an expression of keen anticipation.

The troopers headed down the ravine, still at a gallop. When Lieutenant Pitt spotted the dead soldiers, he threw up his hand to halt the patrol. Cyrus and a soldier dismounted quickly and crossed to the bodies.

"Never mind them! They're beyond help," Pitt barked as he dug his spurs in and wheeled his buckskin back the way they came.

"No you don't, blue boy." Windy cranked the machine gun with a vengeance. The first shot hit the lieutenant, knocked him off his horse, and then the horse went down—the big .45-70 rounds continued to stream out of the Gatling at almost 400 rounds per minute.

Horses reared and screamed in pain as the troopers tried to get to cover. Men and their mounts fell to the ground as the murderous fire raked the gully. Troopers at the tail end of the patrol turned their horses back up the creek bed away from the devastating Gatling fire.

The other outlaws fired rapidly, working the levers of their Winchesters with deadly precision, knocking the panicked soldiers attempting to escape from their horses.

Pink levered off shots as fast as he could. Bully got off one round to every four that Lee fired—he stopped and looked up. One trooper was still mounted and riding hell bent for leather for safety—three shots echoed across the creek. He was dead before he hit the ground.

Suddenly, there was eerie quiet as the huge cloud of gunsmoke slowly drifted away on the soft breeze. The bodies of the troopers and numerous horses were scattered all over the ravine—several floated slowly away down the creek. A few surviving horses tried to scramble up the slope. None of the soldiers moved.

Windy walked out from behind the bushes, waving his hat and yelling gleefully, "We did it, sweetheart!" He patted the big round muzzle that held the ten barrels. "Ooo, a bit warm...Ain't she sweet, Pink? Spits like a mad mama bobcat!" He waded across the creek toward the scene of the carnage.

Dallas and Bully walked down into the ravine—Humby looked bleakly at July. "Likes killin', don't he?"

July just nodded.

Lieutenant Pitt was near death, but he managed to get his Colt in his hand. He lifted it slowly as Windy crossed the creek—pulled the hammer back and steadied the weapon as best he could. Folsom was less than a second from being a dead man—a shot rang out and the young lieutenant on his first deployment slumped over like a rag doll.

Pink shuffled down the last part of the slope and levered a fresh shell into the chamber of his Winchester. Windy walked up, vastly pleased with himself. Lee scowled at him, and then glanced around at the bodies.

"If you're through braggin', let's change horses...the ones you didn't kill...and clear out."

He bent down, took the Army Colt from Pitt's bloody hand, straightened up and slipped it in his belt. Behind him, Dallas and Bully led two horses. Windy—his hands on his knees—leaned over one of the troopers, who was still groaning.

"Hey, Pink! This yahoo's still alive."

Ten feet away, another member of the patrol painfully raised himself on one elbow. Pink walked toward him, turning his head to Windy as he did. "Finish him."

Windy grinned, pulled his .45 and fired.

Lee reached the other wounded trooper, looked down at him for a moment and raised his Winchester high.

Bully flinched and turned his head away at the sound of the crunching skull as Pink brought the rifle butt down forcefully on the hapless man's head.

Fifteen minutes later, as the sounds of the outlaws pulling the caisson toward their semi-scattered herd of cattle diminished, a figure lying partially in the water stirred. He lifted his head slightly and with the smallest of movements, looked around, and then shakily rose to his knees. The man pulled his jacket away, and then his bloody shirt from the hole in his side just below the ribs. *Huh, go clean through...big bullet.*

The Chickasaw scout, Cyrus Maytubbi, reached down under the water and grabbed a handful of the bottom clay and dead leaf mixture from the creek bed and stuffed it in the bleeding holes—front and back. He tore several strips from the bottom of his once-white cotton shirt and wrapped them around his waist. *Have to do.*

Cyrus got to his feet, glanced around again and whistled like a meadow lark. In less than a minute his dark gray Appaloosa with a spotted white blanket over his haunches, trotted out of the brush and snorted when he spied his master. He loped over to him, stopped and nuzzled his shoulder. "Kneel down, Cloud, kneel down."

The well-trained Indian pony did as he was told. Red Eagle grunted, picked up the reins and eased his leg over the McClellan saddle and took in a ragged breath. "Up...We go. Sheeah."

***

CHAPTER FOUR

DEXTER, TEXAS

A little cotton-headed, pigtailed girl in a light blue calico dress skipped a rope being turned by two other similarly dressed little girls near the side of the dirt road.

"One...two...buckle my shoe; Three...four shut the door; Five...six...pickup sticks; Seven...eight...lay them straight; Nine...ten...a big fat hen..."

A young boy in short pants with a small *T* shaped crossed stick rolled a barrel hoop past the girls.

Behind the children—several hundred yards down the road—a big black man with a leather eye patch over his left eye on a light dapple gray horse and a white man on a paint approached the town at an easy collected trot. They were dressed like working cowboys, jeans stuffed in their boots, boiled shirts, canvas jackets and worn, sweat-stained dirty hats. The black man wore two rosewood handled Colt Peacemakers in reverse grip strapped around his slim hips while the white man only carried a single Russian belt gun on his right. Well-used batwing chaps were tied on top of the soogans behind their six inch cantles.

"Eleven...twelve...Dig and delve; Thirteen...fourteen...Maids a-courting; Fifteen...sixteen...maids aplenty..."

The two men crossed a bridge that spanned a narrow, muddy-looking creek, only glancing at the three young girls. Two small colored boys in straw hats sat on the bank fishing with cane poles with short sticks for bobbers. They looked up at the sound of the horses clopping over the wooden bridge and curiously watched them pass.

SUGAR HILL SALOON
DEXTER, TEXAS

The two cowboys pulled rein in front of the saloon, dismounted and loosened their horses' girths. The black man surreptitiously glanced up and down the mostly empty street and nodded to his partner. They stepped through the nine foot tall double doors—their jingle-bob spurs tinkling slightly—into the combination saloon and store, ringing a two inch brass bell attached to the header.

Most of the mercantile occupied the left side of the fifty foot wide building while the saloon with its thirty foot long bar and seven round tables, the right. At the back was an elevated stage with an upright piano on the right front of the unpainted wood plank floor. The air was permeated with the fresh odor of cedar oil floor sweep which somewhat alleviated the stench of stale beer and vomit.

As they approached the bar, the rotund bartender with mutton-chop whiskers, white shirt, black bow tie and black sleeve protectors looked up from drying shot glasses. "What'll you have, fellers?"

"You serve my kind in here?"

"An' just what kind would that be?"

"A manumitted darkie."

"You got silver or gold money?"

"I do."

"Then we serve you...Don't care what color you are. Hell, even serve Injuns...What do they call you?"

"Ben Glass and this here's Babe Hodges...He's mostly that Injun you mentioned...Creek."

"I'm Ed Stein. Run the place. Well, like I said...What'll you have?"

"Beer fer me," said Ben.

"Got'ny Old McBrayer sour mash?"

"Slap out...Got some Old Taylor though."

"That'll do," replied Babe.

A husky man in a dark gray sack cloth jacket at the end of the bar nursing on a mug of beer, glanced up in the big mirror on the back wall. "Ed might not mind, but I damn shore do. I don't drink with niggers…or Injuns." He straightened up his six foot two frame and turned to face Glass and Babe.

"Now Rube, this here is my place, I decide who I'm gonna serve."

"Said I don't drink with niggers or Injuns."

"You want him or you want me to handle it?" Hodges said.

"I got it, you took care of the last one."

Ben stepped down to the end just as the big man reached for the Remington strapped to his right side. Like the strike of a cottonmouth, he snatched the pistol and twisted it out of the man's hand with his left just as it cleared the holster, and then slapped him back and forth across the face three times with his right so quickly it sounded like only one smack. The big white man staggered back and sat down heavily on his rear. Glass pitched his shooter back in his lap and stood calmly in front of him with his hands loosely at his side.

"You satisfied…er you want to go fer two?"

Rube wiped the blood trickling from his nose and rapidly swelling upper lip with the back of his hand and looked at it. "Naw, I'm good."

"I think we're due an apology, Ben…What do *you* say…Rube?"

"I'm sorry," he whispered as he staggered to his feet holstering his gun as he did.

"What was that? Couldn't quite hear," said Babe.

"Said I was sorry."

Glass turned to the bartender. "Pour the man another beer...on me, Ed."

Rube frowned and got a puzzled expression on his face.

Stein grinned, drew two mugs of beer, set a shot glass in front of Hodges and filled it. "There you go, boys, six bits."

Glass pitched a silver dollar on the bar.

Ed deposited the Morgan in a cigar box, laid a quarter back in front of Ben and threw a bar rag to Rube for his nose. "You fellers lookin' fer work?"

"Could say that," replied Babe.

"What's yer specialty?"

"Cattle, horses...'bout anythin' you can name, 'ceptin' chickens...Don't do chickens," said Ben as he took a deep draught of his beer, and then wiped the foam from his thick mustache.

"Look like you might be handy with those irons as well as your fists."

"Could say that too," said Hodges as he threw down the whiskey in one gulp, closed one eye, shook like a wet mule and wheezed, "Smoooth."

"See that feller over yonder in the corner next to the stage by his self?"

They glanced over at the table.

"I hear tell he might be a hirin'...Name's Tom Lee."

LOOKOUT HILL,
CHICKASAW NATION, IT

Cyrus sat propped under the shade of a solitary sycamore tree next to the hill the trail drovers used to check the area in front and the status of the tail-end of the herd on the old drives. It was the tallest hill north of the Red in what would later be known as Jefferson County, Oklahoma.

He grunted and looked down at the blood stain on his shirt. "Red Eagle may not make Healdton, Cloud."

His horse looked up from cropping grass nearby and nickered.

"I know you can, but I'm startin' to feel poorly."

The Appaloosa's head snapped around, he flicked his ears forward and locked his gaze almost due north. In a moment, the head of a star-faced chocolate sorrel followed immediately by a wide straw sombrero type hat appeared at the top of a nearby wash. A smallish man was astride the horse's back as it emerged. He wore trail clothes—faded jeans, blue striped collarless shirt, red wild rag and a canvas vest—a bird's head Colt Thunderer was strapped around his hips.

Cyrus eased his .44-40 Peacemaker from its holster, eared back the hammer, held it hidden beside his right leg and waited...

SUGAR HILL SALOON
DEXTER, TEXAS

Tom Lee watched the two men as they sauntered toward his table, carrying their drinks.

"Mister Lee, I'm…"

"Heard you at the bar, Glass. Have a sit…Looks like you need a refresher there, Hodges."

Babe looked down at his empty glass. "'Peers you'd be right."

"Nice work with Rube there. Don't believe I ever seen anybody that quick…He works for me…Good man, but occasionally needs a bit of an attitude adjustment." Lee nodded at Ed as the two men pulled out a couple of bow chairs from the table. "Where you boys from?" He motioned to Stein to fill the glass.

"Most recent, Catoosa, up in the Cherokee Nation," said Glass.

"Familiar with it. Call it the Hell Hole as I recollect."

"Did…Parker's marshals cleaned it out a while back…Babe and me just happened to be away relievin' the Katy of some excess money they had just layin' around…You understand."

"Oh, I fully understand…Who all did they get?"

"Mostly the Griffin gang…He was the tall hog at the trough 'round there…But he finally bit off a little more'n he could chew."

"How's that?"

"Reeves, Lindsey, McGann and a couple others come waltzin' into town, purty as you please. It was all over in less than ten minutes."

Babe continued the story, "Don't do to have Bass Reeves on yer tail. Felix was the only one left standin'…Hear tell he soiled his pants before Reeves put the shackles on him…Took him to Judge Parker. Due to hang next month."

"Me and Babe decided Texas might be a bit more to our tastes fer awhile…You understand."

"Understand that too…We're in the horse and cattle business…Texas and the Nations. We, uh, appropriate horses in Texas and exchange 'em for cattle we acquire in the Nations. Bring them back down the old Chisholm Trail into Montague County…Sorta a laundry job, so to speak."

"Well, now, ain't that slicker'n a greased pig," Babe said.

"Get bills of sale, goin' and comin'."

"Who gits the horses in the Nations?" asked Glass.

Tom glared at first Ben and then Hodges for a moment. "Don't really think that's any of your business…You?"

"Reckon not. Long as we be gittin' paid, don't matter much to us where they wind up. Right, Babe?"

"I mind that'd be right."

"Everybody works off a percentage. That suit you?"

Ben and Babe glanced at each other and nodded.

"Where you stayin'?"

"Got a camp west of town next to a creek," said Babe.

"That'd be Rock Creek. Most of the other boys are makin' a delivery. Should be back by tomorrow….Send my little brother out to see you."

"What's his handle?"

"Pink."

LOOKOUT HILL
CHICKASAW NATION, IT

The smooth-shaven man drew rein near Red Eagle, leaned forward and crossed his arms over his saddle horn. "How do?"

"Not good as like."

"Noticed...If you'll uncock that shooter you got on the other side of your leg there, I'll step down and take a look."

Cyrus's eyebrows went up ever so slightly. He raised his pistol, let the hammer down easily and slipped it back into his holster. "What are you called?"

"Bill Roberts or Brushy Bill...Most of the time...You?"

"Osí Hommá...Chickasaw scout for the 2nd Cavalry. Christian name, Cyrus Maytubbi."

Bill stepped down and dropped his reins to the ground. "Well, Red Eagle, how'd you get in such a fix?" He opened his saddle bags and took out a small black leather kit.

His eyebrows went up for the second time. "Speak the people's tongue."

"'Nuff to get by. Prefer English or Spanish though."

"English odd tongue, but do."

Bill pulled the bloody shirt away. "Reckon you can roll over to your other side?"

Cyrus nodded, gritted his teeth and moaned slightly as he shifted his hips to better expose the exit wound. Bill gently scraped the mud and leaves off away from the ragged holes with his bone-handled belt knife.

"Damnation! Them holes weren't made by no handgun."

"Gatling gun, .45-70. Detachment take to Fort Washita. Cowboys drivin' herd of cattle south…kilt 'em. Kilt 'em all…and then kilt all of the patrol followin'…all but me." He grunted as Bill washed the rest of the clay away with his canteen, and then sprinkled some powered alum from a packet on the wounds. "Ambush, three mile or so back down trail toward the Red."

"Yeah, been followin' that bunch from Healdton. They're horse thieves too."

"They do all…steal, kill…Take big gun with them."

"Not really what I wanted to hear…Well, they'll have to wait. Gotta get you to a doctor."

"Red Eagle does not think he can mount horse…You make travois?"

"I can…" Bill took his blanket from behind his cantle and ripped several long strips and bound the Indian's wounds. "Here take the canteen while I go down toward that creek yonder and cut some saplin's…Got a pint of whisky in my saddle bags if you'd prefer…Might dull the pain some."

"Could use shot of fire-water…You do not mind?"

Bill walked back to his horse and pulled the flask from his saddle bags. "Naw, have one with you when I get back," he said as he handed him the pint bottle, and then turned and eased down the still lush blue stem and buffalo grass covered slope to the small tree-lined creek.

SKEANS BOARDING HOUSE

Bodie slipped a dollar to the cabbie after he unloaded his and Annabel's luggage from the back of the two-seat style buck wagon with a fringed top. "Much obliged."

"Ya'll have a nice day, hear?" The driver flicked the ribbons over the single bay horse's rump. "Come up there, Daisy."

"Well, Missus Hickman, this is home for a while." He picked up their four bags under both arms.

"It's a beautiful house, Mister Hickman...Reminds me of homes back in Montgomery."

"I'll come back and get your trunk."

"Do you think it'll be all right?"

"Pretty, we could leave it out here for a week and it'd be alright...'cept for gettin' rained on."

She looked up and down the pleasant tree-canopied street at the big, well-kept Victorian houses built along both sides. Some were red brick from the local plant and some were wood sided—mostly painted white—with elegant columns up to the second floor.

"Oh, my goodness!"

They turned to see Faye stepping down the steps from the porch—her full length forest green lindsey-woolsey skirt swishing as she moved.

"Faye, this is..."

"I wasn't expecting ya'll until tomorrow." She quickly stepped up to Annabel and gave her a hug. "You're every bit as pretty as Bodie said you were and then some...I'm glad I already aired out ya'll suite upstairs and put fresh flowers in it."

"Oh, bless your heart, Faye, that's so sweet. You didn't have to do that."

"I also moved the rest of your things, Bodie. I had to rent your old room. It was only for two days though."

"Oh?"

"A cowboy from south Texas, Walt Durbin, by name. But he found work at the Sullivant ranch. It was such a shame, rustlers murdered four of Tom's men a few days back."

"Dang! Reckon I'll have to be headin' out there."

"You won't be going anywhere, mister, until we get settled in and you eat something. I'll not have you traipsing around the country on an empty stomach."

"But, Honey…"

"No 'but, Honey' about it. You heard what I said."

"Yes, Ma'am."

"See she's got you trained already." Faye grinned. "Supper will be ready in just a bit…Besides, Tom Sullivant and his daughter, Francis Ann, are coming over. They may bring Walt along too, he left some of his stuff here. You can talk to them while you're enjoying my fried chicken."

"Do you need some help in the kitchen, Faye?"

"You get unpacked first and then I'll be happy to accept your kind offer. I've already got an apple pie in the oven, but need to peel some potatoes to put on to boil for smashing. I add chopped chives and crumbled bacon, make patties, roast them and put a dollop of sour cream on top."

Annabel grinned. "Yummy…My grandmother used to make those…I'm an old hand at peeling potatoes."

Bodie shook his head as he hitched up the bags and headed toward the porch. "Think I'm gonna be outnumbered."

Faye and Annabel glanced at each other, winked, nodded and walked arm in arm up the steps.

ROCK CREEK
COOKE COUNTY, TEXAS

Bass set about building a fire for their evening meal while Jack scrounged around for deadfall. He walked over next to the pit and dropped an armload of dry wood.

"What do you think?"

"'Bout what?" Bass replied without looking up from constructing his tinder base.

"Reckon they bought it?"

"Who?"

"Now don't pull that horse crap on me...You know damn well who."

Bass got his starter pile lit and as it blazed up he looked at Jack and flashed a big toothy grin. "Well, 'spect we'll find out soon enough when that Pink feller comes out."

"Hellova name for a man...Pink."

"Meby it's short for Pinkerton."

Jack cast him a rolled eye look. "Not likely."

"Don't know...I've heard of the Lee brothers, they's another, named Jim. Nefarious boys if they ever was any...Stealin', killin'...Just never enough evidence to get paper on 'em." Bass added some larger pieces of wood to the fire and set the coffee pot on a flat rock at the edge of the pit.

"Things go right, might remedy that."

Bass' big gray stallion blew and looked off to the east.

"What's botherin' Smoke?"

"Somebody comin'." Bass nodded toward a large red oak at the edge of the camp.

Jack nodded back—since years with Bass had made a lot of words unnecessary—pulled his Marlin from the boot on his saddle next to his bed roll and stepped over behind the big tree.

In a few minutes, a voice came from a thicket of cedars. "Haloo the camp."

"Come on in, but keep yer hands where I can see 'em. Would surely hate to punch yer ticket 'fore supper," said Bass as he readjusted his eye patch.

Rube stepped out from the shadows, his hands well away from his sides. "Wouldn't be real high on my list neither."

Jack walked out from behind the oak the same time the man entered the camp. Rube glanced his way and noticed the big lever action rifle in his hands.

"Ya'll play it cautious, don'tcha?"

"Experience," said Bass. "Have a sit, just put the coffee on to boil. Be ready in a bit."

Rube nodded, pulled his battered hat from his head, wiped the band with his red paisley neckerchief and sat down on a log the two men had drug up close to the fire pit. "'Bliged."

"What kin we do you for?" asked Jack/Babe.

"Reckon I owe you," he said looking at Bass/Ben. "I knowd you could have kilt me...if you'd been of a mind. Hell, thought I was purty fast with a gun...but, by God, today I seen a man."

"It ain't the fast...it's the want to. An' you didn't really want to shoot me...You had a notion, but it just wadn't in you. You was just tryin' to make a point...out of ignernce er foolishness...an' if everbody in the world was kilt fer bein' ignernt on one thing er another, er a fool...why I 'spect they wouldn't be many folks left."

Rube came close to smiling and nodded. "Well, taught me a purty good lesson an' I'm glad I'm still around to use it."

"An' that would be?" asked Babe.

"Don't judge a cow horse er a man...by his color." He stuck out his hand.

Ben nodded, grinned and pumped his hand. "It's a sad day that passes when a man don't learn somethin'...How 'bout some coffee?"

"Don't mind if'n I do."

Ben poured some of the stout trail brew into a blue and white speckled graniteware cup and handed it to Rube.

He blew across the top and took a sip. "Umm, good coffee." He exhaled. "Now that's off'n my chest..." He paused and looked off into the gathering shadows and then back. "...they's somethin' else..."

SKEANS BOARDING HOUSE

"Pass the chicken, please Miz Floyd."

79

"Bodie Hickman! You've already had three pieces."

"It's all right, child, let the boy eat. You forget he's sat at my table before."

"This is mighty fine chicken, Faye. Believe I'll have another piece myself," said Tom Sullivant.

"Daddy!"

"Now Francis Ann, we've been tryin' to teach Sing Loo how to make fried chicken for over two years…he's still puttin' soy sauce in the batter and tryin' to roast it…I'm goin' to enjoy this while I can…So there." He bobbed his head one time at her for emphasis.

"Well, ya'll just save some room for my apple pie."

"Miz Faye, if I had to holler out a leg, I wouldn't miss your pie."

She blushed. "Why thank you Mister Durbin, that's very kind."

"And it's still just Walt, Ma'am."

"It is 'hollow out', Mister Durbin, not 'holler', if you must insist on using such metaphors."

"Yes, Ma'am, Miz Floyd…I apologize."

"Gentlemen, I brought some fine Cuban cigars, if you'd like to join me out on the porch for an after-dinner smoke…We can talk about this rustling plague and how to end it."

"I'll be joining you also, Daddy…but without one of those smelly cigars. After all, I do run the horse operation."

"Yes, sweetheart, I was going to invite you…of course."

She cocked a shapely red eyebrow. "Uh, huh."

ROCK CREEK

"I know who you are."

"Oh, an' just who would that be?"

"You'd be Bass Reeves..." Rube looked across the fire. "...an' that'd make you be Jack McGann, Deputy United States Marshals out of Judge Parker's court." He blew on his coffee again and took another sip. "They cut 'em wide and deep where ya'll come from."

Bass and Jack exchanged looks.

"Why didn't you say nothin' back in town?" asked Jack.

"Didn't come to me 'til later on...after I thought on it some. Seen you in Sand Springs one time...without the eye patch. Put a hellova whuppin' a big giant of a man..."

"That would have been Bear Man Bannack. He stung me once er twict."

"But you dropped him like fellin' a tree...You coulda arrested him fer assaultin' a law officer...but you didn't."

"Figured he'd been punished enough...plus it was a straight up fight...just knuckles and skulls."

"You're a fair man, Bass Reeves...not like a lot of lawdogs I've had truck with."

"Well, sir, meby the law ain't perfect, but it's the only one we got and without it...we got nuthin'."

Rube nodded.

"Once you figured out who we was, how come you didn't tell Lee then?' asked Jack.

"Well, one, guess mayhap you're right, Bass...Ain't really got the stomach fer killin'...leastwise, not in cold blood like some of the others...They kilt four men workin' fer the Rafter S last week, rustlin' some horses...Never seen a horse yet worth killin' a man over. Two, Pink and them made it back just a little bit ago...Heard Tom tell him 'bout ya'll...He'll be comin' out of the mornin'." Rube stopped, grabbed the handle of the coffee pot with his kerchief and refilled his cup. "They're gonna have you kill that young Ranger that's been snappin' at their heels to prove yerselves..."

Jack and Bass exchanged glances.

"...An' three, been lookin' fer a good reason to head on down the trail and git a real job brush poppin' on a cattle ranch down south."

Bass took out his old worn rosewood pipe from his vest pocket, filled it from a doeskin pouch, grabbed a burning twig from the edge of the fire and lit it.

Jack grinned as he knew when Bass pulled out his pipe—he had some thinking to do.

He puffed a couple of times on the sweet smelling aromatic mix, and then blew a big blue cloud over his head. "Tell you what do, Rube...believe I got a better idee."

HEALDTON, IT
CHICKASAW NATION

Doctor Chadwell pushed his Ben Franklin glasses back up on his nose, grabbed a white cotton towel from the cart beside the stainless steel table and wiped his hands. "Well, Cyrus, Mister Roberts did a fair-to-middling job on fixing you up good enough to travel. You were lucky that slug didn't hit anything vital. You'da bled to death."

"Red Eagle been a whole lot luckier not to have gotten hit at all."

"Those Gatling guns are nasty. Hard to miss with one," offered Bill.

"Need to take those stitches out in about a week to ten days...Other than being sore as a risin' for a while, you should be able to travel by tomorrow." He handed him a small green bottle of laudanum. "Take a bit of this if it gets to paining you. just be sure to drink lots of water...you lost quite a bit of blood."

Bill nodded. "Need to get to Ardmore soon as we can and report what happened to Marshal Lindsey so he can forward the information on to Colonel Scott at Fort Sill...The man won't be pleased."

"I'll notify the sheriff, he'll want to send out a wagon crew for the bodies," said Chadwell. "'Spect I'll have to write a mess of death certificates."

Bill nodded.

"Ardmore less than twenty miles, Bill, Red Eagle make...Can see Chickasaw shaman, Anompoli Lawa there if need more medicine...We cousins."

"Winchester Ashalatubbi? Hell of a good doctor...I think he's cousins to about half of the Chickasaw Nation. Go to him myself when I come down with the croup or something," said Dr. Chadwell. "Be sure not to get those bandages wet when you cross Walnut Bayou."

"Not over belly deep to a horse right now, Doc, just crossed it yesterday…Well, Cyrus, let's go over to May's Cafe and get some supper. Big bowl of chicken soup will go a long way toward fixin' you up and take care of this grumblin' in my stomach."

"How much Red Eagle owe?"

"Oh, I expect two dollars will cover it."

Cyrus grunted and fished out two silver dollars from his money pouch in his vest and handed them over. Bill assisted him in putting on a new shirt he had picked up from the mercantile and then his vest.

"Give Winchester a howdy for me."

SKEANS BOARDING HOUSE

"So now ya'll know," said Walt. "Got here quick as I could when I got the word from Bodie." He drew on the expensive Cuban cigar and blew a cloud of smoke downwind, away from Francis.

She winked at the ranger and mouthed, "Thank you."

Walt ducked his head and blushed in embarrassment. "Yessum."

"Can't be helped. What happened, happened," added Tom, ruefully. "But it's nice we're gonna have two rangers workin' on this."

"Well, we'll keep Walt's identity and presence here quiet." Bodie paused for a moment. "It's like they waited 'til I left town for the Nations before they hit...Can't figure out how they knew."

"It wasn't a big secret, Bodie. Think everybody in the county knew you were getting married." Francis grinned and took a sip of the brandy she had brought out on the porch. "...And that we got in some new brood mares from south Texas. They just picked the wrong herd to hit."

"I know Fran...but, something just seems a bit antigodlin."

***

CHAPTER FIVE

ROCK CREEK
COOKE COUNTY, TEXAS

The sun threw crimson and purple arrows across the eastern
horizon and had just climbed above the trees when four men
rode up to the camp.

"Step down, gentlemen, coffee's still hot," Bass said
without looking around as he poured himself a cup.

Pink Lee, Bully Jack, Windy Folsom and Rube Carter tied
their horses to some saplings at the edge of the clearing next to
the creek and walked toward Bass and the fire. Jack stepped out
from his place behind the tree with his rifle—Lee turned in his
direction.

"Won't be needin' that…Take it you're Babe."

"You take right."

"Help yerselves to the coffee, if'n you brought cups."

"Had some, Glass."

Windy, Bully and Rube started to separate away from Pink to spread out.

"Don't think I'd move any further, boys...Wouldn't be real healthy," said Bass/Ben.

"You think you kin take the four of us, do you?" asked Windy.

Ben grinned as he rose to his feet. "You feel lucky enough this mornin' to find out, slick?" There was an unmistakable trace of ice in his voice.

Babe slowly pulled back the hammer to full cock on his Marlin—the click was audible in the brief silence.

"Pink?" asked Bully.

"Better do like the man says...Think they mean business."

"Tend to live longer thataway," said Ben. "Now, what do you have for us...or are you just lost?"

"You got a real mouth on you, boy."

"Just cuttin' to the chase...an' I'm not yer boy," he hissed as his obsidian eye locked on Pink.

Pink held his hands up in front of his chest and took a half step backward. "Alright, no reason to get hostile...Got a little somethin' I would like for you...men to do. Call it a right to passage."

"Right to passage? What the hell does that mean?" asked Babe.

"Means you have to prove yourselves...See if you kin foller orders."

"Uh, huh...So what's the job?" inquired Ben.

"Well see, there's this here Texas Ranger that's gettin' a mite too close for comfort...Kill him."

Ben and Babe exchanged glances.

"If it's anythin' like killin' a marshal up in the Nations, ain't the brightest thing to do. Kill one, the judge sends four," said Babe.

"Purty much the same with the Texas Rangers, 'ceptin' the new one's would have to start all over...an' we should be done by then," replied Pink.

"Sounds reasonable. What's this here ranger's name?"

"Bodie Hickman...He's a second generation ranger and tough as ten year old rawhide."

"Don't mean he's bullet proof," mumbled Babe.

"Exactly...Well?" questioned Pink.

"We kin do it," said Ben.

"You can take these three with you."

Ben chuckled and pitched the rest of his coffee into the fire where it sizzled on one of the logs. "Don't think so. Don't need 'em or want 'em...just be in the way."

"How am I gonna know the job is done?"

"You kin see whose lips is movin' when yer told." Ben looked the three men over. "Or you can send the big dumb one there. I already got his attention back in town yesterday...Didn't I, Rube?"

Carter looked ashamedly at his feet.

"I heard," said Pink. "Alright, just do it…the ranger got back in town with his new wife yesterday. Stayin' at Skeans Boardin' House in Gainesville."

"We'll find him. Just keep the rest of yer men outta our way…Oh, by the way, we git a hunderd dollars fer killin' a lawdog…Twenty in ad-vance."

Pink looked at the big black man for a long moment. "Done." He fished in his vest for a double eagle, pitched it to Ben and nodded to the others—except for Rube—as they stepped to their horses. "We'll be in touch."

"Nope. It'll be the other way around," said Ben.

ARDMORE, IT
CHICKASAW NATION

Bill and Cyrus slowed from an easy jog trot to a walk as they entered Main Street from the west. The steel shoes on their horses' hooves made clicking sounds on the recently red bricked boulevard.

Roberts glanced at his Chickasaw companion. "You hangin' in there, Cyrus?"

He reached in his vest pocket and removed the small green pharmaceutical bottle, pulled the cork and took another swig of the light brown cocaine-based laudanum and wrinkled his face. "Worse than spoilt bear meat, plus Red Eagle can't think when take. He will call it stupid syrup."

"But it does dull the pain, don't it?"

"Does that…But not sure it worth being like have blanket cover head."

They reined up in front of the US Marshals Office just one block off Main Street on Jefferson. Bill tied off and stepped around to help Cyrus from the saddle just as Deputy Marshal Loss Hart opened the door and stepped out on the boardwalk.

"Dang, Bill, why didn't you holler or somethin'?"

He quickly moved to assist the smaller man with Cyrus. "Why this is Cyrus Maytubbi, he's a Lighthorse and sometimes scout for the cavalry. Knowed him for years…What's the matter Red Eagle, broke ribs?"

He shook his head. "Two holes in side…Almost see through."

"Doggies, Cyrus, you cain't be feelin' all that rough, crackin' jokes thataway."

"No joke, Loss, Gatling round went completely through just above the hip," said Bill. "Doc Chadwell over to Healdton stitched him up yesterday…Selden around?"

"Inside."

"Need mayhap see Annompli Lawa. Think pulled some stitches loose in ride from Healdton. Front hole bleedin' again," grunted Cyrus through his teeth.

"Ya'll go on in, coffee's on. I'll go fetch Doc Ashalatubbi."

They nodded at Loss as he turned and strode along the boardwalk toward Winchester's office two blocks down Jefferson Street.

Roberts assisted Cyrus through the door. Marshal Selden Lindsey jumped up from his desk on the far side of the room.

"Bill! What happened?" He rushed over and helped move Cyrus to a bunk against the south wall.

The Chickasaw moaned slightly as they eased him down on top of the gray wool blanket. Selden removed his scalloped top cavalry style boots and set them on the floor next to the iron framed bunk.

"Need some coffee, Cyrus?" asked Selden.

"Water will do, Marshal."

Lindsey felt of the man's forehead. "Runnin' a bit of the fever."

"Loss went to fetch Doctor Ashalatubbi," said Bill.

"Good friend of mine...Chickasaw shaman and a licensed physician as well as a doctor of divinity. He can birth you, doctor over you, git you hitched, shoo away the evil spirits and bury you if need be," said Selden.

"Sounds like a man that's good to know," said Bill.

"He is that. Patched up Jack McGann more'n once."

"Bass tell you what's goin' on?"

"Got a telegram, said you'd fill in the details...You know Bass, not one to use a lotta words."

"Don't know him well, but appears he'll do to ride the river with."

"That and then some...Damn sure not a man I'd want to piss off."

"I'll keep that in mind."

The front door opened—Loss and Winchester stepped inside. The doctor carried a small black valise.

"Winchester, this is Marshal Roberts. Bill, Doc Ashalatubbi."

"My pleasure, Doc, heard about you from Doctor Chadwell over to Healton."

"Fine man and physician. We studied together at the medical college...University of Nashville," he said as he bent over Cyrus and started unbuttoning his shirt. He noticed a fresh blood stain about the size of an apple just above the top of his pants. "Well, well, Osí Hommá, looks like you pulled a stitch."

He leaned Cyrus into an upright position and unwound the bandage. "Doesn't look too serious. Chadwell did a fine job...Apparently you did not follow his instructions to rest." He felt of his forehead, reached in his bag and got a small brown bottle. "Drink some of this white willow extract...Help bring down the fever."

MERCHANT'S BANK OF ARDMORE

Two men in dusty three piece dark suits stood watch outside the bank door—both leaned against the side of the building—one casually rolled a cigarette.

"Everybody put your hands in the air. We're making a withdrawal," the burly leader, Wild Sam Patterson, said as he waved his Remington about inside the bank.

The window clerks reacted with astonishment to the two men with guns and shoved their hands rapidly into the air.

Three customers, one elderly woman and two local businessmen at the counter also raised their hands.

"You two, on the floor. You can remain standing, Ma'am, but keep your hands up."

The two men did as Patterson bid.

The president, Tarlton Whipple, got up from his desk. "I beg your pardon..."

"We're holding you up, fat boy...Now, I 'spect you're smart enough to behave yourselves."

"This is an outrage! You can't..."

Sam's younger brother, Henry, stepped up, stuck his Schofield under Whipple's nose and lifted the sixty year old man up to his tiptoes and growled, "Shut up, old man! Git over there and seddown."

Tarlton hastily moved to comply. Henry tossed a cotton grain sack to one of the clerks who caught it, taking a nervous step backward.

Patterson came around the counter toward him. "Fill it! And don't take all day."

The teller's eyes darted nervously from one robber to another as he racked his brain for some way to stall the proceedings. "But...but, I can't."

"What do you mean, you can't?" demanded Sam.

"Well, s'r...I mean...well, there's a time lock on the safe and we just set it...Bein' near closin' time."

Patterson stepped in close to him and shoved the barrel of his pistol hard against the side of his head. "I happen to know better, sonny. Now you got a choice…open up that safe or I open your head…What'll it be? Up to you."

The clerk swallowed hard, knowing that his attempted ruse had failed, he moved rapidly to the safe.

CITY MARSHAL'S OFFICE

A large black man, Pepper Washington, and a skinny, dark-eyed, pock-faced breed, John Shwadlenak, lounged on either side of the door. Pepper noticed the bench beside him, slumped down on it and was joined by John.

MERCHANT'S BANK OF ARDMORE

The first clerk stuffed bundles of money into the grain sack while Patterson kept him covered. Henry stepped to the window and peered around the edge of the shade to see outside while the second clerk stole surreptitious glances at a nearby desk.

"Come on, come on. Hurry it up!" demanded Sam.

The clerk, prodded by Patterson's gun, worked faster.

CITY MARSHAL'S OFFICE

The two outlaws still sat on the bench to the right of the front door. Pepper had a stick of butterscotch candy in his mouth.

The door opened and a white-haired town marshal with a long drooping mustache and his twenty-nine year old red-haired, freckled-faced deputy came out.

"Buy you a cup of coffee down at Sally's. How 'bout it?" the deputy asked.

"Jest take you up on that."

Washington pulled his pistol while the half-breed got to his feet to cover the pair of lawmen.

"Hold it right there, neighbors. The coffee can wait." Pepper stepped in behind them.

"What in Sam hill?..."

"Shut up, grampaw an' git back inside!"

The two lawmen glanced at one another, turned and sullenly went back inside the office, followed by their captors.

They quickly slugged their captives from behind with their gun barrels. Pepper struck the old marshal an particularly vicious blow that knocked his uncreased crown black hat from his head.

A puddle of blood quickly began to spread around the marshal's head as soon as he hit the floor. Shwadlenak holstered his gun and bent down over the old man

"You done kilt yerself a law."

He raised back up, glaring at his cold-blooded companion. Washington's only reply was a loud sucking noise on the candy. The half-breed turned and stalked out the door, leaving Pepper to gaze after him—a smirky grin on his face.

MERCHANT'S BANK OF ARDMORE

The first teller finished putting all the paper money from the safe in the off-white bag. "That's it, Mister. That's all there is."

The leader of the gang, Sam Patterson, grabbed the sack away from the clerk and motioned to the others.

The second teller—a bit older than the first—edged cautiously nearer the desk, never letting his eyes leave the bandits as they rushed toward the door. He lunged, jerked open a drawer and came up with a .38 revolver, took quick aim and squeezed off a shot.

Patterson was almost out the door when the clerk's bullet splintered the paneling near his head. He whirled, swung his Remington around and fired. The .44 caliber round struck the teller squarely in the center of his chest and propelled him violently backward against the near wall.

The portly bank president and the first teller stretched their arms even higher over their heads.

Patterson started to turn and go, hesitated and then changed his mind. He cocked his pistol and coldly gunned down both men. The elderly woman screamed and collapsed to the floor in a dead faint.

US MARSHAL'S OFFICE

"Gunfire!" exclaimed Loss as he jumped to his feet.

"Sounds like it came from down to the bank," added Selden. He grabbed a Winchester and a double barrel twelve gauge from the rack on the wall and quickly headed out the door, followed by Loss and Bill. "We'll be back, Doc!" He pitched the shotgun to Hart.

"In one piece, please, gentlemen."

"That's the general idea," Bill yelled over his shoulder

They sprinted down the boardwalk toward the bank only a block down the street, separating as they ran.

MERCHANT'S BANK OF ARDMORE

The two men outside, Eller Newsome and Hardin Broyles stared excitedly at the bank door, drawing their pistols as the Patterson brothers exited rapidly from the bank and sprinted to their horses yelling at the others to come on.

Washington and Shwadlenak dashed across the street toward their horses as a few curious citizens appeared from doorways along the street. Sam fired his pistol in the air several times to frighten the spectators. The trick had its effect as the onlookers quickly ducked back inside.

Selden ducked behind a water trough, Loss slipped in the doorway of a millinery shop while Bill walked straight down the middle of the street firing his .41 caliber Colt from the shoulder as he moved. His first shot knocked Henry from his feet.

Sam saw his brother go down and wheeled toward Bill. "Damn you!" He cocked the pistol and squeezed the trigger, but his hammer clicked on an empty chamber—he hadn't reloaded.

Bill's second shot from fifty feet away took the leader between the eyes. He got a surprised look on his face as a thin trickle of blood started running down the side of his nose, and then his knees buckled and he fell forward on his face.

Pepper threw a shot at Roberts—the round tugged at the side of his unbuttoned vest. Selden raised up and levered off two quick shots at the big black man, both catching him in the center of his chest no more than two inches apart.

Shwadlenak panic fanned at Lindsey, two shots hitting the side of the concrete trough and whining off and two more impacting the water, drenching the marshal.

Loss dove to the boardwalk, rolled over and pulled both triggers at the same time. The half-breed was lifted completely off his feet and thrown violently to his back as he took both charges of the double-ought buckshot.

Eller Newsome managed to mount his horse and spurred at full gallop—sparks flying—straight at Bill, firing at every beat of his horse's pounding hooves.

Roberts calmly took the old time dueler's sideways stance and extended his right arm as bullets ricocheted from the bricks around him. He fired once. Newsome flipped backward off his charging steed, hit the brick street, tumbled and finally rolled to a stop at Bill's feet as his frightened horse galloped past—he was dead when he hit the ground.

Hardin Broyles threw down his gun and held his hands high in the air. "I give! I give."

Selden and Loss got to their feet—Hart reloaded the shotgun from the shells he always carried in his coat pocket. Bill snapped open the loading gate at the back of the cylinder to his Colt, ejected the empty brass and thumbed in reloads from the rounds in his belt. The three men walked toward the lone outlaw survivor.

Lindsey stuck his foot under the leader's body and rolled him over. "Well, howdy do, howdy do...Looky here, Loss! Wild Sam Patterson...Been looking all over the territory for this nabob and his gang and they try to rob a bank a block from our office and fall right in our laps."

"They's a right smart of rewards on this bunch...'ccordin' to the wanted dodgers," said Loss as he put wrist shackles on Broyles.

"Let's get this mo-ron down to the lockup and send a telegram to the judge," said Lindsey.

"Why don't we give him a call on that new sound telegraphy we have in the office?"

"Don't trust it. What if he ain't there?...Think it's a fad anyway...never last."

"Probably true."

Lindsey turned to Roberts. "Dadgum, Bill, ain't never seen nobody do what you did."

"What's that?"

"Just stand there calm as you please and squeeze off a round at that jasper...him shootin' all the while he was ridin' down on you."

Bill grinned. "I've found that folks don't shoot very straight when they're scared and tryin' to run away, Selden."

"He coulda got a lucky shot off," said Loss.

"Coulda…but didn't."

"Well, none the less, need to send the hostler over fer their horses…Six. Reckon that's two apiece. Bring a nice penny," said Loss.

"Pretty good lookin' stock. Might have to borrow those six for a spell…If ya'll don't mind?"

"That rustlin' thing you're supposed to fill us in on, Bill?" asked Selden.

"Exactly…Bait."

Loss opened the door to the office and pushed Broyles inside. Bill and Lindsey followed with their arms loaded down with guns and gunbelts.

Winchester looked up. "Anybody I need to tend to? Sounded like a war going on out there."

"Reckon not Doc, the rest are past any help…but from the Almighty and the undertaker," said Selden.

"How many?"

"Four citizens and five miscreants."

"Who were the citizens?"

"City Marshal Barton, the president of the bank, Whipple, two of his window clerks and Deputy Rollie Parwell has a goose egg on his noggin, but that's all."

"Pity. Whipple was a pompous ass and a bit prideful on occasion, but otherwise easy to get along with…."

"Pride is a rooster crowin' on a cow pie, Doc," commented Bill.

Winchester grinned and nodded. "So true, so true."

Loss noticed Cyrus snoring on the bunk. "Pass out, did he?"

"Not really, just gave him a double strong dose of laudanum. He won't wake up until in the morning...Needed the rest and I wasn't inclined to argue about it...Gentlemen, if you require anything further...You know how to find me. Guess I should check on the deputy...could have a concussion."

"Thanks Doc, 'preciate it," said Bill.

Winchester nodded, snapped his bag closed, grabbed his tall uncreased crowned black hat from the hall tree and headed out the door.

Selden stepped over to the black potbellied stove in the far corner and filled his white ceramic coffee mug. "You want to bring us up to snuff now, Bill?...Since we were so rudely interrupted before you could get started earlier."

"Yep, but only if you'll pour me a cup while you're up."

Lindsey grinned and nodded. "Take anything in it?"

"Nope, wouldn't want to spoil it."

"Selden made that batch...Don't think you could tell the difference."

"Well you know the old camp rule, Loss...Don't like the cookin', do it yerself."

"Didn't say I didn't like it, just said Bill wouldn't be able to tell the difference."

"Lord have mercy...A Gatling gun!" exclaimed Loss when Bill had finished giving the two marshals the rundown. "They kin hold off an army with that thing."

"That's what Cyrus said…The caisson was loaded with ammunition, too," added Bill.

"Damnation! Not only do we have to figure out all the players at the table, but where they took that gun on top," said Lindsey.

"I suspect we find where it is…we'll find the boss man too," commented Bill.

Selden got to his feet and warmed up his coffee at the stove. "Might be like catching a panther lion by the tail."

"Could be, but as they say in Latin…*praemonitus, praemunitus*," said Bill.

"Come again?" inquired Loss.

"Forewarned is forearmed."

"Why didn't you just say so?"

Bill grinned and got to his feet. "Thought I did…Bass and them will be checkin' in here sometime today…Reckon I'll go down to the depot and send a telegram to Ranger Hickman in care of the Santa Fe depot in Gainesville."

"How come the depot?" asked Selden.

"Instructions from Bodie. Don't know who we can trust and who we can't. Too chancy sending it to the regular Western Union office…too many nosey eyes and ears. There's folks beside the telegrapher who can decipher Morse code when they hear it, you know?…Just like readin' Indian smoke over in New Mexico and Arizona."

"You been to New Mexico?" asked Loss.

"I have…Worked for John Chisum in Lincoln County for a while some years back."

"Used to have a ranch just south of Gainesville...Heard tell he was a hoss."

"He was that, Selden. He was that...Partnered with John Tunstall and Alexander McSween 'til Tunstall got killed by Sheriff Brady...But, Chisum? Hell, quit just wasn't in his vocabulary...Died of the pneumonia though, in '84. Buried him in Paris, Texas."

"Rumor has it that Billy the Kid worked for Chisum, too."

"You don't say?" Roberts grabbed his sombrero and headed out the door.

SANTA FE DEPOT
GAINESVILLE, TEXAS

Bodie walked up to the ticket window. "Got a telegram for Bodie Hickman?

The bespeckled balding ticket agent and telegrapher inside with a green eye shade looked up at the ranger. "Name again?"

"Hickman, Bodie Hickman." He turned and looked around while the little man checked the missives.

"Here we go." He started to hand the yellow envelope through the window, stopped and pulled it back. "Hold on...How do I know you're you?"

"Well if I wern't me, who would I be?"

The little man squinted his eyes underneath the shade and scratched his chin. "I reckon you could be anybody you were a mind to be...Why, any ol' jakeleg could say they were you...Don't you see?"

Bodie pulled aside his vest to show the Texas Ranger badge, custom made from a Mexican five peso silver coin pinned to his shirt, and then unfolded his Warrant of Authority from the Texas Adjutant General's Office.

The agent paled a little. "Oh, yes, sir, Ranger. Sorry, can't be too careful these days. I'm charged with the security of these telegrams by the railroad and to make sure they get to the proper party." He handed the message through the window.

"I'll mention your name in my report. You're doin' a fine job, yessir, a fine job…But keep it quiet that I got a telegram here, if you don't mind. It'll be our little secret." Bodie stuck the envelope into an inside pocket of his vest.

"Yes, sir, Ranger. My name is Percy Gilhooley, sir."

"Percy Gilhooley…Got it." He glanced around again and leaned in close to the window. "Thank you…First Assistant Texas Ranger Gilhooley." Bodie winked, nodded and put his finger to his lips.

Percy also put his finger to his lips and nodded back. "Ranger Assistant…Gollybob!" He watched as the ranger walked toward the end of the depot.

When Bodie was out of sight of the window, he stopped, leaned against the side of the wooden building, opened and read the flimsey. He looked around and only saw a cowboy across the street sitting on a bench under a live oak tree, smoking a cigarette. He wadded up the thin yellow paper and pitched it into a trash receptacle at the corner of the depot in front of the hitching rail.

He cinched up Moon, stepped into the stirrup and lithely swung into the saddle. The dun tucked his nose and backed up five or six steps—Bodie reined him to the right, clucked and trotted over the red bricks toward California Street.

The cowboy watched the ranger until he had ridden past the two story Turner Hotel on the corner. He then got up, crushed the butt of his cigarette out under the heel of his boot and moseyed easily across the street to the trash can. He nonchalantly glanced around, reached in, grabbed the wadded up ball of paper, stuffed it in his jeans pocket and walked to his own grulla horse back across the street.

**

CHAPTER SIX

WOLF RUN RIDGE
COOKE COUNTY

"Dang, looky here, Bass." Jack pointed to a fossilized ammonite shell almost two feet in diameter—from the Cretaceous period—lying on top of the ground near a limestone outcrop at their new camp just northwest of Gainesville.

"What do you suppose it is…or was?"

"I seen somethin' like it in a book once. Some kind of sea shell with sort of a snail inside."

"A snail that big? Musta been kinda unusual," Bass commented.

"Uh-uh. Look around…they're ever size, some littler and by the Lord Harry, look over yonder…A real biggun." He pointed to another outcrop at the edge of the tree line. "Feller could build himself a rock house out of these things."

"Must have been some big critters back then...What do you think, five or six hunderd years ago?"

"Lot longer than that, I'd wager. All this here had to be under the ocean for them kind of animals," Jack said.

"Under the ocean? Yer joshin'. Why we must be eight or nine hunderd feet high up on this here ridge...Looky yonder." Bass pointed to the northeast. "That's the Red way down there. No way this was underwater up here on top."

"What about Noah's flood in the Bible?...Huh? Tell me that. This all would have been underwater, right?"

"Well...I suppose you..."

Bass was interrupted by a hail from down in the draw created by South Fish Creek on the southern side of the ridge. "Haloo the camp."

"Come on up," Jack yelled back.

Rube's grulla picked his way through the scattered limestone rocks and trees up the side of the hill to the top of the bald ridge. His saddle creaked as he dismounted. After tying off the gelding to the branch of a nearby tree, he walked over to Bass and Jack on the other side of the camp where they were still looking at the fossils.

"I'll say one thing, good place ya'll picked for yer new camp...Knew where I was 'til I crossed the old Mormon Trail, then had the dickens of a time findin' it even with the directions an' rock cairn trail markers ya'll left...Don't think anybody is gonna be a sneakin' up on you."

"General idea…Pick up the message?"

"Did…Hickman done exactly like you said he would." He removed the wadded up yellow piece of paper from his pocket, straightened it out as best he could and started to hand it to Bass.

Jack reached out and took it instead. "Bass don't read writin'." He scanned the message briefly and whistled.

"Well? You gonna keep us in suspense all day?" asked Reeves.

"Yeah, yer gonna love this…From Brushy Bill."

After Jack finished reading through the telegram, Bass removed his hat, wiped his brow and then the hat band with his blue kerchief.

"Lordy, lordy."

"My sentiments exactly," said Jack.

"That Gatling Gun puts a whole new slant on this mission…an' I 'spect it may have changed the rustler's end game some, too."

"Reckon we'd better go ahead take care of that other business." Jack pulled a folded piece of paper out of his pocket and handed it to Rube. "Best be deliverin' this to that drop place Bodie picked out…You can count on him a checkin' on it later this afternoon."

"Yep, 'magine so…Don't like goin' there. Think they's haints…Meby I'll have a cup of coffee 'fore I go…'ny left?"

"They's plenty, go ahead…Have one with you," said Bass.

"Hate we gotta do this, but we've already started down the hill...No turnin' back now," added Jack.

GAINESVILLE, TEXAS
PECAN CREEK

It was just thirty minutes before sundown and the shadows were lengthening across the somewhat barren area on the east side of Pecan Creek—bordered on the north by California Street and on the south by Main. Rube's grulla balked at entering the place some folks in town thought to be haunted...

It was in October, 1862—seventeen months after the beginning of what some called the Civil War and others the War of Northern Aggression—that forty Union sympathizers were hanged over a three-week period—often as many as six or seven simultaneously. Known as the Great Gainesville Hanging, all forty were strung up from the same giant elm tree located on the east side of Pecan Creek by a kangaroo court of Confederates—two more men were shot trying to escape during the so-called trials.

Some years after the end of the war—in 1880—there was such growing consternation, guilt and denial throughout the community of Gainesville, that the citizens banded together, cut down and burned the hanging tree—including the stump. They thought that by removing the symbol of their shame, people would forget the tragedy—they didn't. The Great Hanging remained a taboo topic in the area for many generations. It would be called the largest mass lynching in the history of America.

The bonfire from the giant instrument of death had killed several large pecan trees nearby and it was the hollow stump of one of those trees that Bodie picked to be the secret drop for messages.

Rube tied his recalcitrant horse on the other side of the creek and walked across the Main Street bridge to the old hollow stump. *Damnation, this place is spooky. See why he picked it...nobody ever comes here.* He looked around. *Great God in Heaven...forty men died right here where I'm standin'.*

Rube looked over his head just to check there were no ghostly bodies hanging from a phantom tree. He shivered and pulled his jacket tighter around his shoulders even though the late afternoon was still quite warm. Carter removed the message from his pocket, closed his eyes and stuck it inside the long dead tree, and then turned and literally ran back to the bridge. He stopped at the edge, held on to the railing and took several deep breaths. *Jesus Christ, hope he picks another spot next time. Couldn't hardly breathe in there.*

He tightened up his cinch, stabbed his foot in the stirrup, mounted and rode west in the direction of Commerce Street. *I need a drink and I need it now.*

Just after he crossed the railroad tracks, he met Bodie Hickman on his dun, trotting in the opposite direction. The two men nodded at one another as folks will do when they pass. *Hope he don't mind goin' in that place as much as I did.*

The young ranger ground tied Moon just on the east side of the bridge as his horse also was apprehensive of entering the area. Bodie walked over to the hollow stump and retrieved the letter. "Come here, son," he called to the mustang as he folded the letter in half and put it in his shirt pocket.

Lakota Moon pawed the ground several times in protest.

"Well, come on," Bodie insisted.

He snorted, laid his ears back, turned his head slightly to the side to avoid stepping on his reins and walked reluctantly over to his master with a chuff as he shook his head from side to side, leaving no question that he was not pleased.

"Good boy...It's alright." He rubbed the faithful mustang between the eyes to settle him. Satisfied, Bodie flipped the right side rein over Moon's neck, held on to the left, stuck his toe in the leather bound, flat bottomed stirrup and swung easily into the saddle.

He eased back on the reins just as he reached the corner of Main and Dixon and looped the ribbons around his saddle horn as the dun came to a halt. Bodie pulled the letter out and began to read. "Oh, damn...Oh, double damn!" A pained look crossed his face as he dropped his chin to his chest and sighed.

RAFTER S RANCH
COOKE COUNTY

"This is fine horse country, Miss Fran, mighty fine," he commented as he observed the thick, knee high lush native blue stem and grama grass pasture still wet from the morning dew.

"I think just 'Fran' will be better, don't you? Or actually most of my close friends just call me 'Red'," Francis Ann replied as she and Walt Durbin rode along the northern fence line at a collected slow rocking-chair lope.

The ranger blushed slightly under his tan. "Yessum."

"And you needin' be shy about it either." She glanced sideways at the ruggedly handsome man. *This one is all man, plus he's not hard to look at and he knows horses, thank the Lord.* "Oh, no, look!" She pointed at the gap in the new four strand barb wire fence just ahead.

"Wire cutters."

They reined to a stop, Walt dismounted and checked the end of the cut wire. "Fresh cut." He cut about for sign. "Four horsemen, one dismounted, cut the wire and pulled it aside...See how the grass is just now startin' to straighten back up?"

"Very recent then?"

"Yep...came through less than an hour ago, I'd say and unless they went out at another spot...they're still on the property." He mounted Pepper and wheeled him toward Francis. "Why don't you ride back to the headquarters and send some of the other boys this way...I'll follow their tracks."

"Not on your life, Mister Durbin. They're after my bred mares." She unholstered her .44-40 caliber Peacemaker, opened the loading gate and added a sixth round from her belt.

"Alright, but stay behind me, please."

"Of course."

"Tracks are easy to follow through this fresh grass... Unusual they're hittin' in daylight."

"Maybe that's why they're doing it...because they think we won't be expecting it."

"Could be...How big is this pasture?"

"Between four and five hundred acres all told, in six open meadows. Probably another hundred in scattered timber."

"Which meadow do you reckon the mares are in?"

"No telling...It's obvious they hadn't been along the north line. I'm guessing the far west meadow...It's adjacent to the yearling trap. Horses are herd animals, they like to be together."

"Uh, yes, Ma'am...I know."

"Of course you do, how silly of me."

"No, Ma'am, horse people like to talk about horses. They're God's special creatures."

Francis glanced over at him as they nudged their mounts into a faster canter. "I like you, Walt...like you a lot."

"Uh, yes, Ma'am, I...uh like you too."

"I mean, anyone who understands and cares for horses like you do, is...well...you know."

"Oh...Yes, Ma'am."

They rode down a trail through a wooded creek bottom, ducking branches as they splashed through the shallow water and up the other side to the next meadow.

A shot rang out and a bullet slapped a tree trunk beside Walt's head as he broke from the woods. He drew his Colt and nudged Pepper into a gallop toward the four horsemen near the center of the meadow gathering a group of seven mares.

"Stay back, Red!" he shouted over his shoulder as he charged straight at the rustlers, firing at the run.

"Like hell!" She spurred her buckskin mare into a full gallop, matching Walt's gelding, firing her pistol in the same manner.

Durbin, glanced at the woman riding and firing almost abreast with him on his right. Her hat had blown off and was bouncing on her back, held there by its stampede string—her long flaming red hair streaming behind her. *Damn, that's a real woman.* He had a grim smile on his face as he turned back to the outlaws, fired his last round, holstered that gun and drew the matching ivory-handled pistol from his shoulder holster.

Simultaneously, two rustlers pitched from their saddles as both Fran and Walt hit their marks. The other two threw parting shots at the charging duo, wheeled and spurred their mounts toward the nearby woods in an effort to escape. Durbin scored again and a third man tumbled from his saddle, rolled several times and came to rest at the base of a large red oak in the tree line. The fourth disappeared into the dense woods.

"Let him go…Too dangerous to try to chase him through there." He reined Pepper to a sliding stop and turned in the saddle to watch her horse slow less dramatically. "You alright?"

Francis' alabaster skin turned even more pale as her blue eyes rolled back up into her head—she slowly slid from the saddle and fell to the ground. Her buckskin immediately stopped and stood dutifully next to her master. She reached her nose down to nuzzle the unconscious woman.

"Francis!" Walt shouted as he bailed from the saddle, rushed to the inert form and dropped to his knees. He gently rolled her over and cradled her in his arms. There was an ever-increasing circle of blood saturating her white blouse on the upper right side of her chest. "Oh, dear God!"

He whipped off his bandana, folded it and stuffed the red cotton cloth inside her shirt and over the wound—holding it there as he applied pressure to stop the bleeding. "Please, God, no...Please."

CHISHOLM TRAIL
CHICKASAW NATION

Bill studied what was left of the intermittent dim tracks of the caisson carrying the Gatling Gun. *Uh, huh, figures. Drove the cattle herd behind...pounded out most of the tracks, but couldn't have been more than fifty or so...Plus, that thundershower last night didn't help much.* He got to his feet, stared south toward Texas and imagined the thousands upon thousands of longhorns that had been driven north to Kansas over this very route sometimes called McCoy's Trail, but mostly known as the Chisholm Trail.

He turned to his chocolate sorrel gelding. "Well, Tippy, I expect if we follow the cattle tracks, we'll eventually find the gun or at least where they deviated from the trail...Betcha it's south of Saint Jo, though. What do you think?"

The fourteen-hand Morgan turned his big brown eyes to him and blinked.

"Yeah, me too." He mounted in one easy move and squeezed the horse into a road trot toward the Red.

A little over an hour later, Brushy Bill pulled rein at Heaton's Ferry—a flat-bottomed chain barge that crossed the Red River a little over a half mile from the town of Red River Station on the Texas side.

"Howdy. You Heaton?"

"Nope, he retired. Name's Gilbreath, John Gilbreath. Wanta go across?"

"Why I'm here. River's up a mite after that rain last night."

"Yep, wouldn't recommend tryin' to swim 'er...The mighty Red is a livin', breathin' thing and must be handled with the utmost respect at all times...She can be a vengeful mistress."

"I believe you. Not near as big in New Mexico where she starts."

"Shoulda been here..." Gilbreath spat a long stream of amber tobacco juice into the muddy red water. "...durin' the great flood of '91. She went over forty feet above flood stage. Washed away bunch of folks and livestock and some of the finest corn and wheat you ever seen."

"Had to have been a sight to behold."

"That it was...She was over two miles wide fer a while."

"How much?"

"How much what?"

"To cross."

"Oh! Plumb fergot...Guess I got carried away with my storytellin'...Be a dollar."

Bill stepped down and led Tippy onto the ferry deck. "Like you said, swimmin' ain't a real good idea...What did they do with all the cattle when the Red was on a rampage back in the day?"

"Had to hold 'em on the Texas side 'til she went back to normal...Why, one time in '68, had over 60,000 head millin' around all the way over by Spanish Fort for three days...Took purtnear four weeks fer the stink to go away."

"Don't say."

"I do say...Well, grab aholt, we're off...Ain't much left of Red River Station."

"How so?"

"Wells'r, first they ain't no more cattle drives, second...ol' Mother Nature sent a tornado back in the '80s that wiped out about half the town and then to top it off, the railroad went through Nocona and Saint Jo...Red River Station jest kindly died on the vine, so to speak...Becomin' a real ghost town."

"Pity...Been much traffic lately?"

"Funny you should ask. Some cowboys swam a small herd of mama cows across the other day, headed south, before the rain. They rode the ferry...had one of them fast shootin' guns with a whole rafter of barrels...You know?"

"A Gatling Gun?"

"Yeah, that's what they call it. It was mounted on a two-wheel cart...They was mighty partic'lar with it."

"I can imagine...Wouldn't happen to know where they were headed, would you?"

"Nope, they might have stopped at Tom Pollard's Saloon and Tradin' Post though...Might check there."

"I'll do that," Bill said as the ferry bumped ashore in Texas. "Much obliged." He flipped him a dollar, led Tippy onto the bank and mounted. He tipped his straw sombrero to the man as he rode west toward Red River Station.

RAFTER S RANCH
COOKE COUNTY

Pepper slowly walked into the headquarters with Walt carefully cradling Francis in his arms—Buttermilk, her mare, trailed along behind.

Sing Loo, opened the screen door at the far back side of the house to throw out a pan of dish water and saw them coming through the front gate. He dropped the pan and ran toward them. "Missy Flan, Missy Flan!"

The front door burst open when her father, Tom, heard the Chinese cook yelling. "What...Oh, God!"

"Send somebody for a doctor, quick!" Walt said as his gelding stopped at the hitching rail in front of the rambling ranch house.

"What happened?" Tom asked as he reached up to take his unconscious daughter from Durbin's arms.

Several hands started running from the round pen near the barn to the house.

"Jefferson, go fetch Doc Wellman!" yelled Tom.

"And get Ranger Hickman too!" added Walt

The black wrangler slid to a stop, turned and sprinted toward one of the saddled horses tied to the corral next to the working pen. He mounted, spun the animal around and spurred to a gallop through the front gate working the split reins over and under, urging his mount to greater speed—all of the hired help on the Rafter S worshiped the red-haired beauty.

Walt took Fran's limp body back from her father after he stepped down. "Where?"

"Her room," Tom said as he was already up the steps and holding the white painted gingerbread trimmed screen door open as Walt carried her through. "Sing, bring some towels and hot water...chop, chop."

The ranger carried her through the wide hallway, followed Tom upstairs into her bedroom and placed her on top of the pink chenille bedspread that covered her cherry wood four poster bed. He eased her boots off as her father unfolded a patchwork quilt that had been laying on top of the cedar chest at the foot.

Walt took the quilt and laid it gently over her legs and then began to unfasten the dome-shaped bone buttons on her blouse. He did the same for the four smaller ones on the long cuffs on her bloody blouse, before he tugged the tails out from underneath the waistband of her split riding skirt.

"Tom, help me lift her up…have to get this shirt off and clean the wound."

The distraught father did as he was asked. They carefully lifted her to a sitting position. Walt moved quickly to ease the blouse over her dainty shoulders.

Tom winced as Francis' head flopped forward, the sight tugging at his heart. A tear ran down across his cheek.

Walt glanced quickly at her back. The ivory-colored camisole she wore was unstained there. *No pass through. Bullet must have hit the should blade. Doc's gonna have to dig it out.*

They gently laid her back down as Sing Loo entered the room carrying a blue china wash basin in his hands and a small stack of cotton towels tucked under his right arm.

Tom brushed a few strands of long red hair off Francis' face as she moaned softly. "Oh, baby girl…I'm so sorry." His voice cracked.

"Set the basin right here," Walt said as he pointed to the night stand. He reached under the camisole and carefully lifted the red wild rag he had first used to stop the flow of blood. The ranger dropped it on the hardwood floor on top of the blouse.

He took a clean towel and dabbed it into the bowl. Holding the camisole up slightly, he gently wiped up the caked reddish brown blood off her upper chest, being careful not to break the clot that had already formed on the puckered nearly dime-sized entry wound. "Girl, why didn't you listen to me?" His eyes rimmed with tears.

Without looking up, he continued to clean the wound. "Found the north fence cut about two miles from the house. Fresh tracks leadin' west." He returned the red-streaked towel to the basin and wet another corner of it. "Tried to get her to go for help and let me handle it..."

"I can hear her now...She's a strong willed little filly."

Walt nodded. "Tell me." He took in a deep breath. "Anyhow...tracked 'em a couple of miles and caught 'em in the act in the west pasture next to the fillies. Dropped three of the four and then..."

Tom shook his head and stared at his daughter as her chest rose and fell—her breathing weak, but regular. "Dammit, Little Bit. I would trade all the horses we ever owned for you to make it though this. They're just horses..."

"Doc's gonna have to go in there and dig the slug out...Think it clipped the top of her lung."

"How can you tell?"

"Got a few tiny bubbles in the blood coming out of the bullet hole at the side of the clot. See?"

Tom watched as Walt sat on the side of the bed, finished cleaning the wound and used his strong hands to rip a second towel into thirds.

He folded the soft cotton cloth into a makeshift bandage and placed it under the camisole atop the hole. He stood up and dipped his hands into the basin and washed the blood away. The wash water had taken on a distinct pink color. As he dried them on a third towel, he turned to Sing Loo. "We'll need to toss this out and be ready to bring in some more hot water when the doctor gets here."

"Me got boiling in kettle on stove." The small Chinese man grabbed up the bloody shirt and kerchief, and then carefully lifted the basin and left the room.

Tom glanced over at the tanned horseman who was focused intently on his daughter. "You seem to know your way around a gunshot wound."

Walt nodded and looked Tom straight in the eye. "Comes with the territory, I reckon. Folks I deal with don't always come in peaceful like…'bout once a month somebody gets a hole in 'em…Sometimes it's one of them, sometimes it's one of us. Never had to patch up a lady before…" His voice trailed off.

The look on Walt's face was not easy to parse. Tom was not certain, but he swore he saw something there that was more than a ranch hand tending to his employer—or a law officer. He lifted the quilt and pulled it up to Fran's chin and then patted her on the cheek.

"Hold on, baby girl…Doc's on the way."

Walt reached into his vest pocket and pulled out a silver plated timepiece. He touched the release button, flipping the cover open. *Ten fifteen. With any luck at all, the Doc should be rolling in around noon time…hopefully with Bodie in tow.*

"What can we do now?" Tom asked.

Walt pondered his question for a moment. "Join me in a prayer…she's gonna need it." He dropped to his knees at the edge of her bed.

Tom followed suit.

Walt entered the bunkhouse and quickly walked to his bunk. He laid his saddle bags on the gray wool blanket covering the mattress. Above, on the bare wood wall over his bunk was an unpainted pine shelf—just like that of all the other working wranglers. There were a couple of fresh shirts and a clean pair of pants stacked on top as well as a full box of Western brand .45 Colt.

Fats watched him from his bunk where he was resting, still recouping from his own gunshot wound.

"How's she doin?" one of the other hands asked.

"She's hanging in there, Little John...'bout all I can say for now. Doc should get here in an hour or so."

The short man nodded and looked on as Walt took the extra clothes down, folded them tightly and stuffed them into the well worn saddle bags.

"You fixin to pull out on us?...With Miss Fran laid up and all?"

Walt shot him a look that would melt steel. His jaw muscles visibly tightened. "Not likely," he hissed and took the long black coat hanging from the hook below the shelf, folded it lengthwise and wrapped it up in the bedroll he kept stashed below the bunk. He used four narrow strips of latigo to tie the roll tight.

Little John crossed his arms and stared at him with a growing look of disgust. "Shore looks like you're a planning to cut an' run...from where I stand...And I thought I heard you were a man that rides for the brand."

Walt didn't even look up. He reached for a tattered cigar box he kept next to his soogan, laid it beside the bulging saddle bags, and then flipped the top open. Inside, were some writing materials, two pencils and what looked like a large Garrett Snuff tin. He opened the lid and took something from it.

Little John couldn't make out what he was fiddling with. The tall man placed his hand on his vest and pulled down smartly. When Walt stood back up, Little John was eye level with a distinctive silver icon. *Holy Hanna.* "Uh, Ranger, I'm…I'm powerful sorry. I didn't mean what I said," he stammered.

"Yeah you did…and I'm right proud of you standing up for her." He stuck out his hand. "I ain't plannin' going anywhere…excepting to do my job."

Little John shook Walt's hand vigorously as he looked him in the eye. *May God have mercy on the man that shot Miss Francis… 'cause he won't.*

***

CHAPTER SEVEN

WOLF RUN RIDGE
COOKE COUNTY

Bass flipped his rope over a thick horizontal limb sticking out from the side of a large burr oak at the edge of the campsite. Jack threw a half hitch around the hocks of a young spike deer, and then Bass hoisted the animal he had shot earlier that morning up into the air and tied the end of the rope off while Jack pulled his razor sharp belt knife and moved to cut its throat.

"Hold on there, pard. Mayhap we oughta save some of that blood fer our little project...reckon?"

"What'er we gonna put it in, Bass?"

"Uh, don't you got a bottle in yer saddle bags?"

"Well, yeah, but its still got whiskey in it."

"I 'spect we kin remedy that…Don't you?"

"I mind you got a point there." He sheathed his Bowie, stepped over to his saddle laying at the head of his bedroll and retrieved an almost a third full of a pint of Old McBrayer sour mash whiskey. He pitched the bottle to the big man.

Bass uncorked it and took a swig. "Tad warm, but it helps clear the phlegm from yer throat." He handed it to Jack who took a healthy slug and gave it back.

"Damn, that's good," he wheezed. "Don't suppose they's enough in there to get us spiflicated…do you?"

"'Spect we'll find out." Bass grinned and turned the bottle up. "Probably a good thing you been a nibblin' on it from time to time." He passed it to Jack.

"Only to cut the trail dust." He took another big swallow and handed it back. "Ever since I washed over them falls and had to drink that joy juice Angie give me, I started havin' a taste for sour mash…Saved you a touch."

Bass drained the last. "Sometimes less is more."

"You wanna run that one by the gate again?"

"Well when they ain't much left, yer inclined to just finish it off an' that last little swaller might be all it takes to put you in the well…don'tcha see?"

"Uh, yeah…Uh, No."

"Thought you'd understand…Alright, now use yer knife…an' don't cut yer thumb off."

"Wadn't on…on my list…'Course if it was as nuuu…mb as my nose, wouldn't feel it none anyways." He cut the deer's throat and held the empty flask down to catch most of the stream dribbling out—he corked it when it was almost two-thirds full.

"I foller that…Let's git that scudder gutted and skint…We kin broil us up some backstrap steaks…cut the rest into strips fer jerky after we rub some salt an' pepper mix on 'em."

"My mouth's waterin'…already," Jack said as he cleaned out the deer's body cavity. "How's about you cuttin' up the h…heart and liver and then burrryin' the rest of the innards whilst I peel the h…hide off?" He washed what blood spilled down the side with water from his canteen, put the flask in his saddlebags and went back to skinning the deer carcass. "What time we need to be a headin' over thataway?"

Bass took his pocket watch out of his vest pocket, opened it and squinted his eyes at the face. "'Bout three, I 'spect…just gotta meet Selden and Loss first."

RED RIVER STATION
MONTAGUE COUNTY, TEXAS

Bill drew rein in front of Tom Pollard's Saloon and Tradin' Post, dismounted, flipped his lead around the hitching post and pushed through the batwing doors. He glanced around the room, lit only by the light coming through the two good-sized windows at the front and above the swinging doors.

It was still before noon and several out-of-work cowboys were having a late breakfast while a couple of others were making an early start on the day at the bar.

Roberts bellied up and propped one foot on the brass rail at the bottom.

"What'll it be, pilgrim?" the fifty year old bartender with long gray hair tied back in a low ponytail asked.

"Rye."

"Might be a mite early for the hard stuff, but it's your stomach."

"Hair of the dog," he sort of mumbled.

The proprietor nodded. "Understand that." He grabbed a bottle from the shelf behind him, set a shot glass on the bar and filled it. "Two bits."

Bill turned it up and downed it in one gulp and let out a big breath of air. "Dang, that helped…Take another and a couple of them pickled banty eggs from that jar over there."

The barkeep filled his glass again, fished out two of the small eggs from the gallon jar behind him, put them in a saucer and set it in front of Bill. "Two bits…eggs are on the house."

He pitched another quarter on the bar. "'Bliged." He popped one in his mouth, chewed a couple of times and swallowed. "Um, good…May have to have a couple more."

"The next ones are a nickel a piece."

Bill nodded, turned around, leaned back against the bar and surveyed the room. "Kinda quiet…but I reckon it's early…I tell you what, though. Seen a strange sight couple days ago…a small herd of mama cows and some cowboys haulin' a cannon.

Durnedest thing I ever saw...a cannon. Headin' south, they was." He turned back around and ate another egg.

The bartender glanced at him through slitted eyes for just the briefest of moments, and then he too turned around—away from Bill. "Don't say?"

"Yep...See most anything these days, I reckon...Say, I'm headed to Fort Worth...figure to follow the old Chisholm Trail. What's the next town after Saint Jo?"

"That'd be Rosston, I expect."

Roberts finished off his eggs and drink, tipped his hat to the bartender and headed out the door.

The two cowboys who were eating breakfast looked up at the batwing doors swinging closed and then at the barkeep—he nodded. They pushed back from the table and walked out the back way.

Bill cinched up, mounted and trotted out of town toward the southeast. "Well, Tip, we'll see if that bears any fruit." He unstoppered his leather wrapped canteen, took a big mouthful of water, swished it about and spat it to the ground. "Damn, those were the worst pickled eggs I ever had. Be glad you didn't get any, old son...but then again, you don't eat eggs anyway."

RAFTER S RANCH
COOKE COUNTY

Sing Loo lifted the wrought iron rod and ran it around the inside of the forged triangular dinner bell. The distinctive clang did not elicit the usual scramble of hungry ranch hands to the main house. The somber mood had put a damper on that as the young lady of the house lay near death inside.

Several hands made their way to the well and washed up in a galvanized bucket hung on the rock well casing for that purpose. As Little John dried his hands on his tan canvas pants, he heard the distinctive sound of horse's hooves from the road leading into the headquarters—he glanced over his shoulder.

"Hey everybody! Looky yonder! It's the Doc and Ranger Hickman."

The Doc drove a black dray behind a chestnut gelding. Jefferson White was seated beside him—his mount worn completely out from the hard ride into town to fetch the doctor and Bodie. He had left the courageous animal at Pap Clark's Livery to recuperate.

Hickman trailed slightly behind and offset from the buggy to avoid the occasional cloud of dust kicked up from the dirt road. His face was grim, not certain yet if he would be investigating a horse rustling or a murder. The daunting task of what he had to do later that day lay heavy on his mind as well.

Wellman reined up in front of the house. Jefferson hopped out and took control of the lead rope and tied the horse off to the hitching rail just outside the white picket fence. Doc picked up the back leather bag that carried all his medicines and tools and stepped to the ground. He straightened his back and leaned once to each side to try and get the kinks out from the forty-five minute ride. It helped, but only a little bit.

Tom and Walt walked though the front door and met the local surgeon at the base of the front steps.

"Thanks for coming so quick, Doc." Tom extended his hand.

Wellman shook it firmly. "Sorry it is under these circumstances. It seems like only yesterday I was bringing Francis into this world…"

"She's stable. Ranger Durbin cleaned the wound up as well as he could."

Wellman shot a glance at Walt, but said nothing. Tom and the doctor headed up the stairs.

Walt walked over the hitching rail as Bodie swung down and loosened the girth. "Glad Jefferson was able to find you."

Bodie lowered the stirrup and stuck out his hand. "See you decided to drop your cover."

"Yep. They're getting pretty brazen. We killed three, but one got away…I want him, I want him bad."

Bodie nodded. "Recognize any of 'em?"

"Naw. I ain't been nowhere exceptin' the ranch since I hired on…we can check the bodies on the way north…Don't think they're goin' anywhere."

"We best see if we can give the doc a hand. How's Francis doin'?"

"Lost a lot of blood. She was still unconscious last time I looked in."

Bodie nodded. "You gonna be ready to ride after the doc treats her?"

"Yep. I'll have Sing Loo pack us a couple of sandwiches for the trail."

WOLF RUN RIDGE
COOKE COUNTY

"Well, that ought a do 'er," Jack said as he hung the last strip of venison near the fire to smoke. "Hand me that Dutch oven an' I'll put the stew on to slow cook...By the time we meet Selden and Loss up to Frog Bottom with them horses and git back, it oughta be ready."

Bass brought the cast iron pot over and set it on a flat rock next to the fire. He looked around over his shoulder. "'Pears Rube's back."

"How do you do that?...Oh, never mind, I already know. That dang Injun nose of yourn...Wonder how come I cain't do that? I got Injun in me."

"You never had to practice it like I did when I lived with the Creeks and Seminole. Yer grandmother didn't live in no village and was civilized."

"Yeah, but..."

"Comin' in the camp," came the shout from the woods.

"Come on," replied Jack.

Rube entered the clearing, leading his horse. He had a raw bruise on his cheek.

"What happened to you?" Jack asked as he finished arranging the drying rack he had made from green willow limbs next to the fire with the venison.

"Well, see it was like this. After I dropped off the note...damn that's a spooky place...I felt the need for a drink and went down to the Painted Lady on Commerce…an' well, one thing led to another."

"This is gonna be good, Bass," Jack said.

"Cain't wait."

"I had a couple of drinks…you know, to settle my nerves…"

"Uh, huh," grunted McGann.

"…an' I started singin' 'She'll be Comin' Round the Mountain', an' this ol boy next to me…he said 'shut up'…an' I thought he said 'stand up'…Never seen that right comin'…Made me swaller my chaw…Throwed up most of the night."

"We git the picture," commented Bass with a grin.

"Come to find out, he was a flat-lander…an' he was wantin' to sing 'Buffalo Gals'…How was I to know?" Rube rubbed the side of his face. "Got one hell of a headache…Not to say nothin' of still bein' a mite queasy."

"Well, we got to go meet some fellers, you kin stay here an' heal up…Oh, while yer a restin' you kin mind the fire. Got some jerky smokin' an' a heart an' liver stew on to cook," said Jack as he lifted the lid to the Dutch oven.

Rube looked in the pot, turned pale, wheeled and ran over behind a tree. Bass and Jack looked at each other and grinned as they heard him throwing up what was left in his stomach.

"It ain't done yet, Rube!" Jack yelled at him.

WALNUT BEND
COOKE COUNTY

The sole surviving would-be rustler spurred the bay mare viciously, but she stopped and refused to move.

"What in tarnation is wrong with you? You been draggin' your sorry ass for almost an hour as it is." Windy Folsom swung out of the saddle and held on to the reins as he stepped aft and checked the security of both rear shoes. They were not the problem. A trail of mostly dried blood on the inside of her right leg caught his attention. The high grass had wiped it clear below her hocks, but from the knee joint up, it was quickly evident she had taken a round in the running gun battle.

The bullet had stuck the inner upper hind quarter and penetrated to her pelvis bone. She was in pain and every step had increased her agony.

"Ain't it just like you to leave me shanks mare in the middle of nowhere? I'd put another bullet in your sorry carcass, but I cain't afford the noise." He checked his back trail, and then studied the rough terrain a quarter mile to the west. A sharp bluff dropped off some eighty feet and then the next half mile tumbled down another 300 feet to the Red River. It was covered in many areas with scrub oak and infested with giant ragweed higher than a man's head as well as green briars that would rip a man's clothes from him in the first hour. Beyond that lay the Indian Nations.

To the north, almost twelve miles away was Horseshoe Bend. The broad grassland covered almost 3,000 acres and the river crossing itself was one that was quite familiar to Windy.

He and the other men in the Pink Lee gang used it often. He unshucked his '92 Winchester and let the horse's reins fall to the ground. *I ain't totin' that no account saddle all the way to Dexter. Only slow me down...'sides, reckon I'll steal me a better one 'afore the next job.*

Keeping a eye on the south horizon, the high binder lit out for the gang's hideout.

COOKE/MONTAGUE COUNTY LINE

Roberts held his gelding in an extended road trot at about sixteen miles per hour across the rolling grassland. "Well, look here, Tippy." Bill pulled rein and looked down at a set of grooves some four feet apart running southwest to northeast cut in an expansive exposed outcropping of limestone. "Dollar to bear sign that's from the old Butterfield Stage road. Been enough coaches over this rock, the iron wheels cut permanent tracks...Times they are a changing...Means Rosston ought to be just on the other side of that creek up ahead."

A bullet whined with an evil sound off the rock only two feet to his right followed immediately by the boom of a long gun from the creek bottom. Tippy shied hard to the left almost dumping Bill from the saddle. He wheeled the quick Morgan and spurred toward a copse of cedar trees he had just passed. Another shot rang out and the second bullet also ricocheted from the rock—right beside the flying hooves of his mount.

He reached the shelter of the trees before a third shot could be fired. "Well, think we got our answer, Tip...I say we're gettin' close to the honey pot…Let's head to Gainesville before they get our range." He looked back at the creek through the cedar branches, turned and squeezed his mount into a canter to the northeast, keeping the trees between them and the creek. "We might'ov been up the hill and over the mountain if they had been better shots, ol' son."

RAFTER S RANCH
COOKE COUNTY

With the drapes pulled back on Francis' bedroom window, the noonday sun afforded appropriate light in the room for the country doctor. Wellman had taken a pair of scissors and cut away the camisole before wiping her upper torso with alcohol. A clean towel had been draped over her bare, well formed breasts in a nod to the Victorian modestly of the day.

"You Rangers hold her shoulders steady…I've got a bottle of ether handy, if I have to anesthetize her, but I'd rather not take that risk." He sat on the side of the bed as Bodie and Walt did his bidding, standing on either side of the four poster.

Wellman took a slender polished steel rod that had one end rounded perfectly to follow the bullet's path into her body. A sharper tip might cut its own path like a needle would be expected to do. He envisioned the beautiful redhead sitting astride her horse leading forward slightly—into the gallop—and turned a few degrees with her Colt in her right hand.

Then, he projected the bullet's path through the air and impacting the slender young woman at a slight downward angle.

Compiling these images, he deftly held the eighteen inch long probe over the entry point and did his best to recreate the slug's angle of entry. He placed his index finger atop the rod and gingerly held it between his thumb and middle digit. "Here we go, gents."

Walt winced involuntarily as the probe slowly depressed the clot into the wound and created a small depression in her alabaster skin. Under the doc's careful ministration, the rod slowly disappeared into Francis' chest.

Bodie glanced over at Walt. He noticed a bead of sweat run down his friend's forehead and into his left eye. Walt blinked, but did not move a muscle.

The probe stopped. *Has to be the scapula.* Wellman retracted it one inch and tilted the end a few degrees before he eased it back deeper. Three drops of crimson, mixed with a few tiny bubbles, oozed to the surface and dribbled down to the once pristine white towel.

The doctor's face was etched with intense concentration as he slowly eased the tool down. The contact with the pure lead slug was different that that of the scapula, or shoulder blade. His practiced hands knew the target and when the probe touched it. The sixty year old physician had gotten ample practice as a young field doctor in the War Between the States.

"That's it. No doubt about it...Bodie, hand me those long forceps...the thing that looks like those new pointy nose pliers."

He nodded as he reached over and lifted up the instrument by the handle and handed them to Wellman.

The doctor carefully took control and holding the probe exactly where it was, matched the pitch and inserted the forceps into the entry wound.

Walt forced himself to look away, choosing to focus on the angelic face of the young beauty. He could scarcely breathe until the distinct sound of the slug clinking into the wash basin released him from his transfixation.

"Thank you gentlemen for your help," Doc Wellman said with a sigh of relief as he washed the blood from his hands. "I'll get her stitched up and bandaged. Imagine you boys have something important to attend to."

Walt leaned over and gave Francis a gentle kiss on the cheek and then looked the good doctor straight in the eye. "That we do, Doc...That we do."

Bodie reached into the china basin and retrieved the slug. After blowing the water off, he studied the shape of the nose and judged its size. "Ain't big enough for a forty-four or forty-five. I mind it's from a .38-40." He handed it over to Walt.

"I reckon you're right. 'Bout a hundred and eighty grain, all right. Lot's of folks use 'em in their saddle guns as well, starting back with the Winchester '73."

"Bass likes that cartridge as well...Carries a pair in reverse grip. You ain't never seen nobody quick as him."

FROG BOTTOM
COOKE COUNTY

"Bass, Jack, over here!" shouted Selden from the trees bordering the Red.

The two lawmen had tracked along the sand bars on the Texas side up to a wide area of dunes formed by the eddy of the river when she turned back west from Sivells Bend.

"There they are, Bass," said Jack, pointing up at the tree line.

The turned their mounts and met Selden and Loss as they led the string of six horses toward the river.

"Good to see you, Selden, Loss. Who's yer friend?" asked Bass.

"This here's Red Eagle, Chickasaw Lighthorse and Army scout...Christian name of Cyrus Maytubbi. He was the sole survivor of that Army patrol with the Gatling Gun that got wiped out. Been recuperatin' from a hole in his side at the office."

"An' this here's Marshals Bass Reeves and Jack McGann."

"Heard you good men from cousin Ben Sixkiller."

"Ben was a fine law officer an' good friend," said Bass.

"Dang, Red Eagle, that's only been, what? Four days ago?" exclaimed Jack as he leaned over and stuck out his hand.

"Anompoli Lawa have strong medicine, he fix. Plus Osí Hommá tough Chickasaw an' tired of sittin' around Marshal Lindsey's office listenin' to him and Hart fuss like old women...Need fresh air." He grasped McGann's hand firmly and gave it one hard pump.

"I heard that. Doc Winchester patched me up a time or two," said Jack.

"We needed the help with the horses, anyhoo," offered Loss.

"How many was in the bunch that dry gulched yer unit, Red Eagle?" asked Bass.

"Count four, but with big gun, same as many."

"Well, we need to be gittin' them horses back to camp. Gotta meet Bodie over near Drippin' Spring with one of the horses 'bout three. Purty long haul around the river over to Horseshoe Bend."

"Red Eagle show better way. This Chickasaw country. Me know."

Bass and Jack exchanged glances.

"Believe we'll just take you up on that, Cyrus. Figured we might git lost if we tried cuttin' across. Don't know this area from Adam's ox," said Bass.

"Osí Hommá no git lost…born near Nashoba."

"Nashoba?" asked Jack.

"You call Thackerville."

"By the Lord Jim, yer handier'n handles on a jug."

"Not know what that means, but Red Eagle show way."

WOLF RUN RIDGE
COOKE COUNTY

Bass, Jack and Cyrus led the string of six horses into camp. Rube looked up from where he was sitting on a rock next to the fire, drinking a cup of coffee.

140

"Well, see you come back with mor'n you left with," he said as he pitched the last of his coffee into the fire.

"Rube, this here's Chickasaw Lighthorse Cyrus Maytubbi, also known as Red Eagle. Cyrus, meet Rube Carter."

The two men shook hands.

"How do," said Rube.

"How do what?" answered Cyrus.

"It's just an expression. He's askin' how you feel," said Jack.

"Oh, he should just say that...Red Eagle still a bit sore, but it will pass."

Rube glanced at Jack, somewhat confused. "Uh, well, uh, that's good..."

"Hope you ain't drank up all that Arbuckle," commented Jack.

"Nope, I was just down to the grounds, fixin' to pour me another cup."

"Have to wait. Need you to string up a picket pen with all these lariat ropes on them saddles fer five of these extry horses..."

Rube interrupted Bass. "Where'd ya'll git 'em? They're all tacked an' everthang."

"Sam Patterson's gang had the bad judgment to try to hold up the bank in Ardmore. They didn't know it was only a block down to Marshal Selden Lindsey's office...They ain't gonna need these horses no more...nor anythin' else, fer that matter," said Jack.

"Dangnation, heared he's purty salty," replied Rube.

"Had a little help, Marshals Loss Hart and Brushy Bill Roberts," added Bass.

"Heared of them too. They say Roberts is some fast with a gun."

"Yeah, well, strip their gear, take 'em down to the creek fer water, then put 'em in the rope trap...They's plenty grass and they'll be close to water. Leave all the tack up here at the camp. We're takin' one with us. I'm assumin' yer 'bout over yer katzenjammer?"

Rube nodded. "Had 'bout half a pot of Arbuckle while ya'll was gone...Helped with the jimjams too."

"Red Eagle no understand katzenjammer or jimjams. What is?"

"Too much firewater," replied Jack.

"Uhhh, understand. Evil spirits want come out."

Bass grinned. "Could say that."

"Should be back 'bout dark, dark thirty. We'll have some of that stew then," said Jack.

Rube blanched again.

"That is if Carter don't eat it all."

Rube shook his head. "Ain't no worry 'bout that. Guarantee I won't be botherin' it none."

"What kind stew?" asked Cyrus.

"Venison heart and liver with blood thickener," replied Jack.

Rube turned and ran toward the tree at the edge of the camp.

"Where you learn to cook blood stew, Jack McGann?"

"My grandmother was Creek."

Red Eagle nodded knowingly.

NORTHERN COOKE COUNTY

"Damn all this deep grass!" Windy Folsom cursed the natural asset that made the Rafter S such a productive ranch. Bluestem mixed with broom weed and bunchgrass provided plenty of forage for their livestock, but made it difficult walk though for a man. Folsom quickly tired from the additional effort and stopped to take a breather. He glanced over his shoulder. His tracks were easily discernible from the vegetative furrow left in his wake. "Sumbitch...might as well put up a sign *He Went Thataway.*"

Windy looked for any major change in the terrain to the east, but saw rolling prairie grassland with a few trees for the next mile or two. In some of the deeper ravines, stands of Cypress or cottonwood trees had taken hold—relatively impervious to the purposely set fires the Indians had used for centuries to renew the grasslands for buffalo and deer. He took a swig from his half-empty canteen. *Better refill this thang when I can.*

He jammed the cork back into the spout and draped the strap over his left shoulder. "Gotta say, I've had me some better days." His temper quickly got the best of him. Only four steps back into his journey, the inter-grown bunchgrass tugged mightily at his right boot. He kicked hard to free his ankle and suddenly felt a sharp shooting pain in his right upper thigh.

"What the blazes is that?" he yelled. He touched his hand to where his thigh joined his hip. A shooting pain rivaling that of a sprained ankle emanated from his hip flexor. He didn't know his human physiology, but the pain from what's commonly called a groin pull got his rapt attention. It hurt to even to lift his leg—a lot. What he did know was that his ability to move normally was severely compromised. With luck, he could manage about one mile per hour, each right step a repeat of the last one.

RAFTER S RANCH
COOKE COUNTY

"Here's where we found the fence cut," Bodie said. "We tracked the four rustlers to the west pasture."

"You don't know this place well enough yet to go directly to where the shooting occurred?"

"Not with any certainty. Lot of it looks just like the rest."

"If you say so. We can track the six of you pretty good." Bodie reined left and urged Lakota Moon into a collected easy lope.

"Hey, there's the first one up ahead," Walt said as they rode into the fifty acre meadow.

The riderless horse had made its way back to its owner and was grazing nearby, as the thick set man slept an eternal sleep. Durbin dismounted and turned the body face up. Rigor mortis had set in, making the somewhat gruesome task slightly easier. Green and black flies immediately began to circle the rustler's carcass. "Anybody you recognize?"

Bodie leaned in closer, without leaving the saddle. "Yep. Always suspicioned that young peckerwood, but never had no proof. Seen him over in Dexter the day they ambushed me and my posseman."

Walt went though the man's pockets looking for anything that would link the body to a name. A silver watch in the man's vest pocket was engraved on the inside of the lid—*For Long and Faithful Service.*

Durbin chuckled. "Musta stole it. His kind don't fall in the long...or faithful category."

"Probably some poor bastard's retirement award."

Walt stood up and looked around the grass, moving it around from side to side. Only five feet from the man's body, his Schofield was laying upside down. Walt spun the cylinder and found three shots fired, with three loaded rounds. He stashed the watch and revolver in his saddle bags and pulled the buckle tight to close it. "The other two should be nearby...one about sixty yards right or left and the other up by the tree line." Walt hopped into the saddle and reined right.

Bodie went left without being told. A few second later. He hollered over to Walt, "Here he is."

The man was laying face up and blow flies were already busy laying their eggs in the nose and mouth. Bodie swung down and took off his hat. Fanning it back and forth close to the dead rustler, he caused the swarm of flies to buzz off for a few seconds and took a look at the pock-faced man. "Yep, seen this scum-sucker a time or two...Good riddance."

Walt rode up. "Shoot...That one was butt ugly, even when he was alive." He noted the blood stain on the shirt—just an inch or two off the centerline and starting between the third and forth button from the top. A ragged hole indicated where the .45 cal slug had exited. "Either Francis or I musta clipped his heart. Both these two jaspers got hit at 'bout the same time."

"You don't remember which one you were shooting at?"

He shook his head as he tried to remember. "All happened too fast."

"Ain't tryin' to bust your chops or nuthin', but my daddy taught me to remember every little detail. Never can tell what's gonna be important in a court o' law."

Walt closed his eyes and tried to recreate the chaotic scene before Francis was shot.

Bodie watched as his head jerked slightly back and forth and then came to a stop. His friend nodded twice and opened his eyes.

"I shot this one here. Fran dropped his runnin' buddy over to the right."

"See? There you go...it's all in there somewhere. You just gotta stop and 'member it all. Grab the reins of that loose horse. May end up needin' a spare 'fore the day's done."

Walt wheeled his mount around as Bodie rifled though the dead man's pockets. He didn't find anything useful and struck out locating the rustler's shooter in the tall grass.

Five minutes later, they had located the third body at the edge of the trees and were on the trail of the fourth man.

"What's that? Does that look like blood to you?" Walt asked as he pointed to a discoloration on the tall grass when they broke back into the open.

"Danged sure does." He dismounted and rubbed the brown stain off the tops of the bluestem. It transferred to his gloved fingers. Bodie sniffed it and then spit on his fingers. Rubbing them together, the dried blood mixed with the spittle soon resumed its previous color. "Good, pardner...Cain't be from the rider though. This blood was wiped off the horse's lower leg. Otherwise, it wouldn't have been so smeared and all." He studied the tracks as he spread the grass apart with his hands. "I'm bettin' it's the right rear quarter that ya'll hit. Four out of four. That's some shootin'."

Durbin nodded but couldn't think of anything worth saying in response. He stared at the horizon to the north for a moment, and then nudged his mount forward into a lope, with the confiscated pony in trail. Bodie forked the saddle and followed suit.

***

CHAPTER EIGHT

GAINESVILLE, TEXAS
COOKE COUNTY SHERIFF'S OFFICE

 Brushy Bill had put his Colt in his saddle bags before tying up in front of the county jail at the corner of Pecan and Dixon. He pushed the door open and stepped inside, removing his straw sombrero as he did. "Sheriff Wacker?" he addressed the heavyset man at the front desk working on a report form.

He looked up. "Nope, Deputy George Rudabaugh...Chief Deputy George Rudabaugh. Sheriff Wacker is through that door there."

Bill tapped on the frosted glass of the door.

"Enter."

He turned the brass knob and pushed the door open. "You'd be Sheriff Wacker, I take it?" he said to the mustachioed middle-aged man behind the dark oak desk at the back of the room as he nervously rotated the brim of his hat.

"Well, I won the election and they gave me the badge, so guess that's me." He pushed a stack of wanted dodgers to the side.

"I don't guess your first name is Tal..."

"No, it's not! It's Taggart...How can I help you?"

"I, uh asked a gentleman over at the court house where your office was and he directed me here." He looked up. "Jail upstairs?"

"Yep. If you're here to visit anyone, my steel hotel is plumb empty. Just had some drunk cowhands and I turned them out this morning after they sobered up."

"Oh, no, sir...I just came to report a crime...Well, I suppose it is a crime to git shot at in Texas."

"Shot at?...What's your name, friend?"

"McCarty...Henry McCarty...sir."

"Henry McCarty? Henry McCarty? Where have I heard that name before?" Wacker took a sip of his coffee. "Sounds familiar. Wasn't that Billy the..."

"McCarty is reasonably common name where I come from...sir."

"And just where would that be?"

"New York."

"You're a long way from the house."

"Yes, sir, I know. I'm writer and I'm doing research for a paper I plan regarding the history of the Chisholm Trail. It will be presented at Columbia University in New York...when I complete it. I...uh have been following the route from Abilene, Kansas."

"Uh, huh...Where did this purported shooting take place?"

"Over near the town of Rosston, which I am led to believe is in Cooke County, sir."

He nodded. "Tell me what happened." The sheriff took out a small note book and began writing.

"Well, like I said, I was following the cattle trail and had just reached some old wagon tracks etched in the limestone that crossed..."

"Yep, that would be the old Butterfield Stage road."

"Really?...Facinating...Well anyway, as I was studying the tracks...someone took a shot at me...For no reason at all...I thought the country was supposed to have tamed some."

"Maybe it was just a deer hunter with an errant shot."

"My first thought also, Sheriff...but they did it again a few seconds later...I got out of there as fast as my horse could run...I don't like guns...they frighten me...I do have a pistol, for protection on the trail, but this is the first time I've ever been shot at. It was unsettling, to say the least...I felt obligated to report it to the top law enforcement in the county."

"Well, that would be me all right. I'll go out there tomorrow and take a look. I have a buggy ride with a lovely widow lady I know this afternoon. She might be upset with me if I canceled." He winked at Bill. "If you know what I mean."

"Oh, I do indeed, sir. 'When Love speaks, the voice of all the gods makes heaven drowsy with the harmony.'...Shakespeare, Love's Labour's Lost...It does spring eternal." He paused. "But that notwithstanding, I'm sure that the brigands are long gone by now anyway...I intend to stay in your lovely town a few days...to settle my nerves, you understand."

"Certainly, don't blame you." Wacker got to his feet and grabbed his gray Homberg from the peg on the wall by the door and flicked the dust from the center creased crown with his white kerchief. "Thank you for reporting this, Mister..."

"McCarty, but please call me Henry."

"Henry it is."

"I need to find suitable accommodations, do you have any suggestions?"

"There's the Turner Hotel down by the depot, the Chickasaw Parlor House on Commerce...primarily a bordello...or Skeans Boarding House just down a couple of blocks on Dixon if you want good food in addition to the room."

"Thank you, Sheriff, I will certainly look into it...Have a nice buggy ride." He put on his Mexican style straw sombrero, nodded his head and exited the door.

Wacker shook his head. *Talk about sissies, he takes the cake. Have to check out that shooting...in a day or so.*

NORTHERN COOKE COUNTY

"Looks like we found the one that's carrying a bullet," Bodie said as he lowered the binoculars. The distant mare was standing still as a statue in the open prairie grass. The young ranger lifted the field glasses once more and scanned the surrounding terrain. "No sign of its rider at all. Think you might have clipped him as well?"

"Anything's possible. What say we spread out a bit and ride in real careful? No sense loping into an ambush like a couple of rubes."

"Got a point there." Bodie secured the field glasses in his saddle bags. "I'll drift left."

Several minutes passed before they approached the wounded bay, long guns at the ready. Walt slid his '95 Winchester into its boot, dismounted and eased up to the mare. "Hold on girl...just let me check you out." His soothing manner did not alarm the stressed horse, in fact the presence of three others of her kind seemed to help. Walt took hold of the reins and then stroked her as he loosened the girth and pulled the saddle and blanket. "No sense in making her carry this tack around if she's shot up."

He moved to the hind quarters and surveyed the entrance wound. "It's survivable. I don't think it penetrated the gut. She'll be sore for a week or so, but should be all right once the muscle grows back together. Seen some of 'em recover from a lot worse."

"Might as well pull the headstall as well. That way, least she won't get hung up on somethin' when she starts movin' about."

"Was planning on it...noticed the scabbard is empty and there ain't no canteen." Walt glanced over at the obvious trail leading northeast. "Seems our boy changed his mind about the Nations. What's over in that direction?"

Bodie looked around. "Dexter...That place where I told you I saw one of the other rustler stiffs. 'Pears he's running for home." He took a drink from his canteen.

"How far is that from where we're supposed to meet up with those Deputy Marshals?"

"Less than an hour by road."

Walt dropped the mare's bridle on top of her saddle and mounted up. "We may be a little late for that there meeting time. Now that we know this hombre is shanks mare, I'm bettin' we can catch up with him before he gets there."

"Let's get this low life into custody. Ain't all that fired up 'bout getting me killed off in the first place...even if it's just for show. My bride's gonna skin me alive for doin this to her."

"You? I have to be the one to tell her...I'd trade places with you anytime."

Bodie took in a deep breath and let it out slowly. His eyes narrowed at the sight of the wanted man's track. He nudged his lineback dun into motion.

Windy Folsom limped down the hill to the wet weather creek at the bottom of the draw. A few persimmon trees and an older black walnut surrounded a spongy seep and a rocky limestone outcropping that dripped a steady stream of fresh water. He made his way to the small clear pool, fell exhausted to his knees, and then rolled over to his side. After a few seconds, he took his canteen and dunked it in the water to refill it.

He took a long pull on the cool water and wiped the excess off on the back of his arm. Tossing his black hat aside, he poured the remainder on his head and neck, languishing in the momentary relief. A long as he was not trying to lift his right leg, the pain was almost unnoticeable—but when he tried to walk, particularly through the ever-present deep grass, it was like laying a branding iron on his groin. "Dammit to hell. I sure could use me a bottle of whiskey right now."

"Should have thought about that before you cut the fence at the Rafter S."

The booming voice from behind him caught him off guard. He glanced over his right shoulder and spotted a tall, tanned man wearing a gray Stetson with a shiny Texas Ranger badge proudly pinned to his vest. He was only thirty yards away and had a rifle to his shoulder. It was obvious it was pointed right at him.

"Put your hands up and keep 'em up. You're under arrest for larceny of horses and attempted murder."

Windy turned around farther and spotted a second ranger that had given the order. *That's that Hickman sumbitch from Gainesville...Ain't gonna go without a fight. No law dog gonna string me up with a damn hemp necklace.* "You bastards ain't never gonna take me in alive!"

He lunged for his rifle.

Walt fired a round from his—the .30 Army round caught Windy square in the left side of the chest just as he grabbed hold of his carbine.

Bodie touched off his big bore Winchester. The massive .45-90 slug spun the outlaw's body half way around in the blink of an eye—the echo of the two nearly simultaneous shots faded across the sparsely populated grasslands as the gunsmoke drifted up the ravine.

Walt jacked another round into the chamber, but it was unnecessary—Windy Folsom had ridden his last ride.

Durbin lowered the hammer. "You got your wish, whoever the hell you were. If that's the way you want it…that's the way I want it more." He reached down and pulled the Colt from the dead man's holster and held it up. ".38-40."

RED RIVER
CHICKASAW NATION

Red Eagle led Bass and Jack across the ten miles of Love County just north of Nashobi or Thackerville, I.T. through coolies, draws and rolling grass land. The Red was just ahead. Their crossing point was to be just north of Walnut Bend.

"Shore is good lookin' cattle country, Cyrus."

"Was better buffalo country until white eyes killed all for hide and bones. Leave meat to rot. No understand."

"Me neither, Osí Hommá, me neither. Like killin' the goose that laid the golden eggs," said Jack.

"Goose lay golden eggs?" he said with surprise.

"It's an expression, Red Eagle, like pissin' in yer water jug," commented Bass.

"*Pisa tohbi* have too many expressions. No understand why not just say what mean."

"Got a point there. Never thought of it thataway." said Jack. "What's *pisa tohbi*?"

"White eyes."

"Right."

"Uhh...Where need go in Texas?" Cyrus asked as they waded their horses across the Red and up on the sandy bank.

"Place called Dripping Spring, in the neck of Horseshoe Bend, know it?" asked Bass.

"Red Eagle know. Be there soon...Not far."

GAINESVILLE, TEXAS
COOKE COUNTY

Sheriff Wacker reined up the one-horse black buggy in front of the Cooke County court house. The two story brick and limestone building with the church type steeple in the center had been built in 1878. Clock faces adorned the copula on all four sides and chimed on the hour.

Millie Malena exited the door on the east side of the building, carrying her black clutch. She was wearing her usual dress for her job at the county clerk's office—a light gray lindsey-woolsey full length full skirt, a white ruffled front blouse and a forest green wool shawl. He dark hair was done up in a bun at the top of her head. She quickly skipped down the steps and out to the cut limestone curb where the sheriff was waiting.

"Right on time, I see…I like that," Millie said as Taggart took her hand and assisted her into the open-sided surrey with the fringed canopy.

"Yes, Ma'am. Being late for a lovely lady just wouldn't be proper."

"And he has a velvet tongue also." She smiled as she positioned herself on the tufted black leather seat.

"Just speakin' the truth, Ma'am, just speakin' the truth…How did you manage to get off early? I thought the County Clerk was a cranky ol' curmudgeon," he said after he had walked back around to the driver's side and stepped in.

She giggled. "Mister McCain is certainly that, but it just happened that he is home with a case of the gout…The Deputy County Clerk is my cousin…besides, I was all caught up with my work."

"Well, then, I think a picnic out at Dripping Spring would be a great reward…don't you?"

"I do indeed, kind sir, I do indeed." Millie suddenly went quiet as a dark cloud crossed her face.

"What is it? Did I say something?"

She broke her reverie with a bit of a start and turned to him. "Oh, no, I'm sorry…My son and I used to go on picnics out there quite often. I was…"

"Let's go somewhere else, then."

"No, no, it's all right…I feel close to him there." She scooted over next to the sheriff and wrapped her left arm around his as he flicked the reins lightly over the mare's rump and clucked at her. "Come up, Susie."

DRIPPING SPRING

Bass and Red Eagle looked up the hill and spotted two riders.

"Better late than never," Bass muttered.

Jack had been resting his eyes as he lay against a hollow log. He lifted the brim of his hat and sat up slightly. "Got to have me a talk with that godson of mine 'bout bein' on time."

"Two men have something on other horse."

Bass squinted a bit. "Know something, Red Eagle? Believe you're right. Cain't quite make it out. My eyes ain't quite what they used to be."

The riders were still almost 200 yards away. "Don't make no sense bringin' a pack horse to this little play actin' charade," Jack said as he tried to make heads of tails of the situation. He got to his feet and brushed the bits of bark off his shoulders.

The horse trailing the two rangers suddenly drifted to the left and was more clearly visible as the distance closed.

"Hell, that ain't no pack…them there is a pair of boots a hangin' off to the side," Jack said. "Young 'uns musta got in a scrape on the way here."

"Looks like they did, all right," Bass concurred. He looked back north to make sure no other riders had stumbled upon the clandestine meeting place, and then raised his hand. "Howdy boys. We was wonderin' what was takin' you so long."

Walt and Bodie reined up and swung out of the saddle.

"Uncle Jack, Bass...Sorry 'bout the hold up. This here's Ranger Walt Durbin. He's the one gonna have to tell Annabel you killed me."

Once the introductions were made, Walt filled in the undercover marshals and their Lighthorse friend about the rustlers and the unfortunate wounding of Francis Sullivant on the Rafter S.

"Sorry about that young lady," Jack said.

"I hope she recovers," Bass added. "Hear that sawbones in Gaineville is a good one." He glanced over at the body tied to the saddle. "Ya'll got any idea who he was?"

Walt shook his head. "No name, but the gun he carried was the same caliber of the one that shot Francis."

"I seen him up by Dexter the day my posseman got shot."

Osí Hommá walked to the far side of the spare horse and lifted the man's head by the hair. He bent over and studied the face. "Red Eagle know this one...Him called Windy Folsom. Talks much. Trades many horses in the Choctaw and Chickasaw Nations. Me think he steals horses for living."

"Dying ain't much of a way of living...Didn't turn out too well for him, now did it?" Jack spat out a stream of tobacco juice as he checked out the bullet hole in the body.

Walt took out a small spiral notebook out of his shirt pocket and wrote down the man's name. "One more piece of the puzzle. I don't think this guy was the sharpest tool in the box...Gave him a chance to surrender."

"That's the way it works out sometimes. You got the body and there may be a reward dodger out on 'im," Jack said.

"Maybe so, but I'da killed him for free." Walt looked away to the north for a moment. "How we gonna set up the murder of my friend Bodie?"

"There's a cliff over yonder about three-quarter mile," Bass said solemnly. "I mind we'll touch off a couple shots, have Bodie here and you fire one or two, and then we'll fire one more rifle shot to finish off the whole shebang. That way, anybody inside of three or four miles that heard the shots will 'member 'em good...Should make folks believe it, 'specially when they see the blood on the dearly departed ranger's saddle."

"Blood?"

"Didn't tell you 'bout that? Huh." Jack chuckled. "No need to get yourself all nervous, boy." He smiled broadly and winked at Bodie. "We got us some bottled deer blood that should do the trick."

"Figured out a way for me to hang on to my rifle? Kinda partial to it, you know."

Damn, Bodie," Jack said gruffly. "Ain't my first rodeo...Walt will say you pulled it out after you two got shot at, but once you were hit, you and the .45-70 fell off the cliff into the river...You never came up and he couldn't find your body." He glared at Walt. "Think you can 'member all that, son? Me and Bass would be mighty appreciative if you don't go and blow our cover...Don't need any more holes in me that I already got...Purty sure Bass feels the same way."

"Reckon I can tell that lie good enough. Damned sure not wanting to have to ride into town to face his new wife, though. That's a low-down thing to do to young woman."

Bass nodded. "Yes, sir, I will grant you that, but seeing as how our lives...and Bodie's as well, are ridin' on you doing 'xactly that, I reckon we best get on with it...Saddle up boys. Now is as good a time as any."

Once mounted, the five turned north and headed for the nearby bluffs. A light breeze picked from the northwest. A lone American bald eagle passed overhead and screamed, looking for a new stretch of the Red River to scavenge.

GAINESVILLE, TEXAS
SKEANS' BOARDING HOUSE

Bill climbed the steps to the front of the boarding house and rapped on the white painted ginger bread screen door. Faye stepped over from the parlor with a feather duster in her hand.

"Yes?"

Bill whipped off his sombrero. "How do you do, Ma'am? Are you Miz Skeans?"

She nodded and brushed a wisp of hair from her face. "How can I help you?"

"My name is Henry McCarty, Ma'am, Sheriff Wacker sent me over..."

"Well, that was nice of Tally, I mean Taggart."

He grinned. "I had a hunch folks called him that, just not to his face...Actually you were on the list along with the Turner Hotel and The Chickasaw Parlor House..."

"And you figured you'd rather have good food rather than..."

"Yes, Ma'am. That's pretty much the size of it. I'm a writer headed south doing research on the Chisholm Trail."

"Chisholm Trail or the Chisum Trail as in John Simpson Chisum?"

"Uh, Chisholm...Jessie B. Didn't know there was a *Chisum* Trail...Interesting."

"John Simpson used to live down near Bolivar, between here and Denton. He started the Chisum Cattle Trail and it linked up with the Jessie B. Chisholm or what some called McCoy's trail coming up from south Texas. It wasn't actually called the Chisholm Trail for Jessie B. Until it hit the Indian Nations. There's still some confusion...A lot of people talk about the Jessie Chisholm Trail in Texas, when they really mean the John Chisum Trail"

"Why is that?"

"Jessie B. never drove cattle over it, he just set up trading posts along the way through the Oklahoma Territory and the Nations for the drovers. So the cowboys took to calling it the Chisholm Trail. It kind of stuck and since the two names sound the same, but spelled differently...you can see the problem."

Bill whipped out his notebook and jotted down what Faye had said. "You have been a valuable asset, Ma'am, thank you."

"Now I'm sure you didn't come here to talk about cattle trails, I take it you need a room."

"Yes, Ma'am, for a few days. I got shot at over west of here and I need to settle my nerves and rest a few days before I continue my way south."

"Well, I do have a vacancy. Dinner is at seven. I expect you to be presentable, although I'm sure I don't need to tell you that."

"No, Ma'am. Coat and tie. I'm familiar with dinner dress codes."

"Follow me and I'll show you to your room." She laid her duster on the hall tree and led the way to the stairs. *An interesting man, to say the least.*

NORTHERN COOKE COUNTY

"Whoa up there Susie," the sheriff said as he eased back on the reins at the ornate wrought iron gate entrance to Orlena Cemetery. "Would you like me to go in with you?"

"Not really, thank you. Just give me a moment alone with my son so I can place these flowers you were so kind to stop and let me pick...I won't be long."

"I understand. Take your time."

He watched as Millie knelt at the grave and laid the daisies, Indian paint brushes and buttercups at the base of the headstone. The inscription read:

WILLIAM JEROME MALENA
BELOVED SON
An Angel Gone Too Soon
1877 - 1896

She got to her feet, crossed herself, turned and headed back to the buggy.

A mile down the wagon road toward Dripping Spring, she finally spoke. "Thank you so much for stopping. I make it a practice to visit his grave every Friday, put fresh flowers on it and say a prayer for him. "I hope it hasn't spoiled your day."

"Not at all, we all have family we miss…"

"You've never married?"

"No. My mother and I came from Tennessee when I was a youngster…She, uh, passed away just after we got to Texas."

"Oh, I'm so sorry."

"Long time ago."

"What about your father?"

"Never met him. He ran off before I was born. Folks said he came to Texas. That's why we moved here when I was seven or eight, after the war. Mama was lookin' for him and well, her being a school marm, she could work most anyplace."

"I always wanted to be a teacher, just never could afford to go to a college."

"She was good at it…But, to change the subject, next week I'll take you out to the ranch I'm building down toward Decatur. It's going to be the finest cattle operation in the country when

I'm finished. Another couple of years toting a badge for Cooke County and it should be ready."

"Moving there by yourself?"

He turned and looked into her soft brown eyes for a long moment. "I hope not."

RED RIVER BLUFFS

Walt pulled out his field glasses and scanned the river carefully before he turned in the saddle and did the same to the open grasslands covering Horseshoe Bend. "Nary a soul in sight," he said as he stashed the binoculars back in his saddle bags.

"All right then," Bass said. "You men give us a few minutes to get over to them bushes. Oncet we be all hid out, ride up yonder ways close to the bluff. We'll shoot, ya'll shoot back, but not too close now, hear?…After the fourth rifle shot, Bodie, you act like you's hit and slide out of the saddle and crawl off thisaway in the high grass…Walt, you take off east, on account of somebody we cain't see now might look up after the shootin' starts. Moon should foller yer horse and we'll fire one more."

"Got it, Marshal."

"Let's go ahead on and splatter some of this here deer blood on the cantle and rear skirt." Jack said as he retrieved the re-purposed whiskey bottle. He side-passed closer to Bodie and grinned as he poured the sticky liquid on his fingers. "Lean forward a bit."

Hickman nervously complied, as Jack began flicking them forcefully—distributing a realistic semi-random pattern of blood spatter across Lakota's rump.

McGann smeared a bit on the saddle horn, as if the ranger had touched the entry wound and grabbed the horn before he slid off. He studied his handiwork. "Nah, a liver shot would have more blood."

He took the bottle and poured a bit more blood on the palm of his hand and made a chopping motion with his arm. Larger drops coated the dark dorsal hair of the lineback dun. He glanced at his partner. "Whatdaya think? Look like a liver shot to you?"

Bass leaned over and perused the scene. " Mebe a bit on the blanket and left fender."

"I'd buy that." Jack added the final touches. "You younguns approve?"

"Uncle Jack, you're givin' me the heebee-jeebees right about now."

"You marshals likely have seen more crime scenes that we have," Walt said as he nodded. "I could believe a man got shot off'n that horse, for sure."

"That's the whole point. When you ride up to the ranch house, everybody will only have your word and this here dun to corroborate the story. If you believe it, so will everybody else...We'll fill in Rube with the details so's it will sound like he seen it all when he reports to Tom Lee."

"Let's get to it," Bodie said with conviction. "The sooner this rustling operation gets done with, the better."

NORTHERN COOKE COUNTY

"This is such a beautiful day. Thank you for inviting me to go on a buggy ride and picnic, Taggart." She snuggled closer to him and then jumped back at the sound of a rifle shot from nearby. "What was that? Hunters?"

Another shot, then two more sounded.

"Whoa up there, Susie." The sorrel mare quickly came to a stop from the single foot she had been using. "Not likely! Three different caliber rifles…That's a gunfight!"

Then one final shot sounded.

"Should we go see about it? Someone may be hurt."

"No, Ma'am." He flicked the left rein across the mare's rump and pulled back on the right, turning the horse and buggy around in the road, back the way they came. "Too dangerous. Could be the ranger and some of the rustlers. I'll not put you in jeopardy." He loosened up on the ribbons and clucked at Susie, moving her up into an extended road trot.

"Let's just go to my house, then. We can eat there."

"Probably a good idea, Millie."

She looked back over her shoulder in the direction of the river where the gunshots had come from.

***

CHAPTER NINE

RAFTER S RANCH

As the sun hung low over a sienna colored horizon, Walt Durbin loped up to the hitching rail outside the fence and slowed to a stop. Two of the hands had seen him approach and Little John ran inside to tell Tom Sullivant that he was riding in.

The other wrangler took control of the lead rope tied to the rustler's mount and the loose reins of the lineback dun that came in free behind the ranger. He took a quick look at the man draped over the saddle—his hands and feet tied together underneath the horse's belly—and instantly realized it was not Bodie Hickman.

"Say, Walt…Where'e Bodie? That's his horse!" He nodded toward Moon. "Is this the sorry owlhoot that shot Miss Fran?" He pointed at the body the body.

Durbin did his best to play the part of a bereaved lawman. He held up a gloved hand and shook his head and allowed his shoulders to slump forward.

"That's him…"

The screen door slammed on the ranch house as Little John and Tom hustled out to see what news their former hand had of the rustler that had gotten away earlier that morning.

Tom sized up the situation quickly when he saw Lakota Moon, sans his owner. "Oh my God, son…did something happen to Ranger Hickman?"

He nodded slowly. "Yes…yes, sir…Bushwackers…Up by Dripping Spring. There were three of 'em. Bodie got hit real quick…and fell off the bluffs…He went under…never came up."

"Oh, God, I'm so sorry," Tom said as he took the devastating news hard. "He was so young. And a real fine lawman, to boot…Oh, sweet Jesus. He just got back from his honeymoon…"

"I know," Walt said almost in a whisper, with sadness in his voice. "Little John, can you strip the tack off these three for me?…Tom, I'd be obliged to borrow a couple fresh ones for a bit. Gotta get this stiff to the undertaker…and then have to deliver the bad news to Bodie's widow."

"You bet. Anything you need. Little John, see that those horses get a good brushin'," Tom directed.

"Yes sir." He stepped closer as Walt swung down from the saddle.

"Just these two, if you will," Walt said pointing at his mount and the rustler's. "Bodie's is covered in evidence. Just put the saddle in the barn and Lakota in a stall with feed and water. I got to sketch out the blood spatter when I get back tomorrow."

"Sure thing, Ranger." The short ranch hand took the reins of the lawman's blood bay gelding, Pepper. Almost as an afterthought, he added, "Got some supper almost ready."

Walt shook his head. "Thanks, ain't really got much of an appetite." He took off his gloves and turned to Tom. "How's she doin'?"

Sullivant's face was already etched with worry. "She came to for a while, and then passed out again. The doc says it's from the pain medication he gave her, but she seems to be breathing pretty steady."

"That's a good sign...Mind if I look in on her before I go?"

"Please do. She's sleepin' soundly now, but it might do her good."

They walked toward the porch—Walt turned back in the direction of the hitching rail.

"That highbinder tied to the saddle...He was carrying a Peacemaker....38-40. Most likely the low life scum that shot Francis this morning."

Tom processed the information. "Appreciate that. But it won't help my daughter, I'm afraid. Doc says she's got about a fifty-fifty chance...blood loss and all, and he's concerned about infection in the lung."

Walt's sadness was no longer an act. The thought of her dying sucked some of his spirit away in an instant.

Doc Wellman got to his feet when Walt entered her bedroom. "I'm glad you made it back so soon. Any sign of the rustlers?"

He nodded. "Yep. Caught up with the last of the bunch about eight miles out. In fact, if you don't mind...would you be so kind as to examine the body for me? I'll need a death certificate filled out for my report...not necessary to do the paperwork tonight."

"Don't mind at all. All part of being the coroner and medical doctor, you understand."

"Thanks, Doc."

Tom accompanied Wellman back outside as Walt sat down on the Victorian chair with a needlepoint seat. *I wonder if Fran did that stitchin'?* He gazed at her face, the color still very wan. Both her arms were outside the covers and lying by her side. He lifted up her right hand and held it in both of his. *You gotta get well, you just gotta.* He stroked the back of it, marveling at the silky softness of her skin.

"Francis," he said softly. "Just wanted you to know I got the one that shot you...Tried to arrest 'im, but he made a play for his saddle gun...He won't never...steal no more horses, 'er harm nobody again."

Walt took in a deep breath and sighed as he let it out. He hadn't realized how much he had come to care for that red-haired fireball of a woman. "I got some things to do tonight, but I'll be back by noon tomorrow...Don't plan on leavin' your side until you get back on your feet...There's something I want to ask you, but you got to be awake for that to happen."

He got to his feet and leaned over the young woman. He kissed her gently on the forehead and smoothed a stray strand of hair from her eyebrow. Walt squeezed her hand. He wasn't sure if he was imagining it or not, but he swore he felt her squeeze it back.

DEXTER, TEXAS

The sheriff gazed across the table at Millie after their indoor picnic dinner. "You know, I can't say this tastes quite the same as eating outside on a blanket, but I will have declare that this was the best fried chicken I ever put my lips to."

The thirty-nine year old widow blushed slightly and then batted her eyes. "You flatter me, Sheriff Wacker. It's been a long time since a man complimented me on my cooking...too long, I'm afraid...I'm not sure, after eleven years, I even know how to act around another man."

"Nonsense, pretty lady. If you hang around me, you can expect a never-ending stream of compliments." His eyes sparkled.

Millie smiled back at the attractive lawman. He was slightly taller than her late husband and possibly a tad better looking. She had never thought she would find love again—being a widowed woman—living in a fading small rural town and raising a young boy all by herself. The loss of her only son had been devastating and yet, seated across the small dining table, an eligible man, respected around town with a good reputation was looking at her with eyes that showed he really cared about her. *What was it the priest said at Billy's funeral? One door closes, another opens?*

Taggart reached across the table and took her hands in his. "It must get lonely for a sophisticated woman like yourself living out here, especially now that young Billy is no longer with us."

"I never realized how quiet it was until he..." Tears filled her eyes.

Wacker shook his head. "I'm so sorry...Didn't mean to pour salt on your wounds. Guess I wasn't thinkin'...It's been less than a month."

She nodded. "It's all right. I know you didn't mean to bring me pain. It's not in your nature."

"Billy will always live on in your heart. Things have a way to kinda heal over with time. The love you feel for him will make the pain seem less...day by day."

She sniffed and nodded as she tried to force a smile. "It was like that when my husband died...I thought I would dry up and blow away from the heartache."

"But you stayed strong for your son, didn't you?"

"He was all I had left in the world and I was all he had. Maybe we made it though it because we knew we had to...for each other."

"The Lord works in mysterious ways," Taggart said.

Millie took in a deep breath. "That is so true." A thought came to her. "Sheriff, would you join me in a little after-dinner sherry? I have had that bottle in the cupboard for heaven knows how long…I think it's high time to have a sip."

"Sounds like a wonderful idea, pretty."

WOLF RUN RIDGE
COOKE COUNTY

"How'd ya'll find this place?" asked Bodie as their horses picked the way up the side of the hill toward the top of the ridge.

"Hello the camp," Bass shouted and then turned to the ranger. "Luck mostly. Just looked for high ground near the river and not far from Frog Bottom where we met Selden, Loss and Cyrus to pick up the extry horses…one of which yer ridin.'"

"Lucky me. This is one rough ridin' son of a bitch. He trots like a three legged mule."

"Didn't have the time to test ride 'em…Anythin' else you want to bitch about?" quipped Jack.

"Aw, Uncle Jack, you know what I mean. It's bad enough that Annabel is gonna be thinkin' I'm dead this evenin' when Walt gets into town…Oh, Lordy, Lordy, she's gonna be mad as a wet hen when she finds out it was all just play like. She might just shoot me fer real. Sweet as she is…girl's got a temper."

They dismounted at the edge of the camp as Rube walked forward to greet them.

"Rube, this here's Ranger Hickman, recently deceased. Bodie, Rube Carter, the former outlaw we told you about on the way over," said Jack.

"Musta gone off alright then," said Rube as he and Bodie shook hands. "Howdy."

"'Bout as well as expected. You mind takin' the horses down to the picket pen, water an' grain 'em a bit?" said Bass.

"Shore...They's coffee at the fire and that God awful stew, too," commented Carter.

"Didn't eat it all up?" asked Jack.

"Not much chance of that...had me some jerky," Rube said over his shoulder as he led the horses down the other side of the ridge toward the creek.

"Stew?" inquired Bodie.

"Blood stew," answered Bass.

The young ranger paled. "Think I'll go for some of that jerky."

"Uhh, good. More for Red Eagle."

GAINESVILLE, TEXAS
SKEANS BOARDING HOUSE

Ranger Walt Durbin reined up at the single iron hitching post outside the two story Victorian home. He had dropped off the body of Windy Folsom at the undertaker's and made an unsuccessful attempt to find Sheriff Wacker and brief him on the raid at the Rafter S. He had to settle on giving the report to Deputy Rudabaugh.

Lights were on in several of the downstairs rooms and as well as three of the bedrooms on the upper floor. *That's good. I would hate to wake up Annabel to tell her Bodie just got killed in the line of duty...Aw, hell. Who am I kiddin'? Ain't no easy time to tell anybody that.*

He swung down and looped the horse's lead rope through the ring atop the post and patted the animal on the neck. He stepped through the gate in the white picket fence, and then swatted at the trail dust on his pants with his Stetson. It didn't do much good. Neither did the strokes of his gloved hands on his vest. *Wellsir, I guess this ain't gonna be the first time she ever saw a lawman dirty after a day's work.*

Walt topped the steps, crossed the cypress planked porch and stood before the front door for a moment. *Maybe I can find some way to make it not so painful for her.* He thought for a moment and ran several opening lines through his head. *Dag nab it! That ain't the way to do it...She has to cry and carry on to make the whole thing believable. Wish to hell somebody could have figured out a better way to break that gang of cutthroats. Sure hope Bodie can convince her it was all worth it, afterwards.*

He took in a deep breath and banged on the front door four times—the strength of the blows rattled the glass in the side lights beside the entryway.

"Hold your horses, I'm coming! No need to knock the door off the hinges."

Walt heard footsteps on the hardwood floor as Faye reached the front. The middle-aged lady opened the door and glared at him for a second through the screen door in the dim light before she recognized him.

"Ranger Durbin, why didn't you just come on in?"

"Sorry, Ma'am, thought it best to knock," he replied before he cleared his throat. "Is Missus Hickman avaiable?

She looked at Walt with a sudden expression of concern. "Why, yes, she's still up…Uh, why, do you ask? Is something wrong?"

"Uh, Ma'am. I need to speak with her. May I come in?"

Her expression of concern was compounded with one of puzzlement. "Of course. Annabel has retired for the evening, but I know she was still up. I loaned her my copy of *Frankenstein; or The Modern Prometheus* by Mary Shelly a somewhat gothic novel I was given. I'll fetch her down for you." She stepped aside as he opened the screen door and Faye motioned to a small parlor off the foyer next to a larger sitting area in the downstairs. Have a seat over there."

"Yes, Ma'am." Walt walked across the wool oriental rug and found a seat in a straight-backed walnut chair as Faye ascended the stairs. He focused his thoughts on Francis lying wounded in her bed to keep the proper somber mood.

He heard the knock on an upstairs bedroom door and a muted conversation that prevented him from understanding the exact words used. A few seconds later, he could see a pair of women's legs sticking out from underneath a cotton robe as the lady to whom they belonged began to descend the stairway with Faye. *Oh God, here she comes.*

Walt got to his feet and stood holding his hat in his hands. The beauty of the young woman was remarkable, but he could tell she was nervous by her pursed lips.

177

"Walt, how nice to see you…Is something the matter?" Her brow furrowed as her nervousness increased to concern.

"Yes, Ma'am. Uh, as you know I, uh, I was assigned to work with Bodie under cover." He swallowed hard.

"Yes, he told me after you and the Sullivants were here the other night. "

Walt looked nervously at Faye. "Missus Skeans, could you give us some privacy, please. What I have to say to Missus Hickman is kinda personal…"

"No. Missus Skeans can stay…anything you have to say to me, you can say in front of her," Annabel insisted.

Walt's hands unconsciously rolled up the brim in his hat. He nodded nervously and looked at the floor. "All right, I'll get right to it. Me and Bodie was tracking some rustlers and followed 'em up toward the Red…We found one shanks mare and tried to take him in, but he went for his gun. Both of us opened fire and killed him dead."

"Oh my," Faye muttered as she brought her hand to her mouth.

"Then, an hour or so later…up around Dripping Spring, some others ambushed us."

Annabel grabbed his arm. "Bodie is all right isn't he? He can always take care of himself."

He looked at the floor again. "God, Ma'am, I wish there was an easy way to tell you this…He got hit twice and fell off the cliff into the river…He never came up…"

The piercing shriek Annabel let out was one Walt would never forget. Her fingers dug into his arm, and then relaxed as

178

her pretty cerulean blue eyes rolled up in her head and she fainted dead away.

He caught her around the waist before she could hit the floor and lifted her trim body up in a single swift motion. "Oh my gosh. What do we do now?"

Faye held Annabel's head, her long blonde hair hanging down almost to the floor. "Put her on the day bed for now. That's what it was originally designed for."

Walt swiftly complied and laid the distraught widow on the fainting couch. Women's fashion in the late 1800s enhanced lady's hourglass figures with lace-up corsets—some so tight that they restricted proper breathing and frequently led to the wearer's fainting. The couches were designed to support the person's back and head in an inclined manner and allow their legs to remain comfortably horizontal.

"I'll get some smelling salts!" Faye spun around and headed for the kitchen.

A man with a bushy mustache came quickly down the stairs, followed close behind by an older woman with a disfigured face wearing a flannel robe.

"What's all the ruckus?" he demanded. He held a revolver in his hands.

Walt turned to face him. He held up his hands. "The lady fainted is all...You can put your shooter away."

The man slipped his bird's head six-gun into a large pocket on his robe as he noted the badge on the lawman's chest.

"Sorry, I didn't know what the commotion was all about. I just heard the scream..."

"Where is Missus Skeans?" Miss Floyd demanded.

"I'm bringing the smelling salts, Roberta. Ya'll stand back…give the poor young thing some air, she fainted," she said as she strode back into the room.

"What happened, Faye?" Bill asked.

"Ranger Hickman, her husband, was killed in an ambush by rustlers today. He was working with Ranger Durbin here who had to deliver the awful news."

"Ranger Durbin?" Roberta asked. "I thought you were a horse wrangler?"

"Oh my stars. How unfortunate," Bill remarked.

"You men should move her up to her room and then clear out. This is clearly a time for the women of the house to take care of one of their own," Miss Floyd ordered.

"I think that's a good idea," Faye agreed. "Ranger, do you think you could carry Missus Hickman up those stairs for us?"

"If that is what you want, I surely can. She ain't no bigger than a bar o' soap."

He lifted the waspwaisted beauty up his arms without a sign of a struggle. "Just show me the way."

Walt laid the unconscious girl on the embroidered bedspread, resting her head on the goose down pillow. "Sorry, Missus Hickman. I am really, really sorry."

"You boys scoot now…Mister McCarty, can you show Ranger Durbin where to stable his horse? I assume he'll want to spend the night and talk with Missus Hickman in the morning. Room 4 is open next to yours."

"I will take care of it Missus Skeans. Come on, son."

"Yessir, my horse is tied out front."

Outside, Walt untied the loaned horse and followed the stranger to the small carriage house in the back. Brushy Bill struck a match and lighted a lantern hung inside the door. "There's an empty stall, either end. Take your choice."

"Thanks, mister...say, I never got your name."

"Folks know me here as Henry McCarty." He stuck his hand inside his left robe pocket and pulled out something shiny. "I'm Brushy Bill Roberts."

Walt leaned over to see what it was in the flickering yellow light of the coal oil lamp. "Deputy US Marshal...Indian Territory?"

Brushy Bill nodded and grinned broadly. "I'm undercover, like you were." The smile faded. "Sorry about your partner. Did he die quick?"

Walt held up his raised index finger to his lips and looked to carriage house front door. "Don't let nobody know, but he ain't dead. It's a play-like thing to get Bass Reeves and Jack McGann inside the gang that has been rustling around these parts."

"Whew...Coulda fooled me. I believed you and it was obvious your partner's wife did, too."

"That's the whole idea. Bass and Jack told me that they had a man working undercover in these parts, but didn't know what name you would be using."

"I've used many aliases before. Chose Henry McCarty this time."

"McCarty? Say, isn't that the name you used up in Kansas a while back? I heard you got arrested there 'cause the local gendarmes thought you were Billy the Kid."

Bill chuckled. "Took a rather sizable amount of convincing...Showed 'em my Pinkerton's badge and reminded 'em that everybody knows Pat Garrett killed young Billy way back in '81...right?"

"That's what they say." Walt glanced at him from the corner of his eye.

"I'll bring you up to snuff...

Ten minutes later, Bill added, "I went back out there this afternoon...figured they thought they had me buffaloed and it should be clear...Picked up the tracks again..."

"Where'd they lead?"

"Well, that's the thing. I found what was left of the caisson...burned up in a gully that led down to Clear Creek. There wasn't much left but the metal tire rings and part of the hubs."

"Any tracks leadin' away?"

"Indeed...a set of wagon tracks. I made it a freight wagon due to the width of the iron rim. They led to a big new barn on a spread, that I guessed extended into Wise or Montague counties...or maybe both."

"See anybody?" asked Walt.

"Couple of hired hands. Looked like a typical cattle operation from where I could see. Had some fine stock, no scrub cattle."

"Big place?"

"Oh…A couple of sections, at least."

"What in the Sam Hill would a cattle operation be doin' with a Gatling Gun?"

"Damn sure not for varmint control," offered Bill.

"Ya think?"

"Have to do some more checking. Try to find out who owns it. My time with the Pinkerton Detective Agency should come in handy."

"I'd say…Let me get this tack off of this nag. I'm plum tuckered out, but sure could use myself a bath."

DEXTER

They had been sitting on the back porch for hours after dinner, talking nonstop about things each liked to eat, about books they had enjoyed, and any other subject came to mind. Finally, Taggart slipped his gold pocket watch out of his vest and checked it.

"Miss Millie, much as I hate to do it, I believe it's time for me to bid you adieu. Got a long ride back to town…"

"Nonsense, Taggart. That's silly. Besides, your horse could step in a pothole or rut in the dark and break its leg…It's Friday night. You don't work on Saturday do you?"

"Not usually…just when the need arises." He glanced back in the house. "I suppose you could make me a pallet on the floor."

Millie got to her feet and pulled him up from his rocking chair. A slightly mischievous grin came to her face. "Taggart Wacker. Neither one of us is a child anymore. I could no more get a wink of sleep thinking about you lying in the next room on the floor than the man in the moon." She leaned in and kissed him softly on the corner of his mouth.

He turned his head just slightly and returned the kiss with passion as he gently slipped his hand under her long flowing black hair and pulled her head tight to his. After a long moment, both came up gasping for air.

"Me neither," he whispered.

Her dark eyes sparkled in the glow from the coal oil lamp as her bosom rose and fell with her deep breaths. "It's settled then."

Millie pulled the shades down on her bedroom window and then moved to the Eastlake style dresser with a separate three piece pier mirror mounted on top. She turned the wick down on the lamp, making the light grow smaller until it was barely putting out more illumination than a candle. She turned to her suitor and smiled demurely. "I hope you don't mind...I want to watch you when we make love."

Taggart nodded. "Whatever you wish my dear. I want to remember this night forever."

He kissed her tenderly and began to unfasten the numerous bone buttons on her bodice...

GAINESVILLE, TEXAS

Sheriff Wacker turned the buggy south off the busy California Street onto Red River and drove two blocks to Pecan. He made the right hand turn past the fire station and pulled up in front of the county jail, stepped out and tied the lead rope to a cast iron hitching post.

"Morning, Sheriff," one of the passersby said as Taggart headed toward the jail.

"Morning to you, too, Archie. Beautiful weather we're havin', is it not?"

"It is, it is," he agreed.

Wacker entered the two story building and went straight to the round faced deputy on duty. "Good morning, George. How was Friday night in the big city?"

The bulky thirty year old set down his coffee cup, taking note of the smile on Wacker's face. "Sheriff, you're looking mighty chipper this mornin'...Just like the cat that ate the canary." He chuckled at his own joke. "Nothin' special...a few bar fights and a half dozen drunks...I let em out about ten thirty, once they sobered up a bit. Laid some new dodgers on your desk...nobody I recognize."

"Good work. I did enjoy an afternoon off. Let me just look at the posters and I'll be on my way. Too nice a day to spend inside, I reckon."

A minute or so later, a stocky, well-dressed blonde-haired man entered the building, doffed his black silk top hat and walked up the to reception desk.

"Sheriff Wacker?"

"No sir, I'm Deputy Rudabaugh...Chief Deputy Rudabaugh. May I help you?"

"Actually I was hoping to speak directly with the sheriff himself. It's a matter of some importance."

"Well, sir, you are in luck. He's not usually here on Saturday, but he dropped by to review some paperwork. May I have your name please?"

"Alvin Karl Fleitmann, from Lindsay...President of the Lindsay National Bank."

"Right this way, sir."

The deputy made the introductions and returned to his desk after closing the door to the sheriff's private office.

Wacker leaned back in his padded brown leather chair. "Tell me, Mister Fleitmann, how can I be of service?"

"Sheriff, as you know, Cooke County has become something of a cotton powerhouse in Texas since the war, not to mention the effect the cattle drives have made on the area in years past."

"I am aware of the positive economic impact that the agricultural community has had. Lindsay was situated in a prime location to service the supply needs of the drovers before they crossed over into the Indian Territory."

"That is correct, sir, and although the railroads eliminated the cattle drives, the bounty of our black land cotton crops has presented my bank with a slight predicament..."

"How so?"

"My German friends and neighbors have just sold last year's crop at record prices. You see, they held on after the local harvest, when prices are often depressed due to abundant supply, and recently sold at top dollar."

"That's good, is it not?"

"Of course," the ruddy faced banker agreed. "My predicament, as far as a banker goes, is a simple one. All these crop sales, along with a couple of large ranches and farms which were on the market and closed in the past week or so, put an influx of cash into Lindsay National that far exceeds our ability to lend out locally...As you probably know, banks only make money when they can loan it out and charge a reasonable interest." He smiled.

Fleitmann looked around the room nervously. "The amount of cash that has been deposited recently brings us up to over one million in gold, silver and paper currency. It will be Wednesday before we can get an armed escort to deliver the excess funds to Fort Worth and Dallas banks via the railroad. I have made arraignments with them to act as loan intermediaries in our behalf. What I was hoping from you was to obtain an additional security presence until next Wednesday to protect the interests of my depositors."

Taggart smiled. "Nothing makes me happier than serving the needs of our community...Will two trusted deputies be enough? I'll put my best men on it...round the clock."

Fleitmann was relieved. He jumped to his feet and thrust out his hand. "You don't know what a weight you have taken off my mind. Thank you, thank you, thank you."

Wacker shook his hand firmly. "My pleasure, sir." He winked. "Now don't go and forget me when the election rolls around next year."

"I won't, I promise you that," Fleitmann said with a grin.

Wacker escorted the banker to the front door and bid him farewell. He turned around and walked back to the reception desk. "George, how would like to make a little bonus pay over the next few days?"

"Twist my arm. Either one…your choice."

"Figured as much. I want you and Tyler over to Lindsay from now until Wednesday, 'round the clock at the Lindsay Bank."

"What's up, Sheriff?"

"Just additional security. Seems they have over million in cash in the vault and the president asked me for some help. Is it worth an extra ten bucks apiece?"

"Shoot, sounds like easy money to me. I'll go round up Harold to spell me here and try get a hold of Tyler. Thanks for the extra pay."

"I'll hang around here until you are able to reach Deputy Offner." Wacker grinned and nodded. "Hey, what are friends for?"

SKEANS BOARDING HOUSE

Brushy Bill accompanied Walt Durbin out to the carriage house to saddle up.

"Damned shame about how hard that young Annabel is taking the news about her husband."

"She looked she been dragged behind a team o' mules. Must have not had a bit of sleep and cried her eyes out all night," Walt commented.

"You gonna stop by the Sheriff's office and file a report before you head back to the Rafter S?"

"Got to get the rustling report in and send a telegram to the Rangers first. What are your plans?"

"Cain't do a thing about locating the legal owner of that property until the county clerk's office opens on Monday. 'Til then, I'll keep an eye on Annabel and keep my ears open."

The two shook hands and Walt turned to grab his tack.

COOKE COUNTY TEXAS
CALLISBURG

The moonless night was clear, with the only light provided by the untold millions of stars twinkling like scintillating diamonds. Four men plus the hooded leader met again inside the dusty old abandoned Butterfield Stage way station.

"We have a little change of plans, gentlemen, thanks to Pink's fortuitous and brilliant acquisition of the Gatling Gun on the last trip." He took a draw on his expensive cigar and blew a cloud of smoke toward the other four. His black hood only came to just below his nose, allowing him to smoke.

"It's a sweet piece," said Pink. *Who is this guy? Ain't never seen nothin' but that black hood.*

The leader continued, "We have accomplished our main goal of putting Sullivant into virtual bankruptcy and acquiring most of his prime breeding stock…and, notwithstanding the fact that he now has to spend a lot of his time and remaining resources seeing to his daughter's recuperation…assuming she makes it."

"Pity we lost Windy and the others, but those two new men took care of that ranger," said Tom Lee.

"You did verify?" asked the leader.

"They couldn't find the body, but Rube reported that he saw him get shot and fall off a forty foot bluff into the Red. The hired hand with him hightailed it back to the ranch with Windy's body."

"Excellent…Now, we don't have too much time before they send a bunch of rangers up to find out what happened to him, so, we're going to do one more operation, and then we can all retire…I have it on good authority that the Lindsay National Bank has well over a million dollars in their vault…"

"A million dollars! Jesus, Mary and Joseph!" exclaimed Tom.

"You'll hit it and then scatter and meet back here at the way station the following night to divy up and then scatter again…Let the rangers try to track fifteen men…With Windy gone, who do you have that can operate the Gatling?"

"Con Kilgore, says he can, Boss," answered Pink. "Bully Jack and Dallas can be the rest of the gun crew, reloadin' and such."

"All right, then, here's the plan…"

***

CHAPTER TEN

WOLF RUN RIDGE
COOKE COUNTY

It was Sunday afternoon when Rube rode back into camp. He dismounted and stripped the tack from his grulla.

"Red Eagle take down to picket pen, Rube. There hot coffee at fire."

"Thanks, Cyrus, 'preciate it." He stepped over to the big graniteware pot sitting on one of the flat ammonite fossil rocks next to the pit. He folded one of his gloves and wrapped it around the handle and poured himself a cup of the stout trail brew.

"What'd Tom have to say, Rube?" asked Jack as he held his cup over for a warm up.

"Well, it was interestin'." He blew across the top of his tin cup and took a sip.

The others glanced at one another and shook their heads.

"This another *pisa tohbi* game?" asked Red Eagle.

"No game, just tryin' to figure out how to put this."

"How 'bout startin' at the beginnin'…always a good place," said Jack.

"You know that Gatling Gun?" asked Rube.

"Not personal, but know about it," commented Jack.

"Well, seems like the big boss, whoever the hell that is…says there's over a million dollars in the Lindsay National Bank…and we're gonna relieve 'em of it 'fore they can transfer it to Dallas on Wednesday by train."

"Good gosh amighty!" exclaimed Bodie.

"They have a plan, do they?" asked Bass.

"They do…They've mounted the gun in the back of a freight wagon…gonna cover it with a tarp and have a three man crew. All told, they's fifteen of us an' we're to ride into Lindsay from all four sides just before the bank's closin' time."

"Lindsay ain't very big, cain't be mor'n two or three hundered folks all together…Nothin' there but a Catholic church, the bank, St. Joseph's Convent, a saloon and a mercantile," said Bodie.

"Probably why they picked Lindsay, 'stead of Gainesville. Lotta money in the bank, like in the Gainesville banks, but not too many people around…Good set-up," said Bass.

"What's our plan, Bass?" asked Jack.

"First, just to make everything legal, I'm deputizin' Cyrus and Rube...and Red Eagle, you ain't known in town...need you to go in and bring Walt and Bill back out here and then..."

RAFTER S RANCH

Walt was slumped in a chair beside Francis Ann's bed. His arms were crossed, his chin resting on his chest and showed a full day and a half's worth of dark beard stubble. He didn't even notice when her green eyes fluttered open for the first time and tried to focus on her room. She started to roll over on her side, but the searing pain in her shoulder stopped her cold.

"Ow...What?" She looked down at the bandage as she raised the covers with her left hand.

The weary lawman awoke with a start, almost tipping the ladder-back chair over in the process. A smile came to his lips. "Finally...Didn't think you were ever gonna come to."

"What happened to me? How did I get here?"

"One of the rustlers plugged you and you passed out on Friday mornin'. I brung you back here, quick as I could."

"That would explain why my shoulder hurts..." She looked under the covers again. "Where are my clothes?" Francis quickly pulled the comforter back up to her chin.

Walt grinned somewhat sheepishly. "Doc Wellman and I had to cut 'em off of you. They were bloody and all...and he had to dig that slug outta you."

She eyed him somewhat suspiciously. "You saw me naked?"

"It wasn't like that…you were, uh, disrobed. Yeah, that's it. Disrobed…I didn't look at your…I uh, kept my eyes shut." His face began to blush.

"You mean you did everything by feel?"

"Yes…uh, no! I mean…"

Francis grinned at his obvious discomfort. "Walt Durbin, you look like you were rode hard and put away wet. Didn't anybody every tell you it is rude to go unshaven in polite society? A gentleman must do so…"

"Hold your horses, Red…Now, I shaved Saturday morning at Miss Skeans boarding house. Didn't get any sleep last night watchin' over you…Musta dozed off after lunch."

The redhead was clearly confused. "What day is it?"

"Sunday…Doc Wellman had to get back to town. One of his patients was havin' a hard time with childbirth."

The still very weak horsewoman sank back on the pillow. "Sunday? You mean to tell me I have been unconscious for two days?"

"Two and a half, actually…Bet you're hungry as a panther. You need to eat somethin'." He stood up dropped his arms to his side, exposing the silver Texas Ranger's badge on his vest.

Francis' eyes fell upon the star. "Did the sheriff make you a deputy?" She squinted her eyes and looked closer, read the badges' inscription, and then locked eyes with him. "What's going on? I don't understand…"

"Plenty of time to get into all that. What's important now is to get you back on your feet. 'Sides, your daddy is worried sick about his little girl…Let me get you some soup and tell him you're awake." He smiled broadly, his gray eyes sparkling as tiny crinkles lined his tanned face. He reached down and took her hand in both of his. "Mighty glad to have you back."

She squeezed his hands firmly and softly said, "Thank you."

GAINESVILLE, TEXAS

Red Eagle trotted his red and white Appaloosa east on California Street, looking for the turn to get to Skeans Boarding House, according to the directions Bodie gave him. Spying Dixon, he turned south and in a couple of blocks he noticed the sign in the front yard of the large Queen Anne Victorian brick home. *No know what name Bill using. Will wait across street...he come out, by and by.*

He reined under a large red oak catty-corner from the house, dismounted, loosened the girth and sat down cross-legged in the grass under the big tree and waited with the patience known only to the American Indian. Cloud contentedly nipped at the short Bermuda grass, being careful not to step on his ground tie dangling reins.

Inside the home, Roberta Floyd moved closer to Annabel, who was seated in a dainty settee in the parlor. The young widow's color was still not good and she hadn't really slept in two days—dark puffy circles hung beneath her blue eyes.

"My I bring you another cup of tea, dear?"

"No, Ma'am. I don't believe I'm thirsty, but I do thank you so much for your consideration. That's so sweet."

"As you wish, my child. Heaven knows how hard you are taking your husband's untimely demise."

Faye approached from the kitchen with a tray of finger sandwiches. She set them on the coffee table in front of Annabel. "I know you said you weren't hungry, but I made these for you…even cut the crusts off like you prefer."

Annabel glanced up, and then dabbed at the corner of her eye with an embroidered silk handkerchief. "You ladies are so sweet. I wish I felt like eating something, just to be nice." She sighed and dabbed once again at the other eye. "It seems like I am suddenly all hollow inside…like something has sucked the life out of me…forever."

"Forever is a long time, young lady. You still have a whole lifetime ahead of you," Faye said.

The comment didn't seem to help at all. Annabel slumped even lower. "The thought of a lifetime without my darling Bodie is almost too much to bear…There is nothing for me here any more. I just want to go back to Oklahoma City…My parents are still at my Uncle Bartholomew's."

Brushy Bill passed by the parlor heading for the front door and heard Faye reply, "I'll go down to the depot and buy you a ticket. Now they don't run today, being Sunday and all, but there is a train to Oklahoma City leaving Monday evening at six, I believe."

She nodded. "That would be the best thing for me to do. I want to be with my family now."

Cyrus was chewing on a strip of Jack's peppered venison jerky when Bill stepped out on the verandah, pulled a cigar from his pocket and lit it. As he looked up and shook the match to extinguish it, he first noticed Cloud, and then Red Eagle across the street. He grinned and moved down the steps and toward his friend.

Bill held out his hand as Red Eagle got to his feet. "Looks like you're healing up fine."

"Still sore some, but Red Eagle has things to do."

"Something tells me you're not here on a social visit."

"Not know what is 'social visit', Bill Roberts, but Bass Reeves send to fetch you to camp along with Ranger Walt Durbin...Not know what name you use here, so Osí Hommá wait."

Bill took a draw of his cigar. "Going by Henry McCarty, the writer, here. Glad you didn't ask for Brushy Bill."

Red Eagle almost grinned. "Henry McCarty, the writer. Long name...Like saying me Osí Hommá, Chickasaw warrior and Lighthorse. Too many words...Where ranger?"

Bill chuckled. "Got a point there, my friend...Walt is out at the Rafter S, seeing about his lady friend that the rustlers shot."

"We go."

"Let me get my traps and I'll meet you around back at the carriage house where Tippy is stalled."

Cyrus nodded and called to his horse. "Cloud, come."

The Appaloosa stallion chuckled and stepped over to his master. Red Eagle tightened the cinch and stepped into the saddle as Bill neared the porch.

197

An hour later, Bill and Red Eagle rode through the gate entrance to the headquarters of the Rafter S. Little John, noticing the two, stepped forward from the barn and intercepted them before they reached the house.

"Help you fellers?" he said with his hand resting on the butt of his belt gun.

"Need to see Walt," said Bill. "He about?"

"Meby he is an' meby he ain't. Who's askin'?

"Deputy United States Marshal Roberts and Chickasaw Lighthorse Cyrus Maytubbi. That suit you?"

"Oh! Yes, sir. He's inside seeing to Miss Fran. He just took some hot beef broth upstairs to her. I'll go up and fetch him fer you."

"Much obliged…Mind if we get down and tie up?"

"No, sir, Marshal, sir. Kin I have Sing Loo, the cook, bring you some cool water?"

"That would be right neighborly…"

"John Mayberry, they just call me Little John," the short man said.

"Right."

When Little John went inside, Cyrus asked, "Good name for little man…Like Chickasaw name. Not like *pisa tohbi* names that no make sense…Red Eagle like."

The Chinese cook came out the front door with two pint Mason jars of well water and handed one to each of the men.

He waited as they two law officers downed the water and returned the ubiquitous containers.

"Thank you, Sing Loo," said Bill.

"Velly velcome, Mister Marshal. Velly velcome." He bowed, and then turned and went back into the house.

"Little yellow man with pigtail talk funny. Red Eagle like too."

Walt and Little John stepped out on the porch.

"Bill, something up? Who's this feller with you?"

"Sorry to interrupt, but Bass wants us out to his encampment. This is Osí Hommá, Chickasaw Lighthorse, also known as Cyrus Maytubbi. He's going to show us the way."

"Has there been some development?"

"Bass tell...We go," said Red Eagle.

"No explanation?"

"Explain later, we go...Get horse."

"Man of few words, ain't he?"

The Lighthorse nodded. "Not Osí Hommá's job to talk. Bass also say bring mustang belong ranger. Need extra."

"Lakota? Sure...Little John, you mind tackin' Moon and Pepper while I go back up and say good bye to Francis?"

"Not a problem, Ranger." The little man scurried away toward the corral by the barn.

"Be right back," Walt said as he headed back inside the house and up the stairs.

He tapped on Fran's door lightly.

"Come in," came the response.

He turned the knob and stepped inside and over to her bed. She was sitting up with pillows propped behind her back finishing her broth.

"This was so good," she said as she blotted her lips with her napkin using her good arm. "I didn't realize how hungry I was."

"Would you like some more?"

"Yes, but I think it might not set well, since I haven't eaten for two days."

"I agree," Walt said as he took the wooden breakfast tray from her lap and set it on her dresser. He stepped back over to her bed. "Would you like to lay back down?"

"No, I think I've been in that position long enough. I want to sit up so I can see outside the window."

He plumped her pillows. "Good idea. The doc said you needed to sit upright as much as possible to help avoid the pneumonia setting in due to your damaged lung."

"Guess I was lucky."

"No, if you were lucky, you wouldn't have gotten shot at all."

She grinned and blinked her emerald green eyes.

"I...uh, have to go. The Marshals that came in to work under cover like me, have asked that I come out to their camp. Seems there's somethin' up. Don't know what yet."

Francis nodded. "I understand. I hope they've got a line on the rustlers."

"'Spect that's it. We'll see...I'll brush your hair for you when I get back."

"Oh, that will do me as much good as anything I can think of beside getting out of this bed. I usually brush it one hundred strokes every night before I retire."

"I'll give you two hundred," he said as he winked at her. He stopped when he reached the door and turned back to her. "Uh, by the way, when we get all this rustlin' business put to bed...We're gettin' married."

"Oh, really? You're pretty sure of yourself, aren't you?"

"Yes, I am...about this, anyway."

She smiled big. "You took your sweet time."

"You were unconscious, or I would have told you sooner."

"Don't start making excuses."

"Not. Just statin' facts...When someone really wants to do somethin', they find a way...If they don't, they'll find an excuse."

"You take care out there, mister...You hear me?"

"Yesssum, plan on it. I'm a very careful feller." He grinned and closed the door.

Walt stepped out the front, letting the screen door close behind him with a bang, jumped down the four steps from the porch to the ground and went out the gate to where the others were waiting. He took the reins to Pepper from Little John—Red Eagle was already holding the lead to Lakota Moon—stabbed his foot in the stirrup and wheeled the blood bay gelding about.

"Thanks, Little John."

"My pleasure, Ranger."

"Let's ride, boys," he said as he squeezed his mount into a hand canter out the front gate.

Bill and Red Eagle looked at each other, grinned and kicked out after him.

WOLF RUN RIDGE
COOKE COUNTY

Red Eagle led the way up the incline through the trees and rocks to the camp at the top of the ridge.

"Well, glad to see ya'll finally made it. Thought we's gonna have to send the dogs out for you...but we ain't got any," said Jack. "You must be Walt." He stuck out his hand as the tall ranger dismounted.

"I am, and you'd be Marshal McGann I take it."

"Close enough...That dark complexioned gentleman over there is Bass Reeves, this little feller here is Rube Carter...an' 'course you know the recently deceased Bodie Hickman."

They all nodded at each other.

"Bass, your reputation precedes you far and wide. It's a real honor to meet you." They shook hands.

"Most is newspaper exaggeration, I suspect," Reeves replied with a big toothy smile.

"Not likely," Jack interjected. "The papers ain't even close...Hell, Myra Mabelle Shirley, better known as Belle Starr, turned herself in to Marshal Bud Ledbetter in Muscogee when she heard Bass was carryin' paper on her...That's kindly like fish a jumpin' out on the bank when they see you baitin' your hook."

"Alright, that's enough of that. You boys shuck yer tack off'n the horses, take 'em down to the picket pen by the creek an' give 'em a bait of grain...We'll git the coffee on," said Bass.

"I'll help, need to say hi to Moon and give him a brushin' or he'll be mad at me," said Bodie as he took the lead rope from Red Eagle.

Moon shook his head and whinnied as Bodie ran the curry comb over his flanks. The ranger looked over to his fellow Texas lawman who was hanging a feed sack on his own mount.

"I been wondering how Annabel took it when you told her I got killed."

Walt cut his eyes at him. "You son of a bitch...Don't you even think 'bout askin' me to do nothing like that again." Walt left his mount and moved closer to Bodie. "Like to have killed that pretty little thing. I ain't never heard nobody scream like that...ever and I don't want to again...She fainted dead away."

"Oh goshomighty." Bodie took in a deep breath as a sick look washed across his face. "It weren't my idea, you know. Bass and them needed a way to get in the gang and that was the best way..."

"I got that part. It's just that I hate lying, for one, and having to put her through that all that pain...Tell you one thing, my friend. There ain't no question she loved you a lot. That wasn't no act she put on."

"Think she'll be able to forgive me after this?"

"I reckon as so...but I got to tell you something, partner. She's pulling up stakes tomorrow afternoon...She said there wasn't anything left for her in Texas . Faye Skeans done bought her ticket up to Oklahoma City. Northbound train for Oklahoma Territory leaves at six o'clock."

"Aw, Jesus. I gotta stop her somehow before she gets on that train..."

Fifteen minutes later, the four lawmen trudged back up the hill and over to the fire pit. Each had brought their cups from their saddle bags.

Jack used one of his black leather deerskin gloves wrapped around the handle and his kerchief at the bottom to pour the black trail brew into everyone's cups—he filled his last and set the large blue speckled graniteware pot back on its rock next the fire.

All except Bass took seats on rocks or logs and began nursing the steaming liquid. Being a natural leader, Reeves had assumed control of the operation instinctively—a point no one objected to. He had taken a moment to fire up his old briar pipe and pace a bit. Jack and Bodie knew he did that when he was cogitating what he had to do.

Finally, he stopped, tapped the bowl in the palm of his huge hand and dumped the ashes in the fire. "Gentlemen, we have our work cut out for us. Tomorrow, the Red River gang...that's a name I decided to give 'em...plan on robbin' the Lindsay National Bank of the near one million dollars in cash and gold they got on deposit. 'Cordin' to Rube here, they're mountin' that Gatling Gun in a freight wagon to control the locals."

"Damn, Bass, a lot of folks could get killed with that thing. I was present at a demonstration of the weapon at Fort Sumner for the benefit of the Apaches a few years back. Let me tell you, it put the fear of God in them," said Bill. "I understand it has a firing rate of some four hundred rounds a minute…and those are .45-70s."

There were moans and whistles around the pit by everyone except Cyrus.

The Chickasaw Lighthorse got to his feet, pulled up his calico shirt and showed the newly healed pass-through bullet wounds. "Red Eagle lucky."

More whistles.

"By the Lord Harry, that exit wound musta been big as a baseball…Looks like it taken seven stitches 'er so," exclaimed Jack.

"Unnh, Anompoli Lawa put good medicine he got from Jack's wife…"

"Turpentine and tallow…Damn stuff works miracles, I kin tell you from first hand experience," interrupted Jack.

"Well, the point is, I don't intend for them to use it…if'n we kin help it."

"How're we gonna stop a weapon like that, Bass?"

"That's where you come in, Bodie. You wondered where me an' Jack went while we was waitin' on Red Eagle to get back with Bill and Walt…Well, we took a little ride over to Lindsay to check things out. Seems there's a Catholic church 'bout two hundered 'er so yards west of the bank…It's got a bell tower…"

"I got it! You want me in the tower with my big Winchester…"

"Yep, can't use it if'n they ain't got nobody to crank the handle."

"Hell, Bass, I can drive a nail with that gun at two hundred yards."

"That's the general idee, Bodie."

"Red Eagle, you'll be across the street sittin' 'gainst the wall in front of Dieter's Mercantile pretendin' yer asleep…Walt, want you inside the bank and Bill, you kin be inside Dieters."

"What about you, Jack and Rube?" asked Bill.

"Well, they still think we're part of the gang and we're supposed to enter town from the north 'xactly at 3:30…so that's what we'll do. Rube says the wagon, driven by Dallas Humby with Bully Jack and Con Kilgore ridin' behind 'er is to come in from the south…They're the three man gun crew. The others, includin' Pink and Tom Lee will be comin' in from the east and the west…All told, they's thirteen of them, not countin' me, Jack and Rube, 'course…Plus that Gatling Gun."

"Thirteen to seven…Sounds like pretty even odds to me," said Bill. "Especially with Bodie up in the tower sniping…I'd say they had an unlucky number."

Bass nodded. "Well, let's hope so…and ya'll just try not to shoot one another."

"How we gonna recognize them?"

Oh! Durn, glad you said somethin', Jack...almost fergot."
Rube reached in his inside coat pocket and fished out a wad of
blue cloth. "We's all supposed to be wearin' these light blue
wild rags round our necks." He handed one to Bass and one to
Jack. The third he kept for himself. "'Pears Tom Lee was
concerned 'bout them shootin' each other too." He grinned.

WISE COUNTY

Pink Lee leaned over to look inside the two horse Studebaker
wagon to inspect the finishing touches Skabby Johnson was
putting on the bolts anchoring the Gatling Gun to the bed.

The gang, sans Bass, Jack and Rube were in the center of a
large red barn. The big double doors at each end were open to
allow for maximum light, not to say anything about ventilation
for the stifling afternoon heat.

"You sure those will hold that damn thing to the bed? She
kicks purty good," Pink asked.

"Shouldn't be a problem," said Con Kilgore from underneath
the wagon as he tightened the last of the half-inch nuts
anchoring the thick iron yoke, while Skabby held back up on the
bolt head inside the bed. "We put an extry layer of boards under
the floorboards to bolt to...gives us a full two inches of
thickness."

With the base of the gun fastened to the bed of the sturdy
wagon, the barrels of the deadly weapon just cleared the
seventeen inch high sideboards. The Gatling could swivel
almost three hundred degrees.

Pink turned around to address two other men, Harkey Littlefield and Norman Thurlow, building wooden crates underneath the left side loft. "How ya'll comin' on those crates?"

"'Bout done," said Harkey as he nailed a top slat across one of the three foot square wooden boxes.

"They ain't gonna be too heavy are they?"

"Naw," said Thurlow. "Bein' empty, one man kin chunk the front one over the side and Bully kin just kick the rear one out the back after he drops the gate.

The crates placed at each end on either side of the gun would enable a tarp to be thrown over the entire bed, completely obscuring the weapon.

Tom Lee walked in the north end of the barn smoking an expensive cigar. "How's it goin', boys?"

The other men, Bully Jack, Elmer Simmons, Rad Cullum, Ben Brasher, Bud Stevens, Sawyer Smith and Dallas Humby, were sitting around on bales of hay, most smoking roll-your-owns, answered in the affirmative.

Tom leaned under the wagon. "Con, you, Bully and Dallas practice any on that thing?"

"Fixin' to do some dry loadin' and firin' soon's we git done here. I done showed 'em how to load while I'm a crankin'...Just need to go through a few drills," Kilgore said as he slid himself out from underneath. "Wish we could do some live firin', but one, it's too damn noisy and two, only have those two cases of ammo that was on the caisson."

Tom grabbed a handful of the big bolts from a can, unrolled a two foot square paper he had carried in his left hand and spread it on the open rear gate of the wagon. He placed one of the three inch anchors on each corner to hold it down. "Ya'll gather 'round."

The men crowed as close as they could, the ones in the back looking over the shoulders of those in front at the town plat of Lindsay, Texas.

"Dallas, you'll drive the wagon in from the south, tracking along the Fort Worth and Wichita Railroad after you angle in on the old Butterfield Stage road. Stop in front of Dieters Mercantile like you're going to unload. Con and Bully will dismount and tie up at the adjacent hitching rails."

"Do we pull the tarp then?" asked Con.

"You do not. Wait 'til the rest of us are in place...Understand?"

Kilgore nodded.

"Elmer, Norman, Ben and Harkey will ride in from the west, go around behind Deiters, tie up and saunter down the alley to the front. Rad, Sawyer, Skabby and Bud will come in from the east, go behind the bank, tie up there and drift to the front one at the time...Pink and I will follow and hitch up at the Palace Saloon here." He pointed to the building just east of Deiter's.

"What about them two new guys and Rube?" asked Pink.

"They're to ride in from the north, leave their horses at the end of the street and walk down to the bank from there...All this will take place starting exactly at 3:30. I figure it will take no more than seven minutes for everyone to be in place. Got it?"

"When do I start crankin'?" asked Con.

"I'll wave my hat. Ya'll jerk the tarp off, jump in the wagon and kick the crates out...and then spray a hundred rounds or so across the front of the bank just above head high. The point is not to kill the guy inside who has to open the vault. Swing around and give Deiter's a good spray. That should keep the citizens at bay...Believe me, when they hear that big gun bark and glass goes to flyin', they'll all hit the floor."

"You got that right...It's the scariest thing you'll ever see," said Kilgore.

"That's when we head into the bank, right?" said Pink.

"Right. You, me, Rad, Sawyer, Skabby and Bud go inside. It'll probably take all of us to carry all that money back out to the wagon. You got no idea how big a pile a million dollars will make." He laughed. "Everybody else covers from outside in the event some idiot tries to be a hero...Don't think anybody is going to try to follow us and face the business end of that Gatling."

The others grinned and nodded at each other at that image.

"What if they won't open the vault, er it's got one of them time locks on it when we git inside?" asked Pink.

"That's why Skabby is bringing his special satchel."

"What special satchel?" Harkey quipped with a puzzled expression.

"The one with the five sticks of dynamite and fuses in it...just in case," said Tom.

"Oh! That satchel," commented Brasher with a grin.

"We'll blow the dang door off if we have too...Always come prepared, is my motto," added Tom Lee.

Skabby Johnson touched the brim of his hat and tilted his head.

***

CHAPTER ELEVEN

NORTHERN COOKE COUNTY

Bass, Jack, Bodie, Bill, Walt and Red Eagle had ridden east from Wolf Run Ridge to the Fort Worth-Wichita right-of-way and turned south. The railroad track was a straight shot to Lindsay. It was the same railway the wagon carrying the Gatling Gun was using to move north.

"Kindly convenient that we're supposed to tie up behind the stockyards," said Jack as the group of lawmen hand trotted along the side of the railroad bed.

"I'd say," added Bass as he held his Standardbred to a smooth four beat trot referred to as an amble. "When we git a mile er so from Lindsay, we'll hold up and Bodie kin circle around an' git his self in position up in the tower…See as you kin find a place a little outside of town to leave Moon, Bodie."

He nodded. "Yep. Figured I would…Wouldn't do fer any of the gang to recognize him."

"Believe yer right," commented Jack as he spit an amber stream of tobacco juice at the adjacent west side steel track and hit it. "Damn, I'm good." He wiped the dribble of spittle from his chin with the back of his sleeve.

"Walt, you angle around east and go into the bank and tell the two deputies that you're additional security. Cyrus will go in next to set up outside Deiter's an' then Bill…you go. Me, Jack and Rube will come last…so's we kin be there at 'xactly at 3:30," said Bass.

"You know, I think I've figured out why the 3:30 time…other than thirty minutes before the bank's closin' time."

"Gonna tell us, Bodie, er do we have to guess?"

"Don't git yer tail in a knot, Uncle Jack. I was gonna git to it…They ring the bell to turn school out for the day at 3:30."

"Wonderful," commented Bill. "Not only will there be kids all over the place, but that bell will make a racket that will help cover up the sound of the Gatling…Not completely, but enough to make it confusing."

"Where's the school house?" asked Walt.

"As I recall, 'bout a block northwest of the bank, next to the convent," replied Bodie.

"Well, hell," Bass muttered. "Ain't gonna make our job no easier. The thought of one or more of them kids gettin' shot or trampled kinda makes my butt wanna work buttonholes." He spat a stream of tobacco juice off to his left.

Jack glanced over at his partner. The look on his face was one he had seen before and he knew right away that chances of the bank robbers living all the way to sunset just went down a notch or two. When kids or lady folk get put in harm's way, the big black man tended to get a bit testy.

Bodie spied a cluster of fifteen foot tall cedar trees a quarter of a mile from the church at the edge of town. "Come on Moon. You'll be plumb out of sight in there." He hand loped over and eased up to the outside of the densely packed copse of trees. Pulling rein, he stood in the stirrups and tried to spot an easy way into the brush.

"Not enough room to turn around in there big boy."

He spun the line-back dun around, placed his thumb and forefinger on his withers in front of the saddle horn and lightly squeezed—the subtle signal for the horse to back up.

Moon tucked his chin to his chest and scooted back in a straight line, the branches brushing hard against both sides and then closing in front. He stopped when Bodie released the pressure of his hand and relaxed his legs.

The ranger unshucked the big bore Winchester from its scabbard and stepped down in the small open area near the center of the cedars. Quickly loosening the front cinch, he patted his favorite horse on the neck. "Stay put, son. This shouldn't take too dang long…I hope. Got us a purty important errand to do when it's over." He opened his left side saddle bag, grabbed his binoculars and pulled out a full box of the shiny finger-sized rounds for his rifle. He tore the cardboard flap off one end, and then proceeded to dump the twenty cartridges into his right outside coat pocket. "That outta do…Make every shot count."

He pressed his way out of the brushy hiding spot and began to jog toward the church.

Walt rode Pepper into Schmidlkofer's livery stable a block east of Dieter's Mercantile. A young towheaded boy came out to greet him.

"Say, mister. What can I do you for?"

"Just water him and loosen his girth. I'll be back directly." Walt stepped down and drew the Winchester from its boot before he handed the lad the reins.

"You bet. We aim to please."

Carrying the '95 model muzzle-low in his left hand, the ranger strode purposely past the bustling store and glanced up and down the street for any sign of members of the gang who might have come into town ahead of the designating meeting time. Not a single male wore a light blue wild rag like the ones Rube gave to Bass and Jack.

He walked across the unpaved street and stepped up onto the boardwalk in front of a small barber shop. The sole customer was being given a shave with a straight razor and was covered with a white cotton cloth, pinned behind his neck. He was tilted back so that the barber could better see his throat. Neither seemed to notice Walt's passing.

Arriving at the bank, Walt took his ranger badge from a pocket and affixed it to his vest. He made one more scan down Main Street, and then did the same north and south on Elm. Satisfied with what he saw, he pulled the right side of the eight foot tall doors to the Lindsay National Bank open and stepped inside.

There were four customers in line to see the two tellers working at their positions behind the counter. The two sheriff's deputies assigned to provide additional security tensed for a moment when he entered carrying the rifle. Chief Deputy Rudabaugh thumbed the right hammer back on his side-by-side twelve gauge, but carefully released it back to half cock when the ranger smiled a toothy grin and headed toward him.

"Howdy, boys. I'm Texas Ranger Walt Durbin. Sheriff Wacker asked me if I could stop by and make an appearance with you this afternoon."

Rudabaugh and Tyler exchanged a nervous glance. "He didn't say nothing to us about anybody else working here."

"He didn't know I was in town until today. As you may have heard, one of my fellow rangers got killed up to the river…"

"Oh, yeah. Damned good man, too…I liked old Bodie," Tyler said as he shook his head.

"Appreciate that…Looks like ya'll got everything under control all right."

"So far so good," the larger deputy said as he stuck out his hand. "I'm Chief Deputy George Rudabaugh. This here's Deputy Marvin Tyler."

Walt shook hands with each and sized them up as best he could from the firmness of their handshakes. "Proud to meet you men…They got the vault all locked up?"

"Oh, yessireebob…Tighter than Dick's hat band. Banker's a bit nervous with all that cash in there…as you might imagine." He chuckled. "Bet you couldn't drive a nail in his ass with a two-by-four."

"Yeah, wouldn't know about that myself. Rangering don't pay all that well, so I can't say I've ever had even a thousand dollars to my name." Walt grinned as he looked around the bank. The walls were lined with finely finished oak veneers and the millwork reflected the fine craftsmanship of the local German community carpenters. There were four partially barred teller windows across the back, parallel with the front windows.

His eyes fell on the wall clock affixed between two office doors. *Three ten. All hell's gonna break loose in twenty minutes.* The ranger's face never revealed that secret. "Nice place they got here."

"Shore 'nuff is," Rudabaugh agreed. "Say, we oughta introduce you to the president. Bet he'd like to know they was a Ranger on duty too."

Walt nodded. "Sounds like a great idea…I see why they made you the Chief Deputy."

George beamed at the compliment. "Come on…Mister Fleitmann's a real nice fellow and their coffee is better than any restaurant brew back in town."

SOUTHERN COOKE COUNTY

Just south of Lindsay, Dallas, clucked at the two red mules pulling the freight wagon along the same railroad right-of-way that the lawmen were traveling some six miles to the north—Bully July and Con Kilgore trotted alongside. They had just joined with the tracks from the old Butterfield Stage road.

"How far we out from Lindsay, Dallas?" asked Con.

"Oh, 'bout a mile, I 'spect."

LINDSAY, TEXAS

Bodie reached for the brass knob on the church's back door. Saint Peter's Catholic Church, a good-sized single story wood frame building, sited at the far west end of the community's main street, was the focal point of spiritual life for the close knit community of 400. It had plenty of open ground around it for parking the buggies, wagons and horses of the parishioners and would later be replaced by a series of larger brick structures.

Catching his breath slightly, Bodie turned the knob and was relieved to find it unlocked. *Thank goodness. Guess the good Father trusts his flock.* He pulled the door open and stepped inside. As his eyes adjusted to the darker interior, he found himself in a storage room filled with wooden folding chairs and tables.

He made his way through the room and into a hallway that led past several small meeting rooms. He was headed toward the front of the building where he figured the stairway to the bell tower was when a man's voice stopped him cold.

"May I help you?"

Bodie spun around and found himself face to face with a slightly older man dressed in black with a small tab of white showing at the collar. The priest had his hands behind his back.

"Sorry, Father, I didn't know anyone was here."

"I'm here for my flock almost every day…As I asked before, may I help you?"

"I'm Texas Ranger Bodie Hickman. I need to…"

The priest's eyes narrowed. His hands came from behind his back, producing a .41 caliber nickel plated revolver. "Ranger Hickman is dead, son…One of my parishioners told me that just yesterday. Now I would suggest you lean that rifle against the wall and get your hands up. We gladly share what we have with strangers in need, but don't take kindly to thieves, liars and montebanks…and I do know how to use this, believe me."

GAINESVILLE, TEXAS
SKEANS BOARDING HOUSE

A wan-faced Annabel slowly packed her bag. Her red-rimmed eyes reflected that she was still having recurring bouts of uncontrollable tears. There was a gentle tap at the door to her suite. She softly replied, "Come in."

Faye entered carrying a pot of tea and two cups. "Thought you might like a spot of tea and some conversation."

"Bless your heart, Faye, you're so sweet...but not right now. I have so much packing to do. I only have a couple of hours."

"Don't worry about that. Just take your carry bag, I'll pack the rest in your trunks and send them up on the next train...You need to sit down, have a cup of tea and listen to aunt Faye for a bit."

Annabel looked the older woman in the eyes, saw it would do no good to argue and nodded. She pulled her soft hanky from her sleeve and dabbed each eye as Faye set the tray on a table and poured two cups of her special tea.

They sat on each end of the brocaded settee next to the window.

"Annabel, I know there is nothing in the world anyone can say that will ease your pain...Believe me, I've been there."

"Oh, I'm so..."

She held up her hand. "Let me finish...I lost my husband in 1863 at Gettysburg...We had only been married three months, just enough time for me to get pregnant, before he went off to fight in Lincoln's war. I had a son...and lost him in the Indian campaigns with the Apache at the battle of Big Dry Wash in Arizona in '82...He was only eighteen."

"Faye..."

She shook her head. "So I do know what you're going through and I can tell you from that experience, that this too shall pass...to quote the good book. Time heals all things...It's like crumpling a piece of paper and then straightening it back out. It will be flat again...but it will never be the same as it was before. You won't forget...You'll never forget the good times, but you will find a place in your heart to store those special memories. You have to remember that a joy shared is twice the joy and heartache shared is half the heartache."

Annabel set her cup on the coffee table in front of the settee and hugged Faye's neck. "You are a wonder. Thank you so much...I know I'll be all right. It's just that...that we didn't have much time together." She leaned back.

Faye took a sip of her tea. "I know...Now, tell me, how did you and Bodie meet?"

She nodded. "But first there's something else I have to tell you...have to tell somebody..."

The older woman smiled. "You're pregnant."

Annabel gasped and brought her hand to her mouth. "How did you know?"

"Honey, I knew when I first laid eyes on you. There's just a certain kind of glow..."

"But, I haven't even missed my woman time...I just know that I am. But..."

Faye set her cup on the table next to Annabel's. "Sweetheart, let's just call it women's intuition and keep it our secret, shall we?" She smiled and they hugged again.

NORTHERN COOKE COUNTY

Bass, Jack and Rube sat their horses along the railroad right-of-way. The big marshal pulled out his silver plated watch from his vest pocket, pressed the stem and opened it. "3:20. Everbody oughta be in position 'bout now...better be anyways.

Let's go." He closed the timepiece and replaced it. "Check yer weapons, boys."

They followed his lead, checked their side arms and saddle guns and nodded to Bass. He clicked to Smoke and the three moved out at the trot along the tracks only a few minutes north of Lindsay.

LINDSAY, TEXAS

Dallas Humby reined up just as the mules passed Deiter's, leaving the wagon immediately in front of the twenty-five foot wide general store and catty corner across from the bank. "Whoa up there, boys."

Con and Bully Jack eased in front of the mules, dismounted and tied off their horses. Kilgore took the cotton lead rope from the mule's harness and tied it securely to the iron hitching post on the curb.

"Better tie 'em tight, they'll probably start pitchin' a fit when ol' Betsy starts chatterin'," said Bully.

"My thoughts exactly. Wouldn't do to have a runaway with the three of us in the back."

DEITER'S MERCANTILE

Brushy Bill entered the town general store and glanced around. *Looks like they got just about one of everything in here...including a soda fountain. I'll be darned. Believe I'll*

222

order something. Gotta look like a customer. He stepped up to the counter.

"Yesssir, how can I help you?" asked the young man in a white apron, red bow tie and paper soda jerk hat.

"How's about a vanilla phosphate?"

"With cherry?...No charge."

"Sure, why not?"

"Five cents, sir," the clerk said as he added vanilla syrup and jerked the lever controlling the seltzer dispenser. The tall faceted glass with the footed base rapidly filled up and almost foamed over. He placed a cherry on top, stuck a straw in and handed it to Bill.

Roberts pitched a nickel on the white marble counter and took a draw on the straw. "Ummm, that's good, son," he commented as he glanced out the window and saw Con Kilgore working on the knots holding the tarp on the wagon. *Oh damn.*

SAINT PETER'S CATHOLIC CHURCH

Bodie reached for a pocket on his vest.

"Easy there, son," the padre said as he lifted the gun a little higher.

"Just want to look at my watch," replied Bodie.

"Make sure that's all you pull out of that pocket."

He removed the silver plated timepiece and pressed the stem. "3:28. Da...uh, sorry Father. Dang..." He closed the cover and replaced it in his pocket. "...Is there anything I can do to convince you that I really am Ranger Bodie Hickman in the flesh?"

"Doubt it. We'll just wait until Sister Elizabeth gets here after she turns her class out over at the school. Shouldn't be but another ten minutes or so...I understand she has met the ranger personally and knows him by sight."

"Yes, she will know me...But, Father, people may die in the next ten minutes if I don't get up in the bell tower."

"Oh, really, son. This is 1896 and not New Mexico or Arizona. Don't you think you're being a little over reactive?"

"You just don't understand."

MAIN STREET
LINDSAY, TEXAS

Elmer Simmons, Norman Thurlow, Ben Brasher and Harkey Littlefield had tied their horses behind Deiters and were sauntering one at a time up the alley to Main Street where they nonchalantly spread out.

Rad Cullum, Sawyer Smith, Skabby Johnson and Bud Stevens were already assuming a ragged semicircle around the front of the bank. Cullum and Smith, were leaning against canopy posts, building smokes, while Stevens sat down on the boardwalk with his feet in the street and pretended to be picking a rock out of spur rowel with his jack knife. Skabby just leaned against the wall of the Palace Saloon, with his saddle bags draped over his right shoulder.

Pink and Tom were slow walking their horses down the street and approaching the saloon while at the opposite end of the town—Bass, Jack and Rube had just hitched up their horses. They separated to both sides of Elm and were walking toward the bank.

Bass glanced back up at the church tower trying to make out Bodie.

"See 'im?" asked Jack.

"Naw, must be back in the shadows." He glanced over at Rube across the street, and then down at Deiter's and spied Red Eagle sitting against the store's front wall, his hat over his face, pretending to be asleep. "You best drop on back behind me, ten er twelve yards. What with the three of us wearing these blue bandanas, we'll be a stickin' out like a sore thumb."

"I see you." Jack scanned down the street and could make out the other outlaws scattered about. "Looks like the dance is fixin' to start...Everbody else is in place, Tom and Pink are hitchin' up in front of the Palace whith Bully Jack and the boys standin' next to the wagon. One of 'em 'pears to be untyin' the ropes holdin' the tarp."

"I'd say." Bass began to softly sing, "Nobody knows the trouble I've seen. Nobody knows my sorrow. Nobody knows the trouble I've seen. Glory hallelujah!"

Jack looked at Bass up in front of him as he sang the old Negro spiritual and smiled. He knew the big man was gearing up to do some shooting.

Bass glanced once more over his shoulder at the church just as the school bell rang, dismissing classes for the day.

SAINT PETER'S SCHOOL HOUSE

The schoolhouse doors burst open as a dozen boys flew out as if they had been shot from a cannon. Ten girls followed at a much more leisurely pace, giggling and pointing at one of the young boys that had stumbled at the foot of the steps. He got to his feet dusted himself off, retrieved the books he had dropped and quickly dashed off to catch up with his mates. All the children wore the official Catholic uniforms—white tops and black bottoms. The boys all sported short black ties.

SAINT PETER'S CHURCH

"Thing's are gonna get real bad real quick if'n I cain't get up there to do my job," Bodie reiterated as the echoes of the school bell faded. "Some men are gonna rob the bank. They got a Gatling Gun. You just gotta…"

"Don't move muscle, mister. Sister Elizabeth will be here directly. Just hold your horses. She'll be able to prove…or disprove…that you are who you claim to be."

Sweat began to form on Bodie's brow as the yells of rambunctious schoolboys began to be heard as the fastest ones made their way onto Main Street and turned the corner—headed for the soda fountain at Dieter's. A thought came to him. *Dang it to hell and gone! Why didn't I think of that sooner?*

"Father Felderhoff! What if I showed you my Warrant of Authority from the Texas Adjutant General's Office? That ought to prove somethin', right?"

"You have state papers showing you are a ranger?"

"That's what I'm trying to tell you! It's my commission in black and white. Plumb slipped my mind. It's inside my coat pocket on the left side...Please?"

The priest eyed him suspiciously and raised the Colt to eye level. "My Lord...you're an accomplished liar if there is no warrant in that pocket. I want to believe you, young man. Move slow and easy, now. No funny business, or I swear..."

"As God as my witness, no sir. Just don't get nervous and shoot me by mistake." Bodie deftly used two fingers, lifted the lapel of his suit and held the jacket wide to show that he had no shoulder holster hidden beneath. "Right here it is."

"Lift it out, lay it on the little table."

Bodie nervously complied.

"Now back away. Keep your hands up...don't think about trying for that shooter on your side," Felderhoff ordered.

"Yes sir...I mean, no sir, I won't."

The priest kept his eye on Bodie and lifted the paper by a corner. He shook it twice to make the well-creased commission paper unfold. Glancing back and forth between the ranger and his paperwork, he read the warrant and looked at the date of issuance. "How long have you been a ranger, son?"

"Since May of '89."

The Father jaw dropped. "Sweet Mary, Mother of God...Go! Go! Go!" He pointed at the open stairwell leading to the bell tower.

Bodie stepped forward, snatched up his Winchester and sprinted up the stairs...taking them two and three at a time.

PALACE SALOON

Tom Lee grinned as he watched the throng of children run past. *A man's gotta love it when a plan comes together.* He doffed his hat and casually fanned his face with it.

"Now," Kilgore hollered at his two assistants.

Bully Jack and Dallas jerked the tan tarp covering the Gatling Gun free and vaulted over the seventeen inch high sideboards—quickly dumping the empty crates onto the street. Bully Jack grabbed a 40 round stacked magazine and slammed vertically it into position in the loading slot.

Con swung the muzzle around and lined it up with the Lindsay National Bank's plate glass windows. A sadistic grin came to his lips. Aiming high enough to shoot over the heads of the tellers, he pulled the Murphy lever to cock the deadly weapon and began to turn the crank as quickly as he could, laughing all the while. One after another, each of the ten blue barrels rotated into position and blasted its deadly load with a horrific roar never before heard in that quaint little north Texas town.

Inside the bank, the heavy lead slugs showered the interior with shards of glass as they passed through the front windows and splintered the fine woodwork.

Two women waiting in line began to scream hysterically as the fusillade continued unabated.

Walt Durbin reacted instantly and dove across the lobby. He caught both women in his arms and took them to the floor as he cried out, "Get down! Everybody down!" He glanced over at the two local deputies hired to provide security. Both were curled up in a fetal position in the broken glass. A pool of a pale yellow liquid puddled around Chief Deputy Rudabaugh. *Where the hell is Bodie?*

SAINT PETER'S CHURCH

Bodie glanced up at the remaining ten steps leading to the platform in the tower as the thunder of the Gatling Gun ripped the air. "Oh, God! Oh, God!" He scrambled to the top and circled the single bell to get a view of the deadly scene taking place two blocks east. Not even taking time to catch his breath, he threw the Winchester to his shoulder and took aim at the man behind the crank. Bodie thumbed the hammer back and squeezed the trigger. Nothing happened.

The hell? He glanced down at the external hammer. Tiny bits of green were firmly wedged between the hammer and frame. *Shit...That cedar tree!*

He instantly recalled the moment when he had backed Moon into the thicket and instantly regretted the decision. Pushing on the hammer, he pulled the trigger again and realized the bits of green leaf were locking the hammer back. He dug in his pocket for his folding knife as the magazine of .45-70 ammunition ran dry in the world's first machine gun.

MAIN STREET

"Reload!" yelled Con Kilgore.

Even partially deafened by the gun's blast, Bully Jack did as he was told. A thick cloud of sulfurous black powder smoke drifted around the wagon and down the street on the soft summer breeze. He yanked out the empty Bruce style magazine and replaced it with another full one. "Give'r hell, Con," he yelled as revolver shots echoed up and down the streets.

Red Eagle threw off his blanket, rolled off the end of the boardwalk and ducked into the alley between Deiter's and the Palace Saloon.

Kilgore swung the big gun 160 degrees and began raking Deiter's. "Be ready with another!"

DEITER'S MERCANTILE

Bill threw the vanilla phosphate aside, splashing the remaining sweet liquid against the counter, drew his Colt from his side holster, reached down and grabbed his ankle gun and shouted, "Everybody get down!" He ducked low and sprinted toward the front door as bullets ripped through the store, shattering mirrors and ricocheting off shovel blades sticking out of a wooden barrel. Rows of canned goods exploded, mixing with clouds of feathers as the heavy slugs tore through the pillows in the bedding department.

The freckled-faced soda jerk didn't have to be told twice as he dove behind the counter. Three young boys that had just come through the door to get an ice cream cone, hit the aisle in front—one began to cry. A woman customer at the material rack screamed as she was sprayed with shattered glass. She instantly dropped to the floor and crawled under the table.

A elderly man over at the garden tools section, spun around and tripped over a thirty pound nail keg. "Ach du lieber, mein Gott!" He covered his head with both hands.

A middle-aged floor clerk toppled over him, bleeding profusely from the chest.

SAINT PETER'S CHURCH

Cursing his bad luck, Bodie quickly scraped the bits of cedar jamming the hammer with his pocket knife. Holding the trigger back, he checked the freedom of movement in the mechanism. *Calm down, now. Gotta make this shot count.* He threw the rifle to his shoulder and centered the brass front bead on the far-off target. He touched the trigger, barely feeling the recoil of the big .45-90. He jacked the lever down and reloaded another cigar-sized round in a flash.

MAIN STREET

The booming report was not even noticeable downtown as the constant staccato roar of the Gatling Gun dominated the action. The bullet the ranger fired found its mark, catching Con Kilgore just below his Adam's apple, ripping apart his spine and spraying Bully Jack and Dallas with his blood. His limp body tumbled back over the wagon seat and twitched for a couple of seconds.

Tom Lee mistook the cessation in firing for a magazine change and started jogging across Main Street for the bank. "Close in boys, she's ripe for the pickin'!" His brother Pink ran along beside him. A moment later, Skabby, holding the saddle bags against his chest walked quickly behind.

Rube drew down on Rad and Harkey who were already on the boardwalk at the southeast corner of Elm and Main. "Hold it," he yelled out. Harkey whirled around and realized that their supposed accomplice was no longer on their side. He fired at Rube, but the bullet went high. Rube's shot didn't.

Harkey twisted and crumpled to the street as Rad Cullum fired twice, dropping Rube with the second one.

Bass took Rad with a single shot to the chest.

Skabby turned and fired at the big black man, but was too late. Bass had spied two preteen boys and a girl, frozen in fear in the middle of the intersection.

"Cover me, Jack." He sprinted toward the Blue Bird Cafe and scooped up the children as Skabby fanned multiple shots his way—one striking home.

Bass stumbled to his knees, pushed the kids forward toward the cafe. "Go! Go!" He turned to see Skabby's pistol aimed directly at his head from only twenty paces away.

"Die, you traitorous black basta…"

The outlaw was vaporized in a flash of white light and a tremendous roar that created a cloud of red mist, fire and smoke, knocking Bass to his back six feet from where he had been kneeling as the dynamite in the saddlebags detonated.

The kids were bowled over by the concussion as the plate glass shattered inward on the front of the Blue Bird Cafe.

Frightened horses tied up and down the street pulled out or broke off their hitching posts and dragged them down the street as they sought to get away.

Bass staggered to his feet and started to make his way toward the three children trying to stand up on the boardwalk in front of the cafe. A shot whizzed past his head, he instinctively ducked, drew one of his Colts with his left hand—nearest to the shooter, Ben Brasher—and fired two shots, both hitting him in the forehead. He turned and hobbled over to the children and helped them to their feet and to the door of the restaurant.

Jack ran up. "Damnation, Bass. Sumbitch was carrin' dynamite, sorry. My shot musta nailed a stick dead on….The kids alright?"

"Think so. Just scared a mite."

"What about you?"

"Took one in the thigh."

Bully jumped up behind the Gatling Gun and hefted the fifty pound circular drum magazine into place. He had just placed his hand on the cocking lever when hot lead from the distant rifle lifted him off his feet. His carcass momentarily ended up atop Kilgore's before it rolled off and fell across the wagon's tongue.

Bodie swung his sights over to the third man in the wagon and watched as Dallas crumpled over from a gut shot. *Somebody saved me some trouble.* He knelt down and used the tower railing for a steady rest. The afternoon sun glinted off the brass drum. His third shot struck the magazine, setting off two of the .45-70 cartridges. The explosion, although minor, bulged the brass canister, rendering it inoperable and jamming it in the receiver.

DEITER'S MERCANTILE

Bill ran out the door in a crouch, a pistol in each hand. He saw Bully Jack take a hit and flip out of the wagon and shot Dallas in the stomach before he could take his place behind the crank. A shot slammed into a canopy post beside his head and another splintered what was left of the door jamb behind him.

He turned and saw Norman Thurlow and Elmer Simmons firing in a panic in his direction. He slowly walked straight at the pair, alternating firing his pistols with every step—each shot hitting its target. Elmer sprawled to his face with three bullet holes in his chest. Thurlow—also with three rounds in his torso—managed to get off one final shot as he fell forward to his knees, catching Roberts in the side. Bill put one more bullet into the outlaw's head—sending him to hell. "Son of a bitch...that's number twenty-six," he said as he inspected the blood splotch widening just above his hip bone.

MAIN STREET

Walt Durbin took a quick glance over the three foot high brick sill at the front of the bank. He spotted two armed men running directly toward his position—both wearing the telltale sky blue wild rags Rube had mentioned. He rose to his knees, centered his rifle sights on one of them and fired.

From only fifteen yards away, the .30 Government round stopped the man in mid-stride. His momentum carried his feet out from beneath him and he landed in the middle of the street with a thud and rolled over twice, coming to rest against a water trough.

Tom Lee witnessed his brother's instantaneous death and suddenly lost all interest in becoming rich. He raised his hands and yelled out, "I give up! Don't shoot! Don't shoot!"

Walt scrambled to his feet and stepped through the shattered window. "Drop that shooter! Texas Ranger. You're under arrest!"

Tom shed the sixgun as if were a horseshoe hot off the forge, spread his fingers wide and raised both arms over his head.

From the alley beside the bank, Sawyer saw the young ranger step out onto the boardwalk strewn with broken glass and splintered wood. As Walt stepped into the street, Smith fired a quick shot that caught the lawman in the back. Durbin toppled forward as Brushy Bill and Red Eagle double-teamed the outlaw that shot him. Sawyer staggered and fell onto the boardwalk from the alley and expired.

Suddenly the quiet on the street was deafening. Smoke from the gunfire and explosion slowly drifted east with the soft afternoon breeze.

Jack scanned the streets for any more threats. He saw Red Eagle cross over and take charge of Tom Lee and pick up his discarded weapon. He holstered his Russian and turned back to Bass and grinned.

"About damn time."

"For what?"

"All these years, it was always me that got the short end of the stick…Figured it was yer turn."

Bass shook his head. "Guess that's what friends are for. Angie said she's peel yer head like an onion, you came home with any more holes. Happy to oblige…but I had a worse place on my lip and never quit whistling."

"So you say, now…Speaking from experience, wait 'til tomorrow when the sore sets in."

"We'll see…Make yourself useful. See as you can hire er borrow us a wagon for the ride back to Gainesville."

"Gimme that wild rag. I'll tie it off nice and tight round that leg, don't look like it hit an artery…but it didn't go through."

Bass nodded as Jack applied the tourniquet. "Whil'st you go git that wagon, I be askin' Mister Lee some questions...My gut tells me he ain't the tall hog at the trough."

***

CHAPTER TWELVE

LINDSAY, TEXAS
MAIN STREET

Bass leaned on a cane borrowed from the nearly destroyed Deiter's Mercantile. He looked Tom Lee in the eye. "Mister Lee, just so you know, you'll be a facin' multiple charges, not the least of which will be murder. I spect you've got a hemp collar in yer future. Now I want to ask you one question…Who sent you?"

Lee looked at the heavy steel shackles on his wrists and then back up at Bass, smiled a rueful grin and shook his head. "Of all the people I had to take on, it had to be Bass Reeves. Damn my luck…I'm being honest with you, Marshal…I don't know."

"What do you mean, you don't know?"

"Just that. Every time we met with the man...he wore a black mask. We just stole the horses, took them to the Territory, traded them for cattle...prize breeding stock and brought them back into Texas to Montague County."

"South Montague County, past Roston?" asked Bill.

Lee nodded just as Jack pulled a wagon to a halt in the street with his, Walt, Bill and Bass' horses tied to the back.

Red Eagle brought the last of the outlaw's horses and tied them to the hitching rails that were still standing in front of the Palace Saloon. Up and down the street, citizens of Lindsay began cautiously poking their heads out from stores and alleyways.

Bodie rode up at the same time, having walked the quarter mile to get Moon.

A thirty year old man in a tweed suit and brown bowler hat approached. "Marshal, I'm, Yehudi Krause, town constable, is zhere anyzhing I can do to help?"

Bass nodded and looked around. "Mister Krause, we'll leave the stiffs here, if you'll see to collectin' up. Be sending the county coroner back over. We got to take the wounded and the prisoner to Gainesville."

"Yessir, I'll see to it, yah. Ve got an ice house."

"Need to git Bill, myself and Walt to a doctor...'specially Walt. He's got a nasty hole just under his collarbone. Don't think it's fatal, but needs seein' to, pronto. Then we'll drop this nabob off at the sheriff's office...Oh, anybody checked up on Rube?"

"Didn't make it, Bass," said Jack.

"Damn shame. He was a good man. See that he's listed as a posseman."

Jack nodded.

"Marshal, Bill said Annabel was leavin' this afternoon for Oklahoma City. I got to catch that train before it crosses the Red." Bodie pulled out his watch. "Got fifteen minutes...if it's on schedule."

"The only ones of us that ain't shot up is me, you and Red Eagle and I got to drive the wagon," said Jack.

"Red Eagle help, we take extra horses, belong gang. Ride hard an' switch off. We catch."

Bodie looked at the Lighthorse and nodded. "I really appreciate that, Red Eagle...Let's ride."

NORTHERN COOKE COUNTY

Bodie and Red Eagle hand galloped northeast from Lindsay. The ranger was riding Tom Lee's steeldust Morgan, leading a sorrel gelding and Lakota Moon. Cyrus rode a bay mare that belonged to the now deceased Pink Lee and led two more, including his Appaloosa, Cloud. They were saving their own mounts for the final leg.

"The railroad bends west right at three miles north of Gainesville. If we take the hypotenuse of the triangle from Lindsay to the bend, we should catch the train," said Bodie as they splashed through one of the shallow streams that crossed the rolling grassland in the north part of the county.

"Not know hi-pot-en-use place, but we head off iron horse before get to river."

"I think I said that...At least that's the plan. Train will start to pick up speed after it turns back north and heads down into the Red River valley."

About a mile and a half out of Lindsay, they switched mounts. Bodie quickly loosened the girth on the Morgan and tied the reins to the saddle horn, stepped into the sorrel's stirrup and swung into the saddle as Red Eagle did the same with his second horse.

"They'll probably follow along, but if they don't, we'll have to send somebody back for 'em."

"Osí Hommá take care of horses. Bodie go get woman."

The young ranger nodded and grinned at the Chickasaw. *Nice to have friends.*

A mile due east, they could make out the black smoke belching out of the locomotive as she chugged north.

"Gotta pick up the pace, Red Eagle. Train's makin' good time. We gotta git to the bend, cain't swing north any further...gittin' into the trees."

"Sheeah, we go," he said as he swatted the horse's rump lightly with the poppers on the end of the split reins and quickly caught up with Bodie.

The train's caboose had just passed the bend when they reached the right-of-way—it was picking up speed headed down into the valley toward the iron bridge that crossed the Red River.

Bodie spurred the gelding who was showing a lot of heart, but beginning to flag—the sides of his neck was coated with lather as they galloped full out along the tracks a good hundred yards behind the train.

He tugged on Lakota Moon's lead and eased him up alongside the sorrel as he twisted the reins around the gelding's saddle horn, basically giving him his head. *Oh, boy, here we go.* The ranger kicked out of the stirrups, squeezed his knees, raised up, brought his right foot into the seat and then his left. Just as the sorrel shied to the left away from the charging mustang—Bodie jumped.

He landed square in the saddle, but his momentum carried him to the right, he grabbed a handful of Moon's long black mane flying in the wind, centered himself, reached forward along his neck, grabbed the flailing lead rope and dallied it off. Taking the reins in his left, he leaned forward close as he could to his beloved mount's laid-back ears and whispered. "Come on, son, you can do it. She's on that train."

As if the mustang could understand his master—and maybe he could—he surged forward and slowly they began to gain on the train now making over thirty-five miles an hour.

Foot by foot, the charging horse crept past the red caboose to the last passenger car. Gravel flew from his hooves as they pounded the ground alongside the clacking wheels. *The great Dan Patch got nothin' on you, boy.*

Three hundred yards behind them, Red Eagle had picked up the sorrel and was following along in trail.

They eased up alongside the car, the steel side ladder next to the rear platform was only inches away. As fate would have it, a blond-haired woman passenger dressed in black was sitting at the back of the car on the west side. She happened to glance to her left to see Bodie reaching for the rungs as the line-back dun labored to keep up. She brought her gloved hand to her mouth as her cerulean blue eyes behind the sheer black veil, got big as saucers, and then she disappeared.

The other passengers in the car began to look out the left side and gesture excitedly.

Bodie lunged, wrapped his right hand around the nearest rung of the ladder almost halfway up and let the train pull him out of the saddle just as Moon stumbled in the loose road fill.

He hung swaying by one hand, his boots dragging in the gravel only inches away from the back wheels of the car as the train continued to pick up speed heading downhill toward the river...

GAINESVILLE, TEXAS

Walt Durbin moaned as the wagon rolled over a rock in the roadway. His eyes flickered opened as he came back to consciousness. "What?...Where am I? Am I dead?"

Bass was seated in the seat next to Jack—who was handling the reins—and looked down at the wounded young ranger lying atop a makeshift pallet of blankets in the bed of the wagon. "Naw son, you ain't dead...Least not yet. One of them bank robbers bushwacked you from behind and came close to punchin' your ticket. You been out cold for a spell...Oh, we picked up yer rifle. You dropped it when you got shot. It's in the bed, to yer right along with all the others."

"Thanks Marshal, bought it just before I headed up this way. Today was only the second time I fired it." Walt tried to sit up, but a searing pain in his right chest quickly made him think better of the idea. "Ah, ah."

He lay back down and stared at the afternoon sky. Turning his head slightly, he looked over to the side of the wagon and could see a couple of elm and pecan trees off to his left. He got his bearings somewhat and could hear the hooves of several horses clopping rhythmically behind them. Glancing over his other shoulder, he could see Bass in the seat, and then Brushy Bill leaning against the sideboard in the bed behind Reeves.

"Dang, this bullet hole is more than a mite sore," he said. "How did things work out back in Lindsay?"

Bill looked back at him. "Worked out the way we planned it, 'cepting three of us went and got ourselves shot." He chuckled softly. "Comes with the territory, I suppose."

"Where are we now ?"

"Almost back in Gainesville, son," Bass answered. "They got a sawbones with a good reputation, what I hear tell."

"Yeah...Name's Doc Wellman. He's a good one, all right," said Walt.

"Say, Bill, thought you said you couldn't shoot left handed? 'Peared to me you was doin' purty good," commented Bass.

"Didn't say I couldn't...said I didn't care much for it." He grinned, and then winced.

244

SANTA FE TRAIN

Bodie swung with all his might and grabbed the next rung above his right hand with his left as his hat blew off. He tried to pull himself up, but his strength was fading as his feet continued to drag the ground and he was starting to lose his grip. Suddenly a black gloved hand grabbed the back of his collar. That was all the help he needed. He released his right hand from the ladder and grabbed the vertical iron handrail alongside the back of the car next to the steps and managed to get his right toe on the bottom metal step leading to the rear platform—it slipped off. He tried again and this time, got his entire boot on, and then his left.

The helping hand pulled him on up and then the arm wrapped around his neck, to be joined by the other and Annabel began to smother his face with kisses.

The blue-clad sixty year old conductor—having seen the commotion as he came through the forward door of the car, collecting tickets—burst out the back. "What's all this?" he demanded.

Bodie looked up from Annabel's tear-streaked face. "Bodie Hickman, Texas Ranger. Stop the train."

"Yes, sir, Ranger," he said as he stepped across the coupling to the caboose and opened the door. "Charlie! Signal Joe to stop the train...be quick now, ranger business."

"You got it, Zack."

The brakeman grabbed the red globed lantern, stepped to the rear platform of the caboose, leaned out and waved the lantern up and down in the signal to stop up to the cab of the locomotive.

"Great jubilee! What the…" Joe said when he saw the brakeman's signal in the side-mounted mirror. The engineer grabbed the tall Johnson bar at the side of the cab and eased it full back, releasing the power to the big drive wheels and locking them in place.

Sparks flew from all four five foot high wheels as steel chewed against steel, squalling like a panther. The colored fireman looked up and closed the firebox door. "What's up, Joe?"

"Don't know. Charlie just give me the stop signal."

The seven car train slowly screeched to a stop with the engine, coal tender and two cars out on the bridge over the Red.

Annabel leaned back from Bodie. "How? What? I don't understand." She wiped the tears from her cheeks.

Hickman got a somewhat sheepish look on his face. "It's kinda complicated, hon."

She stepped back and put both hands on her shapely hips. "This better be good, mister…considering what you put me through."

Annabel and Bodie glanced to the right-of-way on the left side of the train to see Red Eagle slow to a halt with Lakota Moon, Bodie's hat in his hand and the sorrel gelding in tow. He was riding his own horse, Cloud.

"Good work, Ranger. Thought you lose it when Lakota stumble," said Cyrus.

Saved by the cavalry. "He alright?"

"Mustang sure-footed, not go down. Just bog up in loose gravel."

The conductor came back out of the caboose. "All right Ranger, did as you asked. What's the problem, we got robbers on board or up ahead?"

"No, sir. Just have to get this lady off the train. She was told that her husband was dead...but I'm, uh...he's not."

"Come again?"

"Yes, I'd like to hear this too," said Annabel—her hands still on her hips and her veil pulled back on top of her head.

"I'll just get her bag," Bodie ducked his head and entered the car.

"You mean there was not an emergency or a crisis?" the conductor asked, scratching his head.

"Oh, there's going to be a crisis, all right...just not here," she said as Bodie came back out of the car with her carpet bag.

"Can you ride in that getup, hon?"

Annabel tilted her head forward and looked at him out from under her furrowed brow. "I'll manage."

He exchanged the bag with Red Eagle for his hat, stepped down and assisted her to the ground, and then on the sorrel.

"Much obliged, I'll put in a good word for the railroad," said Bodie as he swung into Moon's saddle.

The confused conductor watched as they wheeled their horses and headed back to Gainesville—then opened the caboose door. "Charlie, give Joe the go ahead...I guess." He closed the door and headed back into the passenger car. "I'm gittin' too old for this job," he mumbled.

GAINESVILLE, TEXAS
LUCIUS WELLMAN, MD

Jack eased back on the reins in front of the doctor's office on Pecan Street. "Whoa up there, boys."

The front door opened and Doctor Wellman stepped out.

"Heard you pull up, what's going on?"

"Got some wounded folks, Doc. Gonna need some help gittin' one of 'em inside," Jack replied.

"Hilda, would you step out here and bring the wheelchair, please," Wellman called over his shoulder to the still open door.

In a moment, a heavy set, but pleasant faced woman of fifty in a white nurse's smock, came out of the office, pushing a tall wicker-backed wheel chair.

The physician walked to the end of the wagon and peered inside. Lying beside the pile of rifles, belts and wheelguns was a man with a familiar face. "Good Lord in Heaven, that's Ranger Durbin."

Walt raised his head slightly. "Hey, Doc, didn't expect to be seein' you again so soon."

"That makes two of us." He spoke to Jack. "You appear to be the only one in this wagon without a hole in them...besides this man in the shackles...you want to give me a hand getting Walt into the chair?"

"Can do," Jack said as he stepped down, assisted Bass getting on the ground, and then clambered into the bed and helped the doctor move Walt from the wagon to the chair.

"Take him into the treatment room, Hilda, while I help these other gentlemen." He turned to Bass and Bill. "If you men can move on into my office. I'll get to you quickly as I can..."

"I just have a shallow flesh wound, Doc," Roberts interrupted him. "You can put me at the end of the line...Believe Bass' leg still has the ball in it. Right, Marshal?"

"Bass Reeves?" asked Wellman.

The big man nodded. "Yessir, but, I can feel a hard lump on the inside of my thigh just under the skin."

"That's a good thing. Means I won't have to dig around in there looking for it," Wellman said as Bodie, Annabel and Red Eagle trotted up from the north.

"Marshal Reeves, are you all right? Mister McCarty you're wounded also?" Annabel asked.

"Who?" Jack inquired.

"I was using the cover name of Henry McCarty...I'm really Deputy US Marshal Bill Roberts, miss."

"This is getting more confusing by the minute," she said.

"It'll all be clear soon, hon...promise," offered Bodie.

"Ranger Hickman, I understood you to...ah...have been killed a few days ago."

"Long story, Doc," he grinned. "Reports of my demise have been greatly exaggerated."

Annabel elbowed him in the ribs and shook her head. "May I be of any assistance, Doctor? I have had some training as a nurse. My father is a surgeon in Alabama."

"I could use some help, yes. I have to tend to Ranger Durbin first, he's losing a lot of blood. If you can clean Marshals Reeves and Roberts wounds while I'm doing that…it would be wonderful. I have an extra nurse's apron hanging on a peg in cloakroom."

"You don't mind me pitching in, do you darling?" She began to unbutton her sleeves and roll them up.

Bodie looked down at his bride with loving eyes. "No, sugar plum. I think it's a great thing you are so caring."

"Go on, you wild things you…bless your hearts. We medical personnel have more important thing to do than shoot the breeze. Go on now," she said as she motioned them to move along toward the door.

"While ya'll are patchin' everybody up, Bodie, Red Eagle and I will take this miscreant over to Sheriff Wacker's," said Jack with a grin. "We'll come back directly and fetch you men up."

Bass pointed a big finger at his longtime partner. "Don't think for a minute about runnin' over to one of them saloons and wettin' your whistle afterwards. We still got to get us some place to stay tonight…Me, I mind I had all the sleepin' outside on the cold hard ground a man would want for a while."

Jack laughed. "See? I told ya to wait 'til the sore sets in…Come morning, that leg will be all black and blue, swole up and stiff as a board!"

"Mebe so, but you ain't got to be so all fired happy about it."

"Sorry, Pard. You cain't know what kinda feelin' it is that it ain't me getting the slug dug out for a change."

Doc Wellman shook his head and grinned. "Out with the lot of you. Come back in an hour or so. They should be ready to be picked up by then."

COOKE COUNTY SHERIFF'S OFFICE

Jack pulled the team in front of the office as Bodie tied off Moon's lead rope through the ring atop the cast iron hitching post. Red Eagle looped his to an eye hook at the back of the borrowed wagon.

"Me keep eye on guns," the Lighthorse said, nodding to the stack of rifles and sidearms the lawmen had collected from the deceased gang members.

"Good, idea, Osí Hommá. This shouldn't take too long," Bodie agreed. He walked to the edge of the concrete sidewalk and steadied Tom Lee as the manacled outlaw grimly stepped down off the wagon.

Sheriff Wacker had retrieved his hat from the oak stand as he was preparing to leave the office for the day. The hands on the wall clock were almost straight up and down 6 PM when the two men led Tom Lee into the foyer. Taggart caught his breath when he recognized the tallest one immediately—his mouth fell agape.

"Ranger Hickman! I heard you were dead!"

Bodie grinned. "Sorry to disappoint you, Sheriff. Apparently, that dang rumor got passed around purty quick, I understand."

Jack had his right hand on Tom's arm. "Sheriff Wacker, Jack McGann, Deputy US Marshal."

"Ah, yes, certainly. I remember you from that little fracas two years ago at the Painted Lady. Where's Marshal Reeves?"

"Bass is indisposed at the moment…This here low life is Tom Lee…we caught him red-handed in the attempted bank robbery over to Lindsay this afternoon."

"Bank robbery? Over in Lindsay you say? I had two of my finest men on special duty over there. Are they…"

"Just a little cut up from flyin' glass. Those bastards had themselves a Gatling Gun…"

"My God! I can't believe it…And they robbed the bank in Lindsay? How much did they get away with?"

"None, Sheriff. We were waiting for 'em and were able to put the whole Red River gang out of commission in one fell swoop," Bodie said with a touch of pride and a big Texas grin. "I asked Marshal Bass Reeves' and his team to come in and work undercover after Billy got shot…Didn't take 'em long."

"My stars…I can't believe such a thing could happen in my county. Bass Reeves? Hellova man. The Indomitable Marshal from the Territory, my, my…And Tom Lee? Aren't you the man who owns the saloon out in Dexter? Got a brother named Pink?"

Lee glumly nodded.

"Yeah, thought that name was familiar. You say all the rest of the gang is out of commission? How many did you take prisoner?"

"Funny you should ask, Sheriff. The rest seem to have all developed a severe case of lead poisonin'. Came upon 'em real sudden like," Jack said with only a hint of a smile. "We think those boys were the ones responsible for the horse stealing and murders over to the Rafter S and elsewhere around Cooke County over the past few months."

"And you got the whole gang at once? Incredible...The people of Cooke County owe you men a huge debt of gratitude."

"We 'preciate that, Sheriff Wacker. We would kinda like to put this sorry excuse for a human being in your steel hotel for the night. Got us a long list of charges on 'im that will take a while for me write up," Jack said.

"Absolutely, Marshal. I'll take control of him personally and see that he gets put in solitary confinement...Did he make a statement?"

"Not really...Said he had a boss, but didn't know who he was."

"That's real interesting."

Jack nodded. "There's twelve bodies over there that need to be checked for warrants...I suspect they's re-ward money on more'n one of 'em. Let Constable Krause take the whole bunch over to the ice house."

SKEANS BOARDING HOUSE

"I'll be right back, Uncle Jack, just need to take Annabel's bag to our suite," Bodie said as he handed Moon's reins to Red Eagle and walked up the sidewalk to the porch. *Better knock. If I just walk in on her she's liable to have a heart attack.*

He tapped on the jamb next to the screen door.

"I'm coming, just a minute," Faye's voice came from inside the house.

In just a moment, she came to the door, wiping her hands on a dish towel and followed by Tom Sullivant with a glass of wine in his hand. "Oh, my merciful Jesus!" Faye brought her hand to her mouth and took a step backward, her knees sagging just a bit.

Tom quickly grabbed her arm to steady her, spilling a bit of his drink in the process.

Bodie jerked off his hat. "Sorry to startle you Miz Skeans."

"Ranger, is that really you?" asked Tom as he pushed open the screen door.

"Yessir, in the flesh."

"But how...what..." Faye stammered as she fanned her face with the towel.

"Oh, my God!" said Roberta Floyd as she stumbled on the bottom two steps of the staircase and caught herself on the bannister.

"It was an undercover operation, folks...to smoke out the rustlers. I solicited the services of the United States Marshals Service and another Ranger..."

"Walt Durbin," Tom interrupted.

"Right. We killed all but one of the gang this afternoon at an attempted bank robbery in Lindsay...Seems they bit off more than they could chew."

Missus Floyd sat down heavily on a settee in the foyer as she stared at the young ranger just back from the dead.

"Annabel!" Faye blurted.

"I managed to stop the train before it got to the Red, Ma'am. I brought her bag." He picked up the carpet bag he had sat down on the porch.

"Where is she?"

"She's helpin' Doc Wellman over to his clinic with our wounded."

"Who all got hurt?" asked Tom.

"Marshal Reeves took a round to the leg, Marshal Roberts, uh, you know him as Henry McCarty got a flesh wound in the side and Ranger Durbin..."

"Is Walt alright?" Sullivant asked.

"Well, he got the worst of it. Took a round in the back, came out his upper chest. Not fatal, but purty bad, nonetheless...gotta find a place to house 'em while they recuperate."

"I'll just bring Walt out to the ranch. I came in to supper with Faye and have my buggy...We're tendin' to my daughter, he won't be a problem...Fact is, she'll probably insist on it."

"Yessir," replied Bodie.

"And you can just bring Mister McCarty, or I guess it's Roberts and that Marshal Reeves right over here when Lucius is finished with them. I'll set up another bed in Marshal Roberts room...It's not open to discussion."

"Yessum."

"Faye, may I have a glass of sherry. I think I'm getting the vapors and feel a bit faint."

"Of course, Roberta. Let me take Annabel's bag and I'll be right back. I'd better prepare some soup for the wounded men," Faye said as she headed upstairs with the bag.

"We'll be back with the marshals in 'bout an hour, ma'am...Sorry for all the trouble."

"No trouble, Bodie...a little work, but no trouble. I'm just so glad everything has worked out...I imagine you've got some explaining to do to your bride." She smiled.

Bodie ducked his head and crumpled his hat brim in his hands. "Yessum, you could say that."

"I'll follow you over to Doc Wellman's and pick up Walt."

"Just bring him back over here, Tom. He'll need some of my special chicken soup before ya'll go out to the ranch."

Tom grinned. "Was hoping you'd say that."

Faye winked at him.

LUCIUS WELLMAN, MD

The two horse drawn conveyances pulled up in front of the clinic. Bodie and Red Eagle tied their horses to the back of the wagon with Jack and Bass' mounts.

The door to the clinic opened and Hilda pushed the wheel chair with Walt down the bricked walkway. Tom stepped down and motioned for the nurse to bring the ranger to his buggy.

Bass turned a little to the doctor behind him. "Say doc, 'preciate it if'n you was to keep this little hole in my leg under yer hat. I got somewhat of a reputation." He chuckled.

"What hole, Marshal? All I saw was a bit of a contusion."

Reeves nodded and hobbled on out on his cane assisted by Annabel on his other arm. Bill followed behind with Doctor Wellman.

"Tom, you can take the chair to the ranch. You'll need it to get Walt into the house and all. I'll pick it up when I come out to check on him and Francis tomorrow."

"Appreciate that, Doc."

Jack and Bodie helped Bass up into the bed of the buckboard and into a ladder-back chair Wellman had also loaned them so Reeves wouldn't have to lie down and then get up. It was only two short blocks to the boarding house.

SKEANS BOARDING HOUSE

Bass grimaced as he stepped down off the wagon. Jack pretended not to notice as he figured that he had carried on long enough about his partner's first gunshot wound. He handed the cane to the big man.

"Here you go. Take it easy up the steps."

Bass nodded.

"I'll get the screen door for you," offered Brushy Bill.

"Hell's bells, boys. I ain't a total cripple."

"No, Marshal, you ain't. Just being gentlemanly is all. Been there before myself, you know."

Jack reached up, placed his hands around Annabel's waist and lifted the petite woman off the wagon. He set her down by the sidewalk. "Ya'll go ahead on inside. I'll see if Tom needs a hand gettin' Walt situated and such."

All of the boarders, Tom Sullivant and the wounded lawmen were finishing Faye's egg custard desert and starting on their coffee.

"So you see, Annabel, it wadn't Bodie's fault. It was all my idee for him to pretend to be kilt…I been doin' this line of work a right smart of years and the general approach is to get the lawbreakers thinkin' one way and come at 'em another."

She smiled and squeezed Bodie's hand on top of the table next to hers. "Thank you so much, Marshal Reeves. I know you were just looking out for him. If they hadn't of gotten you and Marshal McGann in your undercover roles to do it, they would have gotten someone else…and they might have been successful…It's not something I would ever look forward to again."

"Well, I, for one, find the whole affair despicable. Twelve men killed. For what?" said Roberta Floyd.

"Ma'am, with all due respect, the law ain't perfect. But without it we got nothin'…Nothin' atall. We just as well go back to livin' in caves. 'Sides, them men was a tad arrogant and to me, arrogance serves 'bout as much purpose as teats on a boar hog…If'n you'll pardon the expression."

"Well said, Marshal Reeves, well said," said Tom as he tapped his knife on the side of his tea glass.

Roberta frowned at Bass' butchery of the English language and crude use of alliteration.

After dinner, Jack helped Bass upstairs and got him seated in an embroidered straight-back chair.

"If you think a pair of crutches would work out better for you, I'd be happy to fetch you some tomorrow. Them stairs can be a booger, I tell you what. Been down that road."

"I 'spect so. Never 'preciated how dang much it burns to get shot afore. Gives a man a whole new way of lookin' at it."

"Hurts a hell of lot worse than gettin' your butt whooped up on in some bar fight, now don't it? You'll be fine in a couple of weeks, I 'spect."

"Since you and Red Eagle are headed back to the camp tonight, think you could bring me my shaving kit and possibles? They's all wrapped up in my soogan."

"Was planning on it. We gotta take care of them extry horses anyway. I'm thinking we can bring 'em to town and sell 'em, along with the ones from Lindsay, since this here rustling operation is 'bout shut down. I make it eighteen head all told. Be a right smart fer everybody to divi up...not countin' any re-ward money."

Bass nodded. His face took on a quizzical expression. "You know somethin' funny? Miz Skeans never said nothin' 'bout me being a colored man."

Jack chuckled. "Could be she never noticed."

Bass looked askance at his long time partner.

***

CHAPTER THIRTEEN

RAFTER S RANCH

The sun was setting Tuesday night when the buggy rolled though the gate with Walt's horse, Pepper, trailing along behind. "Hello the house," Tom called out.

Little John was the first one out onto the porch. He spotted the ranger's right arm. "Hell fire! Walt's hurt!" He scrambled down the steps, ran to the hitching post and quickly threw a clove hitch with the lead rope. "What happened?"

"Walt and his lawmen buddies caught up with that gang of cutthroat rustlers that have been bleeding us dry and shot billy hell out of 'em over to Lindsay," Tom called out. "He took one in the back, but Doc says he'll be all right...eventually. Help me get 'im the house."

"You bet, boss." Little John moved to the passenger side of the buggy. "Step easy, now, Ranger. By God, cain't believe you boys caught up with them that fast."

Walt tried his best to smile, but the constant jostling of the eight mile buggy ride had left him feeling exhausted from fighting the pain—Laudanum only went so far. "Sometimes even a blind hog finds an acorn."

He took hold of the shorter man's hand and placed his left boot down on the single metal foot rest. Slowly and deliberately, he swung his right leg around and lowered himself to the ground. Tom went to the back, removed the wheelchair and brought it around to Walt and allowed him to seat himself.

"Don't fret about that horse of yours, Ranger. I'll take good care of him...personal. I'll give him a good groomin', oat him and all. It'll be my privilege."

"Thanks, Little John. You're a good man."

"Let's get you up in the house. Bet you're 'bout worn plumb out, what with all the blood you lost and all," Tom said as he got behind the chair and pushed it across the yard to the front steps.

Walt nodded. "Don't know how much I bled. Could have been more than I thought...I feel kinda light headed and woozy. That musta been what done it...Either that or the doc's joy juice."

Once inside the ranch house, Sullivant began issuing orders to his hands that had gathered to find out the latest news from Gainesville. "Boys, I need you bring the bed from the guest room and put it side by side with Francis Ann's. These two are gonna need doctoring and looking after full time."

As four of them turned to follow his instructions, the two men stood side by side and Tom grinned at Walt.

"She told me after you left so quickly that you had asked for her hand in marriage, well...not exactly asked me, but you did ask the one that's important..."

"I apologize for not makin' it official. But I had things that needed to be done."

"Son, don't ever apologize. Some say it's a sign of weakness. *Son*...kinda like the sound of that. Never had a son...what with my wife passing away when Francis Ann was little, not long after we got here from Tennessee. You know, I tried to make it up to her...be everything for her...I don't know what kind of father and mother I turned out to be." His eyes misted over for a second.

"But I do know one thing...that girl of mine is a ring-tail tooter. Takes a hell of a man to turn her head...and you did. She loves you...so consider the answer to that question you didn't get to ask me...a yes. A big ol' Texas, hell yes."

Walt tried to shake his hand, but held up short when a searing pain shot from his pectoral muscle. "Guess we'll have to shake left hands for the time being." A big smile came to his face.

"Proud to have you in the family, son." The two turned and Tom helped Walt up the stairs one step at a time to Francis' bedroom.

SKEANS BOARDING HOUSE

"It'll be easy to find," Faye said as she cleared the breakfast dishes from the table. "You go up the steps on the west side of the court house and turn right on the second floor. The county clerk's office is the first office on the right. They've got all the records in those great big old ledgers...all the way back to the forties when Gainesville first got started. At least the ones that didn't get burned up in the fire of '79."

Marshal Bill Roberts grinned and got to his feet. "Thanks again for that bell-ringer of a breakfast Miz Faye. You know, if I stayed here permanent, I would have to buy myself a bigger pair of pants."

Faye shook her head. "I do take some pride in my cooking, as you might be able to tell by the care I put into those biscuits. But, you would get used to it after a time...Now when you get to the clerk's office, you want to look for Millie Malena. She's the assistant to the county clerk and a darned good one from what everybody says. Can't miss her. She's petite little thing with dark hair and pretty as a picture...and she's a young widow...Just though you would want to know." She raised an eyebrow and grinned.

"Well I appreciate you thinking about my welfare, Ma'am, but to tell you the truth, I believe I fall into the category of a

263

lifelong bachelor. This life I lead doesn't leave much room for a marriage."

"More the pity. Tell her I said hello, nonetheless."

"You can count on it. I got to keep moving before I stiffen up."

"Take care now. I'll be looking for you about dinner time."

COOKE COUNTY COURTHOUSE

Brushy Bill ascended the cut limestone steps on the Commerce Street side and followed the hand-lettered signs to the County Clerk's office. The short walk from the boarding house didn't seem to bother the lawman a bit and he had a smile on his face when he addressed the pretty brunette seated behind the counter. "Pardon me, Ma'am, but would you be Missus Malena, by chance?"

She rose from her oaken desk and approached the waist-high counter. "Why, yes, sir. That I am. May I help you?"

"Certainly hope so. Faye Skeans gave me directions and she said to say hello."

"She's such a dear."

"I'm Henry McCarty, a cattle buyer and land broker from Wichita and am interested in finding out who owns a particular spread in the southwest corner of the county on the other side of Rosston, bordering right up to the Montague county line…maybe over it." Bill felt a need to hide his true identity until he had more information on the possible landowner where he had trailed the Gatling Gun.

"I'm sure I can help you there, as long as you can read a map. We have the abstracts of all real property in the county and records back to the Republic of Texas and Spanish land grants before that. We'll step into the next room and you can begin with the official county maps and we shall find out which surveys cover that area."

"Splendid. Lead the way."

The process of tracing the ownership of a particular parcel of land was somewhat tedious back in the day of handwritten records. The boundaries of an inordinate number of tracts might be described using a stump or large rock for a corner or a certain creek along one side.

Each sale created a different set of closing papers, each with its own conditions—some required mortgages, others used quit claim deeds, and still others, full abstracts. Many of the older ones were signed with the ubiquitous X as a lot of the early settlers could not write.

It was not Bill's first time to research land titles and he was prepared to take as long as it took to get the information he needed—his time spent with the Pinkerton Detective Agency served him in good stead.

After thirty minutes, he uncovered a bill of sale that conveyed a half section of a parcel of land adjoining the property in question to a T. W. Flowers. The transfer had been for cash, two years earlier.

"Missus Malena, are you familiar with this buyer, by any chance?"

"No, I'm so sorry. Flowers…That name is not familiar to me."

Bill wrote it in a notebook he carried in his coat. "I notice he only listed a post office box in Gainesville as an address. That's not going to be particularly useful in trying to contact him."

"I don't suppose you would want to sit at the post office and wait until he drops in, would you?" she asked.

He shook his head. "Don't believe that would be the most expeditious route. "How about this parcel near Rosston? The one in the John Short survey 241? Can we start to work it next?"

"Certainly," she replied with a sigh. "That is my job, after all." She started to lift a heavy stack of ledgers. Each one of the clothbound books was almost two feet tall and three feet wide and were a good four inches thick.

"Allow me, these are much too heavy for a pretty young thing like you to have to tote."

Millie blushed. "I have to carry these all the time, but, you are so kind, sir…I think we need the one marked number eighty-four."

"The least I can do. This must seem like a wild goose chase to you sometimes." He winced as the act of picking up the big book tweaked the stitches in his side slightly.

She nodded. "I would have to agree with you sometimes. The records are as close to exact as we can make them. After all, legal title to a piece of property is the basis for rightful ownership and governmental taxing thereof."

RAFTER S RANCH

Fran and Walt looked across at each other from their beds. Each was propped up against the headboard and had a tray on their lap.

"Rather odd, don't you think?"

"What's that, hon?"

"We get wounded in exactly the same place."

"Didn't plan on it, believe me. But there is one difference."

"That would be?"

"You got shot from the front and I got shot from the back."

"Same difference...Still the same place." She grinned. "After five days of chicken soup and oatmeal, I think I'm about ready for a good steak," Francis said as she looked at the bowl on her tray.

"I can understand that and know how you feel from the last time I got shot. After a week of baby food, I felt like I could have eaten the whole cow...But for now, I'm still weak as a three day old kitten," Walt replied.

"Your color is already much better."

"Thought I was going to pass out again after climbin' those stairs yesterday. All the blood loss, I reckon."

"Uh, huh...How many times does this make?"

"They say things come in threes and this makes my third. Maybe I've had my quota."

"And maybe not." Fran glanced over at her fiancé. "Honey, would you consider giving up your commission in the rangers?"

He looked back. "And do what? I've been rangering for the last ten years...it's what I do. Not in my nature to run just 'cause I been shot a few times."

"Well, we've got a lot a rebuilding to do here at the Rafter S, breeding stock to replace...and daddy is not getting any younger. I'm not sure he's up to it. He doesn't get around like he used to."

"What are you gettin' at babe?" Walt put down his spoon.

"I'm just saying that I need some help...I've never seen anybody that's as good with horses as you are...and I can't do it by myself."

You little heifer, only been engaged two days and you already know how to play me like a fine fiddle...I love it. "Well, I guess I can take a leave of absence...Not sayin' I'd give up my commission but, you, uh, we do need to get the ranch back on its feet."

Gotcha. "Oh, that's wonderful, darling." She looked out the window at the foaling meadow and smiled.

SANTA FE DEPOT
GAINESVILLE, TEXAS

Jack and Red Eagle waited as the 4-4-2 southbound locomotive bled off steam.

"I see what Bodie meant about that telegrapher, good ol' Percy Gilhooley comin' in handy. Gotta remember to use that First Assistant Texas Ranger ploy sometimes...jest change it to First Assistant Deputy Marshal."

"Unnnh," replied Cyrus.

"Here they are." Jack pointed down to the third passenger car as Selden and Loss stepped down. "This way, boys." He waved his arm.

Marshals Lindsey and Hart walked up and both stuck their hands out.

"Caught the first train south after we got your telegram," Selden said as they walked past the depot.

Jack held his finger to his lips when they passed the ticket window where telegrapher Gilhooley winked back.

"What was that about?" asked Loss.

"Tell you later...bring all yer dodgers?" said Jack.

Selden patted the saddle bags slung over his broad shoulder as they reached the horses tied across the street.

"I made arrangements for a photographer from the local paper to meet us in Lindsay and take pictures of the gang. May have to stand 'em up and throw a rope around 'em to git the whole bunch in one picture...either that or stack 'em like firewood," said Jack as they trotted west on California Street.

"Well, don't have to worry none 'bout 'em movin' an' spoilin' the shot." Loss grinned.

"I 'spect we kin prop 'em against the wall inside the ice house. They'll all be stiff as boards anyhoo," said Selden.

COOKE COUNTY COURTHOUSE

The clock on the wall showed it was almost noon and the two had uncovered three more small purchases by the mysterious T.W. Flowers when a voice from out in the hall called out, "Millie, can you break away for lunch?"

"Excuse me, for a moment. I think my friend has dropped by unexpectedly," Millie said. "I won't be long."

"Take as long as you need. We've been at this for some time and I'm sure you need a break."

Millie stepped into the main office to see Sheriff Wacker standing at the counter with a bouquet of long-stem red roses in one hand and his hat in the other. Her eyes sparkled as she gasped at the surprise. She brought her hand across her bosom as she stammered, "Are...are those for me?"

Taggart smiled broadly and swept his hat in front of him as he bowed. "You don't think for a minute that I brought them for your old crotchety boss, do you?"

"No, it's just that no one ever brought me roses before." She blushed.

"High time to mend that terrible oversight. Here you are, madam, with my warmest regards."

She smelled the scent of the fresh-cut flowers. "They're beautiful," she said. The stems of the bouquet were wrapped in flimsy white tissue-like paper. Attached was a small handwritten note:

To the most extraordinary woman
I have ever met.
Love, Taggart.

270

"What's the occasion?" she asked. "It's not my birthday."

"You'll see. I'm taking us to the Main Street Steakhouse for lunch."

"How wonderful! I always wanted to go there, but it's so expensive...I only have a half hour for lunch."

"I'll square it with your boss. He owes me a favor anyway."

"But I have a customer looking at records..."

"Suggest they go to lunch and come back around one. Customers have to eat as well."

"All right." Millie blew him a kiss and placed the flowers in an unused vase on the window sill behind her desk. She grabbed her purse and stepped into the map room. "Mister McCarty, would it be an imposition if I left for lunch now? I'll return by one o'clock sharp, I promise."

"No imposition at all, madam. Enjoy your lunch with your suitor." He winked at her. "If it's all right with you, I'll just stay here as keep digging. Had a big breakfast at Miz Skeans...Promise not to make a mess of anything..."

"That you for being so understanding." She wheeled away and joined Sheriff Wacker.

LINDSAY, TEXAS

"All ve could find of zat fellow vat got his self blown up, ver his boots, his gun and part of his hat vat vasn't burnt up, yah," said Lindsay's Constable Krause after the marshals had examined all the corpses and had their pictures taken.

Loss had collected their personal belongings, watches, wallets, money, family pictures and the like and put it all in a cloth sack they got from the feed store.

"Reckon we best contact Colonel Scott over to Fort Sill, he can send a detachment and git his Gatling Gun back. Figure their armorer kin prize that ruint drum out of the receiver...looked like that was all was wrong with it. Bodie made a hellova shot."

"That he did, Selden, that he did," agreed Jack.

MAIN STREET STEAKHOUSE

After a leisurely and delightful lunch in the small private dining room, Millie dabbed at her lips with the crisp white linen napkin. The waiter approached with a tray of desserts.

"May I interest either of you with an eclair, crème brûlée or strawberry tart?"

She looked across the table at Taggart. He grinned.

"Whatever your little heart desires, punkin'. I think that crème brûlée would be a great finale."

"I never had one before, but they do look so...decadent!"

"I shall being you each one." The waiter turned and disappeared past the curtain to the kitchen.

Millie sat back and gazed up at the majestic Longhorn steer mounted on the wall. His massive horns were a full nine feet across, tip to tip, and gracefully curved—a reminder of the trail drive days that helped put Gainesville on the map. "That will be a wonderful end to a perfect meal."

Wacker shook his head. "No Ma'am. It will not..."

She looked at him curiously.

"...But this might be." He stuck his right hand in his coat pocket and produced a dark blue velvet-covered jewelry case. He slid the small box across the table. Her eyes grew wider.

"Go ahead. Open it," he said sweetly.

Millie held her breath and her hand trembled as she lifted the lid. The inside of the box was lined in white satin. The name of most prominent jewelry store in town, KINNES, was printed in small gold letters in the top. In the bottom half, was a slot holding a diamond ring set in gold.

Her eyes sparkled as they locked with his.

"Millie Malena, would you do me the greatest honor of becoming my wife?"

Tears of joys rimmed her eyes at the unexpected turn of events. She nodded vigorously and the sheriff reached across the tabletop to take her hands in his. "Yes...oh my...The answer is yes."

COOKE COUNTY COURTHOUSE

Millie glanced up at the clock on the wall. The hands were approaching 4 PM. "Mister McCarty, I hate to sound like a bureaucrat, but the courthouse closes at four."

"No need to apologize, Ma'am. We've been hard at it all day. I can come back tomorrow and finish my search then."

"Very well...I must say, you are the most persistent person I have ever encountered in title searches."

"When I have my sights on something, I admit there is a bit of bulldog in me. Cain't seem to turn loose."

"I certainly hope you find who the mystery person is. See you tomorrow."

Bill grabbed his hat, tugged it in place and tipped it at her. "Good day, Missus Malena. Until the morrow."

COOKE COUNTY SHERIFF'S OFFICE

A few minutes later, the marshals and Red Eagle—along with the photographer and reporter from the Gainesville Daily Register—stopped in front of the brick building after the four mile trot back from Lindsay. The reporter stepped down and tied the single horse pulling their buggy to one of the hitching posts. The rest dismounted, tied up and entered the door.

They met a beaming Sheriff Wacker headed toward the front with his hat in hand.

"Sheriff Wacker, glad we caught you before you went home. You remember Marshals Lindsey and Hart?" asked Jack.

"Certainly." He shook hands with both men. "How can I help you gentlemen?"

"We've been over to Lindsay trying to figure out who all was in storage in the ice house. Marshal Lindsey brought down his stack of dodgers to see how many we had paper on. Need for these fellers from the Daily Register to take a picture of Mister Lee to send to the US Marshals Service for federal warrants...Know there wasn't anythin' on him or his brother Pink locally or in the Nations. Just thought we'd branch out."

"Of course." He turned to Harold Lamkin, the night jailer. "Harold, I'll take the marshals upstairs to the cell area."

"Yes, sir," the skinny-as-a-rail young man replied as he looked in awe at the three federal law officers.

"This way, gentlemen."

They made their way up the stairway to the second floor containing the county jail. There were ten barred cells, five to the side with an eight foot wide aisle between.

Tom Lee was the only occupant...He was in the last cell on the north side, reclining on his bunk, leaning against the brick outer wall.

"On your feet, Lee, the marshals want to talk to you," directed Wacker.

"Got nothin' to say."

"Didn't ask if you had something to say, just said on your feet. Not going to tell you again."

Lee glared at the sheriff, a frown on his face, and then got to his feet.

"Back up against that wall, need to take yer picture," said Jack.

"What for?"

"For I said so...Dang, but yer the most argumentative feller I ever seen...Oh, by the way who was that dumb one carrying dynamite to a gunfight? We couldn't find enough of him to make an identification."

"Said I got nothing to say."

"Pity…Might go easier on you if'n you was to cooperate, but as I recall, believe he would had to been Skabby Johnson…'cordin' to Rube."

"Rube was workin' with ya'll too?…Sonofabitch!"

"Yeah, we had you six ways from Sunday, slick," said Jack.

A look of defeat came over Lee's face. "All right, what do you want to know?"

"Wellsir, like we asked earlier…We know you give the orders to the gang, but who give you yer marchin' orders?…Last I figured, based on what that Chickasaw Lighthorse told me, the dead count is up to twenty-two, countin' the soldiers yer men kilt up in the Nations to git that Gatling Gun…The court kin only hang you onct. Seems like you'd want to share…but, up to you."

"Honest to God, Marshal, if I knew, I'd tell you. He was pretty cagey about letting anybody know who he was."

Jack nodded. "Let's git his picture and git out. The stench is overpowerin' in here."

The newspaper photographer, set up his tripod with the Henry Clay dry plate camera and extended the lens. The reporter held the flash powder tray high for him while the photographer squeezed the rubber bulb, opening and closing the shutter and simultaneously sending a spark to the magnesium powder. There was a blinding white light and a huge cloud of smoke that instantly collected at the top of the fourteen foot ceiling. Everyone blinked and rubbed their eyes.

"How about a picture of all the marshals and rangers that took part? Need to do a story…front page. FEDERAL

OFFICERS AND RANGERS TAKE DOWN THE RED RIVER GANG. That's gonna be the headline," said the reporter, passing his hand in front of him.

"Have to go over to Miz Skeans boardin' house. That's where Bass Reeves is. He runs the show," offered Jack.

The reporter nodded to his photographer.

SKEANS BOARDING HOUSE

Bill walked up from the Courthouse as the photographer was setting his camera up in the front yard. The other law officers were milling about on the porch. Bass was leaning on his cane, clearly not happy with the proceedings.

"This is the only part about marshalin' I never cared for," he whispered to Jack.

"Me neither, but you gotta admit, because of it, when the lawbreakers know it's you or that you got paper on 'em, sometimes makes our job a whole bunch easier."

"I know. Don't mean I have to like posin' for some camera. Makes it harder to go undercover...don'tcha see?...If you say anythin' 'bout all us darkies look alike, I'm gonna whack you with my cane. Figure it's near as good as my ax handle."

Jack held up his hands in mock surrender, grinned and turned as Roberts climbed the steps. "Find out anythin' at the courthouse, Bill?"

"Maybe, gotta go back in the morning...My eyes feel like two burnt holes in a blanket."

"Heard that." Jack motioned to the reporter. "Barney, this here's Marshal Roberts, he's been doin' a little follow up investigation…Just in time for the picture takin', Bill."

"Wonderful."

"Marshal Roberts, it's a pleasure." The young man stuck out his hand.

Bill shook it, nodded and forced a smile.

"Gentlemen how about we have Ranger Hickman and the Lighthorse on the bottom step of the stoop and the four marshals on the top? It's a pity the other ranger can't be here," said the young reporter.

"Don't 'spect he'll be gittin' around much anytime soon," commented Jack. "Got a purty good hole in him."

"Are you wounded too, Marshal Reeves?" asked the young reporter looking at Bass' cane.

Bass shook his head. "Not nothin' worth talkin' 'bout."

"All right then, here we go. After we take the picture, I'd like to interview the participants. This could be a big story, gentlemen, really big."

Bass took a deep breath and moved up beside Jack and got a stoic expression on his face for the camera.

***

278

EPILOGUE

COOKE COUNTY COURTHOUSE

It was close to eleven in the morning when Brushy Bill unfolded a sheet of paper and found a pair of signatures on a simple deed of trust concerning the transfer of a small plot of land. Only eleven acres were involved and at the less than princely sum of six dollar per acre. The seller was a man named Ruben Phelps. But it was the buyer's signature that got his attention. In beautiful flowing script the name he had been seeking appeared:

Taggart W. Flowers

"I got you, you son of a bitch!" Bill blurted out.

Millie was a few feet away and brought her hand to her mouth at the slightly vulgar outburst. "Mister McCarty!"

"Sorry, Ma'am, my apologies. Sometimes I get a bit excited when I get a break on a case."

"A case? I thought you told me you were a cattle buyer and a land broker."

"Yes, Ma'am, I did, and I am so sorry to have misled you. My real name is William Roberts, I'm a Deputy US Marshal...I was sent here to help shut down the Red River Gang."

"That awful bunch killers and rustlers that have been in the paper? Oh, my God...they were the ones who killed my son..."

Her eyes filled with tears as her voice trailed off.

Bill reached into his jacket for a handkerchief. "There now, Miz Malena. I didn't know of your loss."

She dabbed at her eyes. "How could you have known? He was only nineteen..."

"If it's any consolation, I believe I just found the full name of the brains behind the whole rotten mess...He made one little slip-up here." He pointed at the piece of paper in his stack.

Millie blinked away the tears and glanced down at the signature. Her heart skipped a beat as she recognized it—the same flowing signature as on the card with the roses she had received the day before. Her knees became weak as she almost fainted.

Bill's lightning fast reflexes enabled him to catch her by the shoulders. "Ma'am? Are you going to be all right?"

"She gasped a couple of times. "I'll be fine in a few minutes. I just need some air."

Bill released her. She went straight to her desk, picked up her purse and walked a little unsteadily to the door. He dutifully took out his notebook and wrote the man's full name into it.

Wonder where she's goin'? Better check on her and make sure she's all right. She looked a little pale. He closed up the writing pad and stuck it back in his jacket.

Outside the south exit to the courthouse, Bill spotted Millie walking purposefully across the street. Her gait was quick and he stepped off the sidewalk onto the brick street, holding up for a second as a buckboard clattered past. She reached the corner of Main and Dixon Streets, turned and cut diagonally across Dixon. *Looks like she's headed for the county jail.*

Keeping an eye on crossing horse traffic clacking along on the red brick street, Bill kept his distance, but followed discretely behind her. *She's making a beeline for the jail, for sure...interesting.* Just as he reached the corner of Main, Millie entered the front door of the jail. He looked around and moved close to the entrance, but held back, waiting for her to possibly come back out.

Millie walked up to the Chief Deputy's desk. "Is Sheriff Wacker in?"

"Oh, yes, Ma'am. I'll get him for you," said Rudabaugh.

She noticed he had bandages on both of his hands.

Wacker appeared in the doorway of his office. "I thought I heard the voice of an angel out here," he said cheerfully. "How are you, sugar?"

"I wanted to look the man that murdered my son in the eye," she said coldly.

"Sure, honey. I'll take you up there, if that's what you want, but I think seeing him might upset you."

Her mouth tightened. "Too late for that, I'm afraid."

Wacker held out his hand for the set of keys attached to a large welded metal ring. Rudabaugh fumbled with them for a second as both of his thumbs were wrapped with gauze.

"Sorry, Sheriff. These cuts are playin' hob with me."

Taggart ignored his excuse and put his arm around Millie. "Right this way, my dear."

He led her over to the stairway leading upstairs to the cell area and tried to take her arm to assist her. She shrugged his hand away.

"I'm perfectly capable of climbing stairs, thank you."

"As you wish, sweetheart."

He unlocked the thick double panel door at the top and pushed it open for her. Tom, in the far cell, got to his feet.

"Lee, this is the mother of the young posseman that was killed up at Delaware Bend," he said as they walked down the aisle to the end.

Lee crossed his arms and glared at her, not showing any emotion at all.

"So you're the man who murdered my son?" she said icily.

"I never killed nobody, lady. Don't know where you heard that."

"But, you ordered it done. It's the same thing in the eyes of the law...and someone else told you to do it, didn't they?...Answer me!"

"Just following orders, ma'am."

"I know...That's always the way it is, isn't it?" she said with venom dripping off each word.

Marshal Roberts stood outside staring at the entrance to the county jail. *Damn, I just as well go inside...What if she and Wacker are somehow in cahoots? How can I be such a fool? I know better.* He opened the door and stepped in. "Deputy Rudabaugh, is the sheriff in?"

"Yessir, he and Miz Malena are upstairs. She said that she wanted to look the man who killed her son in the eye."

Bill's eyes flew open wide, and then he heard heated voices coming from upstairs. "Oh, Jesus!" He headed across the foyer toward the staircase.

Millie's dark eyes changed to slits of obsidian as she turned her face to Wacker. "...and I know who it was...Taggart Wacker...Flowers." She pulled a short-barreled thirty-two caliber revolver from her clutch, wrapped her left hand around her right, cocked the hammer and pointed it at him.

"What? What are you talking about, Millie? I never..."

"Shut up! Just shut up!" she screamed. "You murdered my only son and then...then you used me...You evil bastard," she hissed. "You have no soul." The muscles in her jaw tightened. "I'll not wait to see them to put a noose around your worthless neck, Taggart…Vengeance is mine, sayeth the Lord…But he was busy, so he sent me."

"The hell you say!" Wacker began to draw his Colt and had only cleared leather when she pulled the trigger…twice.

Both rounds hit him high in the abdomen, one penetrating his liver and fragmenting into three pieces. He folded over in pain as his sixgun discharged once into the floor—his limp hand let it fall to the wood planking with a clatter.

"Oh, damn." Bill moved as fast as his wounded side would let him to the stairs as he heard the three rapid-fire shots. Drawing his sidearm, he hurried to the top and shoved the heavy door open. Millie was standing in front of Wacker, her hand still holding the pistol down at her side.

The sheriff was on his knees holding his stomach with both hands, dark, almost black blood oozing out between his fingers—his .45 on the floor in front of him. There was a splintered bullet hole halfway between the two of them. He looked down at his hands over his stomach, and then up at her, the searing pain clearly etched in his face. "Millie, I'm so…so sorry. I never meant…"

"Sorry?…" she said through clenched teeth. "Sorry…That's the most useless word in the English language…It's better to never do something you'll be sorry for…You burn in hell."

Wacker toppled forward on his face and exhaled the last of his breath with a rattle.

Bill eased up behind her, reached down and carefully took the gun from her hand. "Why, Millie?"

"I had to," she softly said as her eyes rolled back in her head and her legs buckled.

Roberts caught her under the arms and gently lowered her to the floor. "Did she get hit?" he asked Tom Lee.

Tom caught his breath and stepped closer to the bars, shaking his head. "Nope. The sheriff never got off a shot...except into the floor. It was clear act of self-defense, Marshal, no doubt about it. She called him out and he drew on her...But, now I remember where I heard his voice before! He was the man in the black mask."

SKEANS BOARDING HOUSE

The boarders and Faye sat around the long dining table, all having their after dinner coffee.

"I just can't believe it. Millie has always been such a sweet thing. It just doesn't make any sense," said Faye.

"I can still hear her cry of anguish when I was riding off to get the priest to come over and read Billy his rites...Never heard anything like it in my life," said Bodie.

"Grief or betrayal can make folks do things they wouldn't ordinarily do," offered Bass.

"The shock of it made her faint dead away...I'm not sure she's even aware of what she did," said Bill.

"Didn't you say it was self defense?" asked Annabel.

"Yes, Ma'am, but she went there with a gun in her purse and was acting very strangely when she left the County Clerk's office...that's why I followed her."

"Lot of womenfolk carry a gun in their clutch or pocket, I know my Angie does," Jack said.

"I don't understand why you didn't stop her," said Roberta with a huff.

"I waited outside for a few moments so it wouldn't be so obvious, then I went in. Less than a minute later, the Chief Deputy and I heard the shots."

"Where is she now?" questioned Faye.

"I had sent the deputy over to fetch Doc Wellman and he said he would sedate her and keep her under observation at his clinic overnight as he determined that she was in a state of shock."

"Is she still there?" asked Annabel.

Bill nodded. "I had Deputy Tyler stand guard at the clinic until I heard from Judge Miles. He said there would be an evidentiary hearing as soon as the doctor said she was up to it…and that's Thursday morning…"

COOKE COUNTY COURTHOUSE
DISTRICT COURT ROOM

"All rise for the honorable Judge Leander Algernon Miles, III," announced the middle-aged bailiff.

The standing-room-only crowd got to their feet. In the front row, Bass Reeves used his cane to help him stand erect. *Jack was right…sore as a risin'.* His face gave little indication of the throbbing pain that was going on with his recent gunshot wound. He had been seated at the end near the center aisle way.

Beside him sat Jack McGann and to his left were Bill Roberts, Ranger Bodie Hickman and his wife Annabel.

Across the aisle in the front row were Roberta Floyd sitting next to the aisle with Faye and Tom Sullivant on her far side. Everyone looked around the room for the entrance of the judge. Almost without sound, a nearly invisible paneled door in the west wall opened and the imposing figure of Judge Miles swept in wearing a flowing black robe that dusted the floor as he walked. His hair and beard were coal black.

"Kindly reminds me of Judge Parker," Bass whispered as he leaned toward Jack.

His partner nodded slightly. "Sorta has that look, don't he?"

The judge stepped up onto the platform and sat down behind the wide cherry wood bench. He glanced at the bailiff who took in a deep breath and spoke loudly.

"You may be seated."

After things quieted down a bit, the judge addressed the courtroom. "We are here today in what is known as an evidentiary hearing regarding the killing of Sheriff Taggart Wacker. This is not a trial, merely a hearing to establish the facts surrounding the death and determine if there is adequate cause to send the matter to a grand jury."

He let the words soak in for a moment before he continued. The court reporter and newspaper representatives scribbled furiously to take down every word. An artist was busy sketching the aristocratic jurist in pen and ink since flash photography was not allowed.

"You will notice that there is no jury impaneled. I will be the sole arbiter of the facts as presented and will make any decision based upon my many years of jurisprudence. The tragic killing occurred only two days ago and I am aware that emotions are still running high. Nonetheless, I will tolerate no outbursts from the witnesses, the accused or any spectators…Do I make myself crystal clear?"

You could have heard a pin drop as his booming voice faded. His steel gray eyes looked across to the tables where the district attorney sat just a couple of feet from the defense attorney hired to represent Millie Malena.

"Yep, just like Judge Parker…Reckon they're related?" Jack commented softly.

"Mister Prosecutor, you may call your first witness."

The middle-aged barrister rose to his feet. Alexander White was a fifty year old career politician with a heavyset body and wore his sideburns in full mutton chops. The gray whiskers did nothing to enhance his appearance and, in fact, gave his face a comical resemblance to a chipmunk.

"Thank you, Judge. The state calls Chief Deputy George Rudabaugh to the stand."

After the man was sworn in, the DA proceeded with his line of questioning. In a couple minutes, he asked about the three shots that he had heard.

"Can you describe the sound of the gunshots?"

"Well, they were all fair close together, I can tell you that. They kind of took me by surprise, you know. I wasn't expecting to be hearing shots from up in the jail, you know."

"And then what happened?"

"I remember that Marshal Roberts took off like a turpentined cat...ran right up them stairs with his gun in his hand when them shots rang out. The last one was a bigger caliber, you know...louder."

"Did you follow Marshal Roberts upstairs to the jail?"

"Yes, sir. I was right behind him...Well, a few seconds later I reckon, 'cause I couldn't handle a gun." He held up his hands, showing the bandages to the spectators and the judge.

"Could you tell the court what you saw when you got to the cell area?"

"It was terrible, I have to say. Miz Malena was standing there at the far end of the aisle, tears running down her cheeks and poor old Sheriff Wacker was laying there on his face in a puddle of blood. He had been shot two times...both in the belly. They was blood everywhere, I mean everywhere...Never git all that cleaned up."

A murmur spread though out the courtroom.

"I see. Did she still have the gun in her hand?"

"No, sir. I forgot to tell you, I seen Marshal Roberts take it out of her hand as soon as I got the top of the stairs. It was just hangin' at her side. She was standing there, like in a trance...then she fainted."

"No further questions, your honor," the DA said as he turned to take his seat.

"Mister Johnston, your witness," said Judge Miles.

"Thank you, your Honor," Marcus Johnston, the young lawyer fresh out of the University of Texas School of Law replied. He was dressed in a trim fitted black frock coat and contrasting brocade vest. He approached the witness chair.

"Deputy Rudabaugh…"

"Chief Deputy Rudabaugh."

"Of course…Chief Deputy Rudabaugh, did the Sheriff have a gun in his possession when he accompanied Missus Malena upstairs to the jail?"

"Yes, sir, he did. He always carried it with him."

"Can you describe that gun to the court?"

The deputy nodded. Johnston waited for him to continue, but he did not.

"Deputy Rudebaugh, I need for you to answer the question with a yes or a no, and if the answer is yes, I would like for you to actually describe the weapon for us."

Jack McGann tried hard to suppress a grin. He had seen such scenes played out many times before when the witnesses were not the most astute of persons.

"Oh, since you put it that way…Yes, I can." He looked over at the stern face of the judge. "See, the Sheriff carried a three inch Colt Single Action .45 in a belt holster on his right side. They actually call it the Sheriff or storekeeper's model. It ain't got no ejector on the side of the barrel, on account it's too short…the barrel that is."

"Thank you. And did you see the pistol when you went upstairs?"

He nodded.

"I need a verbal answer."

"Oh, uh huh. It was laying right there on the floor just in front of his body."

"I see. The gun was not in its holster, indicating the Sheriff had drawn it?"

"Objection!" the prosecuting attorney called out instantly. "Supposition not supported by testimony."

Judge Miles pondered the matter for a moment. "Sustained, rephrase your question, counselor."

"Gladly, your Honor…The gun was not in its holster, is that correct?"

"That's right. It was laying there like it got dropped. There was a bullet hole in the floor that wadn't there before."

Marcus smiled ever so slightly. "Thank you. No further questions, your Honor."

He sat down beside Millie and patted her hand. Her face was blank and pasty white as if all the life had been sucked out of her. "It's going to be all right, Ma'am. Don't you worry about a thing, now," he said.

Bass glanced around at the others sitting in the front row. Roberta's face, the left side twisted as it was from Bell's Palsy, seemed even more twisted than normal.

District Attorney White called Deputy US Marshal William Roberts to the stand. Brushy Bill got to his feet and walked around the low partition separating the front of the courtroom from the spectator area. He was quickly sworn in and sat down.

"Marshal Roberts, you were the first one to reach the cell area on the upper floor, were you not?"

"That is correct."

"Can you tell the court what you saw when you arrived?"

"Certainly…Missus Malena was standing over the body of Sheriff Wacker. She still had her revolver in her hand."

"What happened next?"

"I took it from her fingers and confirmed that the Sheriff was in fact deceased."

"What was Missus Malena's mental state of mind at the time?"

"Objection!" Marcus said in a loud voice. "Question is related to a medical issue beyond the scope of a law enforcement officer's normal purview."

"Sustained," Miles declared instantly. "Please rephrase the question."

White shot a withering look at young Johnston, who didn't seem fazed from it in the least.

"Marshal, would you be good enough to tell the court what you saw when you took Missus Malena's weapon from her?"

Bill pondered the question for a moment. He looked down at Millie, back to the DA, and then at the judge. "That's a tough one…There were tears running down her face and she was just staring down at the body. But I think I saw heartbreak, betrayal and a deep sadness, and loss…"

The courtroom erupted into a bedlam of noise as spectators began making comments and talking among themselves. The Judge banged his gavel on the bench loudly three times.

"Quiet! I won't tolerate another outbreak like that. I swear before God I will clear this courtroom of all spectators if that happens again!" Miles bellowed. The room fell silent.

"Marshal Roberts," the DA continued. "Did you ask her why she shot him?"

"I did," he replied, nodding agreement. "She said she had to and then she collapsed."

"She did not deny shooting him?"

"No sir, she did not."

"No further questions at this time, your Honor." White glared at the defense table and took his seat.

"Your witness, counselor," the Judge said to Johnston.

"Thank you, your Honor...Marshal Roberts, I understand you were working undercover as Henry McCarty, a land buyer."

"That's correct. I find I can collect more information if people don't know I'm a law officer."

"I see...but you told Missus Malena your true identity at the Courthouse earlier?"

"I did. When I found out what I was looking for."

"And that was?"

"That a Taggart W. Flowers owned the ranch in southwest Cooke County where the Red River Gang was headquartered."

Tom Sullivant in the front row next to Faye, cocked his head at the name Flowers.

"You apprised Missus Malena of that fact?"

"I did. She apparently recognized the signature as being that of Sheriff Taggart Wacker...I wasn't aware that they had murdered her son at the time."

Again, the courtroom burst into a fury of murmuring, gasps and comments.

The judge pounded his gavel. "I've warned you people once."

The room got quiet again.

"Was there anyone else in the cell area at the time of the shooting?"

"Yes, sir. Tom Lee, the titular head of the gang. We arrested him when they tried to rob the bank in Lindsay with a Gatling Gun...He was the only survivor."

"Did Mister Lee say anything when the Sheriff was killed?"

"Well, I asked him if she had gotten hit and he said that she hadn't...and that it was pure self-defense. He also said he finally recognized the voice of Wacker as the leader of the gang that always wore a mask."

"I object, obvious hearsay!" shouted the DA.

Bill snapped his gaze to White. "It was in response to my question, counselor."

"Overruled," declared Miles.

"Then I instructed Deputy Rudabaugh to fetch Doctor Wellman."

"Thank you, Marshal, that will be all."

"The state calls Doctor Lucius Wellman."

The doctor walked up and took a seat in the witness chair.

"Doctor Wellman, did you perform an autopsy on Sheriff Wacker?"

"I did...In my capacity as the county coroner."

"What were your findings?"

"He took two rounds to the abdomen...either of which were fatal."

"How so, Doctor?" asked White.

"One shot entered the central portion of the upper abdomen and clipped his aorta and the second entered upper right side of the abdomen, struck the liver and shattered into three pieces, severely lacerating the organ. With either wound, he would have bled out in forty-five seconds and with both...it was less than twenty."

"No further questions, your Honor."

"Mister Johnston, your witness," said the judge.

"Thank you, your Honor...Doctor Wellman, what was Missus Malena's condition when you arrived?"

"She was unconscious, had an abnormally rapid, weak and erratic pulse rate and her skin was cold and clammy to the touch. She was in a state of severe shock...In other words, her entire system just shut down. I elevated her feet, covered her with a blanket, chafed her hands and arms to stimulate blood flow and then administered spirits of ammonia under her nose.

In a moment she responded. I helped her to her feet and escorted her to my clinic for observation of some twenty-four hours...Actually, we almost lost her. Don't think I've ever encountered a more severe case of shock in all my years of practice."

"Thank you, Doctor, that will be all."

Wellman got to his feet, nodded and smiled at Millie and took his seat in the third row.

"The state has no further witnesses, your Honor."

"The defense res…" Johnston was interrupted by Millie when she leaned over, tugged at his sleeve and whispered in his ear.

"I have something to say."

He whispered back, "You are not required to testify…It's not necessary. We've…"

"No! I want to make a statement." She got to her feet.

Marcus leaned forward on the table and put both hands to the side of his head. "No…no…no."

Bass turned to Jack. "Uh, oh. That ain't a good sign."

The spectators began whispering among themselves. All eyes were on the petite brunette as she sat down in the witness chair.

DA Alexander White shot a glance at the young defense attorney and could not suppress the big grin on his face. As he stood before the witness stand, he pulled at the vest under his unbuttoned long coat and attempted, unsuccessfully, to cover up the starched white dress shirt that was hanging out over his prodigious stomach and gathering in loose folds under the vest.

He set his jaw and inhaled deeply as he laid out his line of questioning in his mind. The unforeseen opportunity to rip apart a confessed murderer on the stand was too juicy a fruit to let lay.

"Missus Malena," he thundered. "It has come to my attention that you and the late Taggart Wacker were engaged to be married. Is that correct?" He turned away from her and faced the crowd.

"Yes," she answered softly.

He turned back to her. "Speak up now, so that those in the back can here you, young lady."

"Yes," she said in a firm voice. Color began to return to her cheeks.

"Would you be so kind as tell the court how long you have been engaged?" He turned to the gallery again to see that they were watching his every move like a major drama was unfolding before them—as indeed it was.

"Tuesday...he asked me to marry him on Tuesday afternoon."

"Tuesday?" White repeated. "And yet before noon the next day you took your Smith & Wesson revolver to the county jail and shot and killed the man you had agreed to marry the day before..." He pointed his finger at her face. "Was that some aberrant form of a lover's spat?...What could possibly have changed your mind in twenty-two hours to do such a thing?"

His words lit a fire within her. Her eyes flashed and shone like black diamonds as she stared at the engagement ring on her finger for a long moment. Suddenly she ripped the offending bauble off and flung it to the floor. It bounced and Jack McGann caught in midair.

A collective gasp emanated from the spectators. Marcus Johnston's jaw dropped as he sat frozen in disbelief.

"Lover's spat! Lover's spat? I'll tell you why I went to face that lying son of a bitch! He killed my son! My only son...and he was just nineteen...Taggart lied about his name. He lied about his life, his plans...He seduced me and took advantage of me." She rose to her feet screaming, "Taggart Wacker Flowers was an evil...scheming...bastard! Everything about him was a lie!"

"Jezzebel!"

The unearthly screech came from Roberta Floyd as she sprang to her feet and pointed a bony finger at Millie.

Her twisted face took on a macabre look. "You ruined everything, you painted up trollop! My plan was almost complete with my revenge on Tom Sullivant and you had to go and murder my sweet baby boy!"

She spun ninety degrees and pointed her finger at the owner of the Rafter S ranch. "You ran out on me thirty-four years ago and left with me to raise our child alone." She almost appeared to snarl. "But I got even..." she hissed.

Tom stared in disbelief. "Rachel?...Rachel Flowers?"

Roberta spun back to face Millie, the veins pounding in her forehead. Her color was a sickly gray—her eyes wide and wild with hate. "You will pay for what you did!" Her hand dipped into the slash pocket on the side of her dress and produced a nickel plated revolver and pointed it at Millie. She squeezed the trigger.

As the hammer fell, a wooden cane flashed from across the aisle and struck Roberta's wrist with a sickening crack as old brittle bones shattered. The shot went high and to the left, just barely missing the District Attorney, as the revolver flew from the her grasp—spinning as it arced into Tom's lap.

Roberta grabbed at her broken wrist as she screamed and glared at Bass Reeves, still holding the handle of his hickory cane. Her face twisted even further into a sardonic mask of vengeance that sent a shiver even through the big black man. A garbled sound rumbled from her throat as she convulsed from a searing pain deep inside her head and foam bubbled from the frozen left side of her mouth. She toppled over the railing and landed face down on the courtroom floor.

"Bailiff! Take that woman into custody!" Judge Miles bellowed.

"Yes, sir," the man replied as he started to follow through as directed. He had to step around a yellow puddle that had formed under the DA's feet following the near missed shot, giving the petrified barrister a dirty look as he passed.

"Stand back! Everybody stand back!" shouted Doctor Wellman as he rushed to prostrate woman's side. The crowd moved back, more from revulsion than anything else.

He rolled her over on her back. She gasped, gagged, and then let out with a long, ragged death rattle. Her tongue was partially protruding and was twisted to the left.

Wellman palpated the carotid artery on left side of her neck. "She's dead. Cerebral Aneurysm." He looked up at the judge. "Stroke, your Honor. She apparently had a weak blood vessel in her brain as a result of her apparent long time affliction with Bell's Palsy. The sudden spike in her blood pressure from the high degree of anger was too much for it."

Judge Miles leaned back in his padded brown leather chair, brought his finger tips together and thought a moment and then leaned forward. "In my opinion, justice has been served. I find no cause to remand Millie Malena over for trial. Missus Malena...You are free to go." He slammed his gavel.

Millie collapsed to her knees in tears. Bill and Bodie rushed to her side and helped her to her feet. She hugged the both of them.

"Humf," grunted Bass. "Works almost good as my ax handle." He nodded to Jack as he looked at the cane.

"But, kiss a fat baby...didn't see that comin', you?"

Bass grinned wryly under his big full mustache. "Just shows to go you. Think you got 'er all figured out and then somebody puts a kink in the rope. Who woulda guessed it was his maw behind all this?...We learned a lesson, pard."

Tom turned to Faye, slowly sighed and shook his head. "I never knew...All the times I had dinner at your table and I never recognized her...suppose because the way her face was twisted from that disease.

"She was my girlfriend back in Tennessee, when we were just kids...Neither of us over eighteen as I recall. I went off to fight in the war. My company wound up in Texas and I was wounded at the battle of Palmito Hill. When the war was over...I just stayed. Fran's mother was my nurse and we fell in love and got married...I just never knew." He shook his head again. "We had no agreement...I never asked her to marry me. I suppose she made more of it than I did."

"I think that's pretty obvious. Bordering on the obsessive, in my opinion," said Faye.

"I guess I'll never understand how some people can carry that much hate around with them all their lives."

"Hate usually does more damage to the one that does the hating, don't you agree?"

"I would think so...Can't believe Wacker was my son," Tom said as he looked over at the pathetic figure on the floor and paused. "I always had a dream about having a top flight horse ranch and this looked like really good horse country."

Faye looked at him and put her hand on top of his. "About the worst thing a man can do...is to let a dream die."

SKEANS BOARDING HOUSE
THREE MONTHS LATER

Flowers decorated the back yard. Tables and folding chairs were set up. A wicker arch festooned with white roses was erected in the center with chairs lining both sides of an aisle.

Angie and Jack McGann with twenty month old Baby Sarah, Bass, his wife Nellie Jennie, and Bill Roberts holding hands with Millie, all dressed in their finest, stood looking at the back of Faye's house. Judge Miles, looking dashing in a black suit was standing just past the rose covered arch with a Bible in his hand.

Osí Hommá, in a ceremonial white doeskin beaded warshirt, stood off to the side looking very uncomfortable and talking to Doctor Wellman and Selden Lindsey.

Bodie and a four month pregnant Annabel were on both sides of the arch with a black-suited Walt Durbin.

Loss Hart began to play the wedding march on his fiddle. Everyone turned to see Francis Ann come out the back door, accompanied by her father and followed by Faye carrying her train.

Fran was dressed in a dazzling white lace and satin beaded full length gown. She carried a small bouquet of white rosebuds in front of her that matched the buds woven through her flaming red hair in a type of a crown. Her emerald green eyes sparkled. There was only the slightest trace of a pink scar where she had been shot showing just above her bodice on the upper right side of her chest.

She, her father and Faye stepped slowly in time to the music being played by Marshal Hart. They stopped at the arch and Tom and Faye backed off to the side. Annabel moved next to Francis as her matron of honor and Bodie stood beside Walt as best man.

After Judge Miles performed the ceremony, Walt kissed his bride—for what seemed to the guests as an inordinately long time—much to their delight. Francis turned with her back to the crowd and threw the bouquet high in the air. It landed directly in Faye's hands. The guests cheered and several nudged Tom.

Baby Sarah, finally became impatient at being held in Angie's arms, squirmed her way down and toddled over to Annabel, reached up as high as she could and placed both hands on the ravishing blonde's slightly swelling stomach.

"Baby," the toddler managed to blurt out. "Baby."

Annabel bent over and picked the little cotton-headed girl up in her arms. "Yes it is, pretty thing, but I don't know if it's a boy or girl."

"It's a boy," said Faye, matter-of-factly, walking up next to them.

Both Annabel and Bodie turned to her and simultaneously asked, "How can you tell?"

Faye winked at the beaming young woman. "Women's intuition, remember?"

****

TIMBER CREEK PRESS

PREVIEW

THE NEXT EXCITING INSTALLMENT IN

THE NATIONS - THE BASS REEVES SAGA

BASS AND THE LADY

CHAPTER ONE

WILD HORSE CREEK
CHOCKTAW NATION

"I'd keep my hands wrapped around that cup…unless you want to make that the last Arbuckle you ever drink," said the voice from the shadows at the edge of the campfire light.

The giant, dark visaged man sitting on a log near the campfire stiffened. His right hand moved slightly down the side of the tin cup—a wisp of coffee steam rose up into the cold night air.

"Unh, uhh. Not smart." A shot rang out from the shadowy figure with long dark brown hair hanging out from under a sombrero.

The cup spun crazily out of the man's hand, splashing hot coffee over his bearded face, legs and arms. He sprang to his feet. Some of the stout trail brew landed in the fire where it hissed and sizzled on a burning log.

"Ow, ow, ow, Gawd dammit!...Jesus Christ!" The man sprang to his feet and looked at his right hand which now only had four fingers. He glared over at the figure standing in the shadows. "Who the hell are you?"

"F. M. Miller...Deputy United States Marshal and I got paper on you. Bosco 'Mad Dog' Walters...wanted for larceny of horses, rape, arson, attempted murder and murder...Seems to me, you've been a bad boy."

The figure stepped into the outer edge of the firelight—a .38-40 Colt Peacemaker with ivory grips, in each hand. "Nice and easy, now...turn this way...slowly."

The six foot four, barrel chested man, held onto his injured right hand and moaned. "My trigger fanger's gone! You shot it plumb off! God damned law dog!"

"Don't think you're in a real good position to go to callin' names right now, slick. Be a real shame to lose another one...or an ear."

He glanced over as the six foot tall shooter stepped nearer—the flickering firelight illuminating under the broad brim.

"You wouldn't do that, wou..." He looked closer as the shadows gave way to a well proportioned face with fair features. "A woman?...I got took down by a split-tail? Son of a green bitch!" He turned his head and spit into the fire. "I thought yer voice sounded kindly funny fer a man."

"It doesn't matter whether I squat or stand to pee...I'm wearing a Deputy US Marshal's badge...and that trumps everything else." She reached into the slash pocket of the long dark brown oiled canvas great coat, pulled out a set of steel shackles and pitched them at the groaning man's feet. "Put those on...Now. I know you've had experience in doing that."

"I cain't...My fanger."

"I'd be for figuring out a way or you're going to lose your right ear. You got five seconds. Two...three..."

"Hey, what happened to one?"

"Four..." Her steel-gray eyes flashed.

"Alright, alright!" He reached down with his bloody left hand and picked up the shackles. Mad Dog slipped one half over his maimed right one and closed the shank. He braced it on his leg, put his left through and managed to push it closed with his right wrist. "There, satisfied?...Lady, you gonna do somethin' 'bout my hand now, 'fore I bleed to death?"

"Don't know...might save Judge Parker's court some money, if you were to bleed out. I'll collect the reward and the two dollars for serving the warrant, in any case."

"Aw come on...You cain't do that...I'll be good. Honest Injun...Uh, what do I call you?"

"Marshal will do just fine," she said as she pulled the flap of her coat back that served as a rain slicker and a cold weather outer covering and holstered her left pistol in a cross draw.

The law officer stepped closer and pulled out a blue bandana. "Hold your hands way out in front of you."

The docile outlaw did as he was told. She stuck out one end of the large wild rag.

"Grab the end with your left hand." She started wrapping the cotton cloth around what remained of his right index finger, and then around his hand and stuffed the end under the wrap. "Now don't move it around much and it might stay on until we get to McAlister. Marshal Cantrell is anxious to have a little word with you," the striking brunette said with just a hint of a confident smile that showed her even white teeth.

ARBUCKLE MOUNTAINS

Deputy US Marshal Jack McGann—accompanied by his big white wolf-dog, Son—worked his red and white Overo paint down the steep slope along the north side of Turner Falls. An eight point buck was draped across the horse's rump—tied on by the long saddle strings behind the cantle—as they headed back toward the cabin.

A cottontail jumped up right between Chief's front feet. The startled horse shied hard to the right, stumbled and flipped over—head first. Jack was thrown forward in front of the tumbling horse and caught his leg under the saddle as the gelding went over—the six inch cantle landing directly on top of his lower leg. There was a sickening snap and McGann cried out in pain.

"Aaaah!"

The horse scrambled to his feet, the deer still tied on, but it had shifted to the left. Chief was further frightened by the antlers of the buck banging against his left flank and headed on down the mountain and toward the security of the barn. Son trotted back to Jack, as he lay writhing in pain.

"Son of a bitch!" He tried to sit up and got high enough to see his lower left leg was bent at an unnatural angle to the right. "Aw, damn!…Go git Angie, Son. Go!"

The big animal spun around and charged down the hill, running around the large gray outcropped boulders and jumping over smaller ones as he made a beeline to home, a half mile away.

Angie McGann, Jack's attractive redheaded wife, and her uncle, Winchester Ashalatubbi—who was not only the shaman of the Chickasaw Nation, but also a trained medical doctor—were sitting on the porch having their morning coffee. They looked up as Chief thundered into the clearing and stopped in front of the big red barn. Son ran right in behind him, cleared the white slat fence around the yard of the cabin and stopped at the bottom of the steps leading up to the porch and barked twice.

"Uh, oh," Angie and Winchester said simultaneously.

"Saints preserve us, something's happened to Jack." She jumped up, handed her twenty-one month old daughter to her uncle. "You watch after Baby Sarah, I'll follow Son. He'll lead me to me husband."

"Child, it would be best if I go. If he's unable to move, you'll never be able to get him back here and if he's badly hurt, at least I can treat him. You go tend to Chief." He handed the baby back to his niece, stepped inside and grabbed the black valise that carried his medical supplies, his black, tall uncreased crown hat and Angie's Irish grandfather's shillelagh. "Got a feeling he may be up past the falls. Need to use this as a climbing stick."

"It's always wise ye are, Anompoli Lawa."

Angie often referred to the shaman by his Chickasaw name which meant, 'He Who Talks to Many'.

"Just common sense, my dear, just common sense...and it looks like it was fortunate I chose today to come by and check on Baby Sarah."

"Aye, that it is."

The native Chickasaw followed the big white wolf-dog up past the roaring falls and halfway up the hill. "You could slow down a bit, Son. I'm not used to climbing around these mountains anymore." The faithful animal stopped, looked back over his shoulder for a moment, and then moved on.

"Winchester! Over here."

He looked up slope nearly twenty yards past Son and saw Jack, propped up on his elbow and waving his other arm above the tall grass. The dog reached his master and licked his face.

"Alright, that's enough, Son." The stocky mustachioed lawman laid back down with a sigh.

"Well, I'm glad you weren't any farther from the house than this, Jack. Where are you hurt?" Winchester asked as he reached the downed man.

"Broke leg."

The doctor looked down at his left leg underneath his right. "Oh, my goodness, Jack, you are correct." He moved the top leg gently off to the side a little, got out his scissors and cut Jack's jeans up from the bottom. "Well, at least it's not a compound fracture, but both the tibia and fibula are broken and will have to be put back in place."

"Wonderful, how lucky can I get?"

"I'm going to have to splint it before we try to get you back to the cabin."

"What do you mean, 'try'."

"You're going to have to put your arm over my shoulder and hobble down to the trail by the falls…That's assuming we don't both fall and that would not be a good thing."

"See your point," said Jack.

"Let me have your Bowie…Got to cut some sticks for the splint."

Jack pulled his big razor-sharp knife from his beaded belt sheath and handed it to the older man.

"Be right back." He reached in his bag an dug out a small green bottle. "Here, take a couple of pulls of this…it'll help deaden the pain."

He took the bottle from the white-haired shaman. "Laudanum?"

"Yep."

"Hate this stuff."

"Beats the alternative."

"What's that?"

"The pain you're going to experience, when I set that leg."

"Cain't wait." He twisted off the cap and turned the pharmaceutical bottle up. "Gag."

"Another."

He did it again and made another wry face. "Why don't you just thump me in the head with that shillelagh?"

"I can do that too." Anompoli Lawa said as he walked toward some willows growing alongside Honey Creek.

After he had trimmed the four three foot long branches, he cut the rest of Jack's jeans off at the knee and ripped the tough denim cloth into tie strips. He handed him a piece of one of the sticks about a big around as his finger. "Here, bite down on this. Even with the Laudanum, this is going to hurt a mite." Winchester grabbed the back of Jack's boot and the top of his foot. "Look! What's that over there?"

"Huh?" Jack mumbled with the stick in his mouth and looked off toward the creek.

The doctor gave his leg a sharp jerk.

"Ahhhhh." The sound came from deep in Jack's throat as both ends of the thick willow branch fell from each side of his mouth. He arched his back, collapsed heavily, spit out what was left and blew his breath loudly three times. "Jesus, Mary and Joseph!...You tricked me!"

"Let's call it a distraction." Ashalatubbi started placing the splints evenly around Jack's lower leg.

They hobbled into the yard at the cabin, Jack had his left arm around Winchester's shoulder and the black shillelagh in his right.

"Woman of the house," McGann shouted with somewhat of a slur.

Angie opened the front door and stepped out on the porch.

"Saints be praised, ye found him." She stepped down the steps and assisted Winchester getting him up the four steps.

"He has a badly broken leg, but I set it. I'm going to have to check it again before I cast it. He's lucky the bone didn't break the skin...won't have to worry much about infection."

"I gotta g...go unsaddle ol' Chief. He's got a buck deer ridin' on the b...baaaack...Hee-hee-hee."

"He's already unsaddled, husband." Angie turned to her uncle. "It's splifficated, he is."

"The Laudanum. Had to give him a pretty stout dose before I set his leg. He still bit completely through a half-inch piece of a willow limb."

"We'll be having to send a telegram to the Judge. He was supposed to meet Bass in Fort Smith early next week for their next assignment."

"Your husband won't be going anywhere for four or five months."

FORT SMITH, ARKANSAS
JUDGE PARKER'S CHAMBERS

"Enter," boomed Judge Parker from his big cherry wood desk when he heard the solid knock at the door. The door swung open and a muscular black man with a full mustache entered, nearly filling the doorway with his six foot three inch frame.

"Mornin' yer honor."

"Morning, Bass. Have a seat."

He hung his black Boss of the Plains type hat on the Judge's hall tree next to the door and strode over to one of the wing backed burgundy chairs in front of the desk and sat down.

"Bass, I got a telegram the other day from Jack's wife, Angie…"

The big lawman shot to his feet. "Jack alright?"

"Well, that's the thing…No. He apparently took a tumble on his horse coming back from deer hunting. Broke his left leg below the knee. Luckily Anompoli Lawa happened to be at the cabin checking in on their daughter. He got him home, set the leg and put it in a cast. The upshot is, Jack is out of commission for the next four to five months."

"Lordy, lordy, and we us got a stack of warrants to serve," Bass said as he shook his head and sat back down.

"I assigned someone to ride with you until McGann comes back. Hell of a shot and damn good on a horse…I'm told."

Bass frowned. "Who is it? Anybody I know?"

"I don't think so…Marshal F. M. Miller."

"Nope, don't know him."

Parker looked up at Bass over the top of his Pince-nez reading glasses with a wry grin.

There was a tap on the door.

***

TIMBER CREEK PRESS

16479597R00194

Printed in Great Britain
by Amazon